FOR BETTE[R]

Miranda was certain what would happen if her cousin Darryl seized the family business that her grandfather had taught her to run so well.

Darryl would swiftly run it into the ground as he pursued his passion for gaming and wenching in fast-living London society.

On the other hand, Giles Lindsey promised to be a most prudent business partner if Miranda agreed to be his wife— strictly in the eyes of the world only, of course.

But by the time she suspected that both Giles and his promises were just too maddingly tame to be true, it became appallingly clear that not only her business but also Miranda herself was in his hands. . . .

*The
Prudent
Partnership*

Ⓢ

SIGNET Regency Romances You'll Enjoy

The
Prudent
Partnership

 Barbara Allister

Ⓢ
A SIGNET BOOK
NEW AMERICAN LIBRARY

SIGNET TRADEMARK REG. U.S. PAT. OFF. AND FOREIGN COUNTRIES
REGISTERED TRADEMARK—MARCA REGISTRADA
HECHO EN CHICAGO, U.S.A.

SIGNET, SIGNET CLASSIC, MENTOR, PLUME, MERIDIAN AND
NAL BOOKS are published by New American Library,
1633 Broadway, New York, New York 10019

First Printing, July, 1984

1   2   3   4   5   6   7   8   9

PRINTED IN THE UNITED STATES OF AMERICA

—1—

"But, Miss Merry, I can find no other solution," stated John Pettigrew, removing his glasses and mopping his brow. "You must realize how little time you have."

Miranda Sommerby regarded her lawyer with affection tinged with impatience. "The cure seems almost as bad as the disease." She paused. "There is no other way?"

At the shake of his head, Merry bent over the tea service, pouring him a fresh cup and adding the two lumps of sugar and the cream he liked before she handed it to him. Only then did she return to his suggestion.

"You know very well," Merry stated rather emphatically, "that I have no intention of marrying anyone— much less a man I do not know."

John Pettigrew, because he knew her background, understood Miranda's position; however, he had many times reminded her of the impracticality of her desires.

"Marriage is a trap for women." Her words echoed those in his memory. "I will inherit part of Grandfather's fortune no matter what I decide?" she questioned.

"You know the problem is not that simple. You will inherit a small yearly income no matter what you decide. However, you will see the remainder of the money and the control of the business pass to the hands of Hugo Darryl, your father's cousin who is your grandfather's closest male heir. Consider carefully—a yearly income of several hundred pounds is far different than that of several thousand."

"If money were the only consideration," murmured Merry, "I would not even consider the idea. But Hugo would ruin the business within a year."

"Only consider it," Mr. Pettigrew suggested. "You know it is the only way to defeat your cousin's plans and keep all this."

Merry frowned, for "all this" to which Mr. Pettigrew referred was her late grandfather's home, an imposing gray stone structure on one of the most fashionable streets in Bristol, her home for the last eight years. Only a year earlier it had been charmingly redecorated by Merry herself in the quiet, soothing colors the Sommerbys preferred. The library in which she and Mr. Pettigrew sat had been her grandfather's favorite, decorated in golds and soft greens with the book-lined walls adding the color accents. "I realize that I must take action," she mused, "but I am not certain your way is best."

But John Pettigrew was a man who never spoke without thinking, and he was ready to present his reasons in the straightforward manner he used in his legal office. "Miss Merry," he said quietly, "you have only one week before Hugo Darryl arrives. That fact makes a decision imperative." Realizing he had to give her a chance to think, he sat quietly finishing his tea and then returned the cup to the tray.

Miranda crossed to the window after ringing for Barrow. She pushed the heavy drapes to one side. "Grandfather buried last week and already the hounds are closing in," she whispered. "They must know what we had been planning." The plans had been made some time before. Mr. Pettigrew, her grandfather, and she had worked carefully, but they had not considered the possibility of her grandfather's death.

"I know you think I am forcing you into a way of life you do not want," Mr. Pettigrew remarked, "but all our careful plans mean nothing now. Your grandfather, as soon as the doctor would allow me to see him, called me to his bedside and suggested this alternative."

The reminder of the situation did little to ease Merry's mind. The entrance of Barrow, her grandfather's butler, caused her to pause. Waiting for him to remove the tea tray, she considered her problem. She knew that her decision would affect her servants' lives too. Her grandfather had made certain that the older servants would be independent if they wished to be. Yet they refused to leave her. Her smile and word of thanks to Barrow were only two of the reasons that the servants had adored her from the moment she had arrived eight years earlier.

Mrs. Barrow, the housekeeper, often remarked, "That young lady has brought a touch of spring to these old walls. Just hearing her laugh makes my day brighter. Since she started planning the meals and supervising the household, my work has been easier."

Even Henning, Mr. Sommerby's valet, who had been jealous of her influence with her grandfather, had to admit that she had not interfered with his duties, adding that the same could not be said for Hugo Darryl. In their fondness for their mistress and their dislike of her cousin, they were united.

As a result, Merry had no doubts about their reasons for staying. She crossed to the chair beside the fireplace, turning to face her lawyer. "My grandfather," she said quietly, "did all in his power to make certain I would be free to make my own life. Did he approve of an action that would severely curtail my freedom before I have had a chance to enjoy it? He often said that freedom and the ability to make one's own decisions were the only worthwhile things in life."

"Your grandfather made plans to protect you, to give you a choice," Mr. Pettigrew said, "because he could not eliminate the threat of Hugo Darryl from your life. But he also trained you to think and to plan for yourself because he knew that even the most carefully determined actions sometimes fail. You are heir

not only to his fortune but also to his mind. Please use
it wisely."

There was little that Merry could contradict about
this statement, since it was only an echo of words she
had heard from her grandfather on many occasions.
He had trained her in logic as well as in business
management, providing her tutors when he was caught
up in business problems. He hoped to help her learn
the problems she would face when he was gone. The
only problem he had never been able to solve was that
of her great-grandfather's will. Even the best legal
minds in England could find no loopholes in that
document.

"Oh, Mr. Pettigrew," she said, "you have my best
interests in mind, I know, yet I chafe at the restrictions society has placed upon me. I long for freedom,
yet I see it slipping farther and farther away."

"And the only guarantee you have of achieving any
freedom at all is to accept Giles Lindsey's proposal,"
he reminded her. "At least let me arrange for him to
meet you to discuss the matter." He paused, recognizing the thoughtful look in her eyes. Perhaps Merry
was closer to agreeing. If he could arrange a meeting,
perhaps Lindsey could convince her.

"Mr. Lindsey is a shareholder in the company, his
shares a legacy from his maternal grandfather. Because he has chosen to explore the West Indies and
America, your grandfather has voted his shares until
recently. As a result, not all partners of the company
are familiar with him. But because of his efforts, the
West Indian portion of the firm has begun to do as
well as the ones your grandfather personally directed.
At least once a year since he inherited, he has visited
with Mr. Sommerby for several weeks and has reviewed the details of the business in England and in
India. Had you not accepted your aunt's invitation to
visit Bath the last few summers you would have met
him."

"A shareholder? Are you certain?" Merry's face
wore a look of surprised thoughtfulness. "He may be

the answer to the problem after all. But I thought all the shares were controlled by the family."

"His great-grandmother and your great-grandfather were brother and sister, she being much younger than he. Although your great-grandfather loved her as a daughter, he refused to leave shares in the company to a woman. Instead, he left them in trust for her infant son, Mr. Lindsey's grandfather," explained the lawyer. "I think you might like Mr. Lindsey. Your grandfather did."

Giles Lindsey might be the solution, thought Merry, but he also could be a problem. Her grandfather had had very catholic tastes in friends, including among them a highwayman, a pickpocket, the Lord Mayor of London, and a former prime minister. "Just because he has a good head for business and amused Grandfather does not necessarily mean that he and I will suit. I must have some time."

Merry could see that Pettigrew believed in Giles Lindsey, and she knew that he would never give up until she agreed to see the man. It might be by meeting Mr. Lindsey she could show Mr. Pettigrew that the idea would never work. "What will happen," she asked, "if I see him and then do not agree with the plan? What alternatives will you then recommend?"

"Then may I arrange for Lindsey to call this afternoon?" Mr. Pettigrew said evasively. "What time will be convenient?"

This obvious attempt to avoid her question caused Merry's brows to slant downward. "What if this meeting does not accomplish what you hope? What then do you suggest?"

"There will still be a little more time. But I fear that this may be the only solution available in the time we have left," Mr. Pettigrew confessed. "Mr. Lindsey's proposal will give you a permanent solution. He is an unexpected advantage that your cousin has no idea exists. With his help you can be free of Darryl."

"Free of him," repeated Merry. "How is it that Lindsey is here now when he usually arrives in June?"

Mr. Pettigrew cleared his throat and straightened the lace at his throat, an action he usually performed when he needed time to consider what he was going to say. "Your grandfather had me write him, asking him to come as soon as possible." He eyed Merry's wrinkled brow anxiously. "I believe he talked to Mr. Sommerby at least twice. He was also at the funeral."

With effort, Merry composed her face. "Why did you wait so long to tell me about him? I think it odd that Grandfather never mentioned him as a possible help. Perhaps he felt Mr. Lindsey was not to be trusted."

The lawyer snapped, "Your grandfather was a very healthy man. He did not expect to die so suddenly. He probably would have introduced the two of you this year. Is it not true that you were to spend this summer in Bristol instead of visiting your aunt?"

Reluctantly, Merry considered his words. It was unfair to blame Mr. Pettigrew for a situation her great-grandfather had created. It seemed to her that whatever choice she made she would be robbed of the freedom she so desperately wanted. What guarantees did she have that Lindsey would not use the situation for his own benefit? "This is the only way?"

"It is the only one I see for the present." Once again he cleared his throat. "The terms of the will give us a year, but your cousin gives us only one week. Already he has your aunt on his side. Will you be able to withstand her pressures as well as Darryl's? You are a loving niece, too loving your grandfather believed. Your mother's sister might just persuade you to accept Darryl's demands."

Remembering the days in Bath when her aunt had urged, persuaded, and continually hammered at her until she accepted whatever new plan had been proposed, Merry capitulated. "Will three this afternoon be suitable?" At least he would not force her to make a decision today; in fact, she knew Mr. Pettigrew would never suggest an idea to her if he believed it to be wrong. The least she could do would be to meet the man and decide for herself.

With a smile, the lawyer said his good-byes and hurried from the room.

As Merry dressed for the meeting, the long look she gave herself in the mirror revealed an image she was familiar with—brown hair, hazel eyes, a figure that was both too rounded and too short for true beauty. "At least," she said to herself, "my hair is neat and my skin is clear." As usual, she had failed to recognize that the combination of clear hazel eyes, a creamy complexion, and wavy brown hair made a pleasing picture. Her sweet expression and voluptuous curves drew many charming glances, and when she spoke, strangers often commented on her clear bell-like voice. Her laugh, when it rang out, reminded listeners of a happy song; her grandfather, hearing it for the first time, had called her "his merry darling," and Merry she had been called ever since. Until recently, her pleasant expression had been dimmed only at the mention of her father or Hugo Darryl. For some weeks, though, her face had been sad and her laughter silent.

Entering the cream and rose drawing room, she thought about the coming meeting. She had just settled her black skirts and picked up her needlework when Barrow announced, "Mr. Giles Lindsey."

Her breath caught as he entered. His black hair curled in spite of his obvious attempts to control it. The snug fit of his dark blue coat revealed the muscles that rippled in his shoulders and arms. His eyes, which had watched her closely since he had entered the room, were a deep blue-green. As he made his bow before her, Merry felt the inadequacies of her inches as opposed to his nearly six feet.

No man should be so ruggedly handsome, she thought. His voice reminded her of why they were meeting.

"I am sorry we have had to meet under such unhappy circumstances, Miss Sommerby. I had a deep

respect for your grandfather. I will miss him as
know you will." Giles's quiet words and pleasant ex
pression were a mask for his thoughts. Was this
Sommerby's granddaughter, this serene, attractive
innocent? As Giles observed her more closely, he no
ticed the white knuckles of the hand holding the
needlework and realized that hers was a surface calm
He also saw the fear and the sadness she tried to hide.

As she murmured her reply, Merry tried to remember where she had seen him before, but her memory
played her false. She asked, "May I offer you tea or
would you prefer sherry?"

Declining either, Giles reminded her why they were
meeting. So intent was she on his quiet, deep voice
she heard Giles say only, "Therefore before we begin,
here is the letter your grandfather gave me to give
you. That was our last meeting."

Holding her emotions under tight control, Merry
reached for the letter, her eyes misting as she recognized her grandfather's handwriting, legible but very
shaky. Hesitantly, as if afraid of breaking the last link
with her grandfather, she broke the seal. At first
unable to read the words because of her tears, she
paused and then read:

My darling Merry,
  I love you, my little happiness. Unfortunately my
love can no longer protect you. Although I know it is
not what you want, I have found someone who can.
  The choice is yours. But I hope you choose to marry
Giles. If you do, the marriage settlements are already
planned, and he has agreed to allow you to control
both your income and your shares. He will have to
vote the shares, but he will vote them as you decide.
  If you choose not to marry Giles, you know that
under my father's will the shares will be held in trust
for your sons in the event that you marry a partner in
the company. Until you do so, Hugo will vote the
shares as if they were his own and give you an allowance to supplement what I can leave you. After your
marriage, your partner-husband will have the right to

vote them. If you marry outside the company, Hugo will hold them in trust for your oldest son.

Darling Merry, put aside those dreadful memories of your parents' marriage and think logically. I know you will make the right choice.

Your loving,
Grandfather

Merry's eyes revealed both despair and sadness as she questioned Giles. "Do you know what the letter contains?" At his nod, she continued, "Why have you agreed to do this? What do you hope to gain?"

Giles knew that she would be hurt if he revealed his promise to her grandfather. And somehow he knew that he wanted to protect her, to remove the fear he saw in her eyes. Giles wrinkled his forehead and moved to sit beside her on the sofa. "I have several reasons. First, I would like to have more of a voice in the company. Together, we could make the changes you and your grandfather had planned." He smiled as she looked at him sharply.

"Next, my parents are out of the country at present. My father is a special envoy to Russia. When they left six months ago, they arranged for my sister Charlotte to stay in Kent with one of my cousins and to be presented during the Season. Now my cousin refuses to do so. Apparently she and Charlotte do not often agree. I must find someone else to undertake this task and rescue my sister."

Merry hastily interrupted, "If I am to be the one to present her if we marry, you should know that I have little experience or interest in society."

Giles reassured her, "All that is needed is a married lady to serve as her chaperone. Several of my friends' mothers who are also presenting daughters this Season will see that she is asked to the proper events." He continued. "The last reason is more personal. For some time now I have been trying to discourage a lady who believes that I will marry her. Recently I have come to the conclusion that I must take drastic action or she will find some way to force me into marriage."

"But your drastic action will involve marriage to me," stammered Merry.

"If I marry you, she will understand that I refuse to be manipulated," Giles snapped.

"But you will still be married!"

"The difference is that the choice will have been mine." Realizing that his attitude might have confused her, Giles explained, "If you and I marry, both of us will understand from the beginning that our marriage is primarily an alliance to gain control of the business. We will be able to continue our lives without much interruption. Also, your grandfather told me you liked to travel. I also enjoy exploring new lands. As soon as my parents return to take charge of Charlotte, we can go abroad—to India, to the Americas, to Greece."

Raising her eyebrows slightly at his persuasive tone, Merry considered once more the letter in her hand. Giles's words echoed in her mind, "Travel, business, life as usual." Finally she broke the silence, uttering the words she had known were inevitable since she had read the letter. "How soon will we be married?"

—2—

The fog and gloom outside reflected Merry's mood as she sanded and sealed the last of the notes. She rubbed her forehead, trying to ease her headache. It had been late when she had finally fallen asleep. As she pulled the bell to summon her maid, she wondered what her Aunt Mathilda would say when she received the news of her niece's marriage to Giles. Knowing her aunt's fondness for tall, dark, and handsome men, she expected her to adore him. Fortunately, Mathilda was visiting friends in London and would not be able to arrive before the ceremony.

As clearly as though her aunt were in the room, Merry could hear her voice droning on, "You are not getting any younger, my dear. You simply cannot expect your grandfather to live forever. Then what will you do? You can live with me if you want, but the best idea is to marry Charles as Hugo suggests. After all, Hugo—a charming man—certainly knows what is best for you." How little her aunt knew of Hugo! (Now Merry would be marrying a man her aunt had never met. Giles wasn't Charles, but all Mathilda would care about was that Merry would be taken care of.)

When her maid entered, Merry thought for a moment before she said, "Pilgrim, please see that both of these letters are delivered. The one to Arabella—Lady Montrose—must be delivered by messenger as soon as possible. Ask him to wait for a reply. The one to my aunt should be sent by post . . . to Bath." At least that

15

way she would have a few more days without her aunt's exaltations and without her telling Hugo about the wedding. Merry knew her friend Arabella too well to think that she or her husband would tell Hugo anything. Fortunately, Arabella and Brandon ran with a younger set than her aunt.

"The third note goes to Madame Camille. Please have it sent immediately. Also, have a footman bring the trunks of fabric to my sitting room as soon as possible. When you have arranged these things, please return. I will need you again." Merry smiled her thanks to the woman who had taken charge of her when she had arrived in Bristol, remembering how horrified Pilgrim had been when she had realized the state of her clothes and the fact that Merry had traveled from India with only a groom for protection.

As the door closed, Merry looked once more at the list she and Giles had compiled the night before. Fortunately, once the decision had been made, both had agreed on what had to be done. She remembered Giles's words, "This marriage will surprise many people. Therefore we must proceed cautiously. Because of your grandfather's recent death, the ceremony itself must be small and private. However, we must notify our relatives and closest friends about our plans. Sir Alex Ramsey, whom I have known since childhood, lives in Salisbury. With your permission I would like to ask him to stand up with me." When Merry agreed, Giles asked, "Do you wish your aunt to attend?"

"Aunt Mathilda is in London now, and we would have to wait some time if she were to be present. But my best friends, Lord and Lady Montrose, have an estate outside Bath and are there now. I would truly like to have Arabella and Brandon at my wedding," said Merry.

"If our letters are delivered tomorrow, then we can be married the next day. But can you arrange a dress? You must not be married in black. And who will give you away?"

Answering the second question, Merry blinked back her tears as she remembered her grandfather's death. "Mr. Pettigrew was my grandfather's closest friend; he will represent him. But clothes—I can wear something I already have."

"Do you want everyone to think that this is an over-the-anvil wedding? Of course you must have something special," Giles thundered. "What will you say when my sister asks to see the dress you wore for your wedding? If we return to Linden Hall, the tenants will expect you to wear that dress for the party there."

Retreating behind the wall of calm she always erected to escape the arguments and loud noises she hated, Merry had agreed. "Perhaps Madame Camille can help. Grandfather and I found her when we visited Paris last year. She was a seamstress in the house of LeRoy but had been fired when some wealthy woman accused her of ruining a dress." Looking at Giles, Merry had realized that he was not interested in her story. "Yes, I will arrange a dress."

Once Giles had her agreement, he went on. "Fortunately your grandfather had already obtained a special license and arranged with the vicar to marry us." Merry's lips thinned as she thought how her grandfather had accurately predicted her actions. Giles asked, "Do you wish to arrange for a caterer, or will the servants prepare the wedding supper? I think, considering your recent bereavement, it need not be elaborate."

Merry had promised to make the arrangements. Her servants would have been offended had anyone else been called in. Together she and Giles had drawn up a list of relatives that would have to be notified. Other than Aunt Mathilda, Hugo and Charles Darryl, and a few distant cousins, Merry had no one, but Giles's list seemed to go on forever. She wondered how she would ever be able to keep the relationships straight. For once she had been glad that neither her father nor her mother had had many relatives.

A scratching at the door announced Barrow, Pilgrim, and three sturdy footmen. The footmen carried one large and one small trunk, which they placed in front of the sofa. "Do you wish the smaller boxes as well, Miss Merry?" asked Barrow after he had assured himself that the footmen had carried out his orders perfectly.

"Not now. I'll ring if I need them. Please show Madame Camille up as soon as she arrives."

Sinking to the sofa in front of the large trunk, Merry helped Pilgrim open the lid, revealing layer after layer of fabric in a rainbow of colors and textures. Remembering her grandfather's delight in surprising her with yet another treasure, her eyes grew misty, but she resolutely blinked her tears away. Lifting out the crimson silk worked with gold thread that her grandfather had wanted her to make into a ball gown, she searched for the softer, quieter, more subtle pieces. Even though her grandfather had insisted that there be no formal mourning period for him, she felt the brighter colors out of keeping with her spirits.

Beneath the layers of crimson, emerald, and sapphire silks lay the ones she was seeking—a soft pearl gray, a clear blue that matched her favorite aquamarine pendant, and a beautiful pale yellow fabric, the color of clotted cream. She put these three pieces to one side. She knew that a Season in London would require more of a wardrobe than she possessed, and continued to sift through the fabrics. Soon Pilgrim had taken charge of a pomona green, a light rose, and a dark blue shot with silver.

As Merry finished sorting through the fabrics, Pilgrim was opening the smaller trunk. She exclaimed over the laces and ribbons it contained. Although Napoleon was interfering with their trade with Belgium, Venice, and Florence, their company was prepared. Her grandfather had taken advantage of the brief peace the year before to invest in hundreds of ells of fabric, laces, and ribbons because as he said, "Wartime or peacetime, every woman longs for beautiful clothes."

"Madame Camille," announced Barrow, ushering her into the sitting room.

"I came as quickly as I could, Miss Sommerby," said the modiste. "Here are the latest fashion plates and *La Belle Assemblage*. As you can see, the new dresses are simpler, softer than before. Recently I received some fashion sketches from my cousin Nanette in Paris showing this new Empire style." She handed the designs to Merry. "She also writes that muslins are popular there, especially with the younger ladies, and that some of the faster ladies are even dampening their petticoats so that their dresses will reveal their figures more clearly."

Merry's eyebrows went up, "I hope that is not what you have in mind for me, Madame Camille?"

"*Mais non!* But the raised waistline of the dresses, the soft gathers under the bust, the lighter fabric, and the long lines will soften your figure, *mademoiselle*. And the décolleté bodice will be perfect for your lovely shoulders and bosom."

Exchanging a glance with Pilgrim, Merry suggested, "Perhaps you would like some tea while I look through these designs. Go with Pilgrim, and I will decide." Eager to discuss what was happening with her friend Pilgrim, Madame Camille agreed.

Merry picked up one of the fashion plates. They were certainly different from the stiffened overskirts and gathered underskirts she had been wearing. Idly, she wondered how her dressmaker could get the latest Paris fashions when England and France were at war. "At least I won't look so much like a ball in these," she mused. As she inspected each, she realized that she was making her selections based on whether or not she thought Giles would like them. She reminded herself that it was she who would have to wear them and selected three she felt would be most becoming, the ones with the least frills. The only problem would be time.

When Madame Camille and Pilgrim returned, Merry was ready with her choices. By this time the modiste knew what had been planned and showed no surprise when Merry said, "One dress must be finished by tomorrow. I am to be married at three. Will this be possible?"

"For you, it will be done," assured Madame Camille. Looking at the sketches Merry had chosen, she suggested, "Perhaps this one in the pale cream. But it must have some trim. The Brussels lace—you remember, I showed it to you when you last were in the shop—that will do nicely. For the hair, more lace and dark cream roses." Once the dress for the wedding had been chosen, the three women rapidly matched the remaining sketches to the gray and the clear blue fabrics. Deep burgundy ribbons were chosen to complete the gray while ribbons of a slightly darker blue than the fabric were the choice for the other. After the wedding there would be time to choose other morning dresses, traveling clothes, and ball gowns. "How fortunate I know your size so well, *mademoiselle*. I will need only to make a few adjustments when I deliver your dress tomorrow. The dressing gown and nightrobe you ordered last week were to be finished this morning. I will bring them with your dress tomorrow. The rest will take a day or two longer."

At first the mention of the dressing gown and nightrobe confused Merry. Then a blush spread up her neck to her face. As she left, Madame Camille said, "Ah, so innocent." And Merry's confusion grew.

Before Merry had a chance to dwell on her thoughts of the intimacies of marriage, Mrs. Barrow scratched at the door. She reminded Merry that they must plan the wedding supper. After deciding on a clear soup to begin, lobster patties as the fish, capon, and beef removes, Merry suggested that her housekeeper complete the menu and present it later for approval. As the woman left the room, Merry heard her talking to herself, "A vegetable, perhaps green peas. Mr. Giles seems to like them. And Cook still has a fruitcake to ice. At least Miss Merry will have a traditional wedding cake." With Mrs. Barrow in charge, Merry knew she would have no problems with the supper.

Merry walked down the stairs after the housekeeper. Before she entered the library, she stopped Mrs. Barrow. "Please send a luncheon tray to the library. There are still some letters I must finish." Noticing the frown on the housekeeper's face, Merry said, "I promise I will try to rest before Mr. Lindsey returns for dinner."

Merry hoped that concentrating on business would keep her from worrying about the marriage. Pausing only briefly for tea and a slice of chicken, she began work on the correspondence that had been sent to the house regularly since her grandfather had become ill. As she tried to plan the letters, she wondered about Giles. What kind of marriage would they have? That was what they needed to discuss instead of those endless lists of relatives and hostesses. Remembering the impish look in Giles's eyes, Merry had second thoughts. He might tell her more than she wanted to know.

She checked the chart of arrivals and departures for the ships the company owned. How proud she had been when her grandfather had incorporated her plan of keeping track of ships and merchandise into the office. The question of how she and Giles would work together made her pause. Her forte was planning and organizing, and now she was expected to introduce someone to society. "How will I ever manage the Season?" she whispered. In Bath it had been her aunt who had arranged their days and the parties.

Dinner that evening was almost a repeat of the one the previous day. Giles, after asking her if everything had gone well that day, began listing what still had to be done for the wedding. "What flowers do you prefer for your nosegay?" he asked. As he glanced at her, he caught her look of surprise. What a wonderful impression I must have made if she is surprised that I would send her flowers for the wedding, he thought to himself. Giles wanted a loving, willing wife, but he knew that he would have to proceed carefully if he wanted to win her. He smiled, a smile that was famous for winning harder hearts than Merry's.

Her breath caught for a moment, and she felt a stirring in her breast. She stammered, "I, I'm not . . ."

"I need to arrange for them first thing in the morning. Do you prefer violets, roses, or something else?" Once again he flashed a smile at her. He wondered if he would ever get her to look at him directly when they were discussing anything other than business.

In a voice that was almost too soft to be heard, she said, "I'm wearing a wreath of cream roses in my hair. I will show you the bushes in the conservatory after dinner."

"Alex has said that he will be happy to second me at the altar tomorrow. He was rather curious and told me to tell you that you might want to wait until you meet him before you make any final commitment." Giles laughed. He wondered if Alex would keep Lady Farrell to himself, but a person could never be certain about Alex. How he wished he could see Denise's face when she read the announcement. He wondered who her next victim would be. Giles asked, "Will your friend Arabella and her husband be here?"

"Her acceptance arrived so quickly that I expected to see her shortly thereafter. Giles, you should know that Arabella loves asking questions. She said they would arrive before noon, and she will deluge me with questions. I wish Mr. and Mrs. Pettigrew were coming before half past two, but I'm not certain their presence would silence her." For a moment the commonplace remarks she was exchanging with Giles seemed familiar, even natural. Then she thought of the long years of such discussions before her and seemed to freeze before his eyes.

Sensing her change in mood, Giles tried to reestablish the easy discussion of a few minutes before. He asked, "When do you expect 'The Swan' to dock? Your grandfather believed that Captain Stone—his first voyage as captain, isn't it?—had some interesting cargo on board." As she answered, she looked straight into Giles's eyes. Her eyes seemed free of sadness and fear at that moment. The meal progressed swiftly with neither remembering much of what was served but able to describe in detail the expressions that had crossed the other's face. At its conclusion, Giles refused his port to accompany her to the salon.

When Barrow entered to remove the tea tray, both Merry and Giles were surprised to hear the clock chime twelve. When the butler was gone, Giles rose, that impish look in his eyes again. "I can see that evenings with you will never be dull, my dear. I will see you at the church at three tomorrow." Grasping the hand she held out to him, Giles pulled her to her feet and into his arms. Before she had time to resist, he bent and kissed her lingeringly. Then, pressing a kiss into her palm, he whispered, "Until tomorrow." The underlying sensuality in her kiss had surprised him. Perhaps the marriage would be more enjoyable than he had been led to believe.

Her response to Giles had startled Merry. For some time after he left, she stood bemused, wondering at the thrills that had run down her spine. Climbing the stairs to her room, Merry kept her hand lightly clenched. Only when Pilgrim asked her to open her hand so that she could remove a sleeve did she realize what she had been doing. Startled, she did as her maid asked only to be stirred once again as the fabric stroked the spot Giles had caressed.

As on the evening before, sleep was a long time coming. For the first time Merry had begun to realize the feelings of which she was capable. The next day she would be married to Giles. Would they be as lucky as Arabella and Brandon, or would their marriage resemble her parents'?

As hard as she had tried, even the last eight years could not erase the years of bitterness and quarrels of her parents' marriage. Robert and Lady Jayne Sommerby had married for love. She had given up the society she loved to marry the merchant of her dreams. But

Robert's possessive nature and his overwhelming love for business caused Jayne to regret her sacrifice. Eventually their marriage had disintegrated into a series of loud quarrels and love affairs with anyone available.

One of Merry's earliest memories was one of her parents' quarrels. She had gone into her mother's sitting room. She had forgotten why she had gone there, but she never forgot the scene she witnessed.

Her father's angry voice shouted, "How dare you ignore the wife of our largest client to dance with that wastrel! And you encouraging him. Flirting with him. The only thing Lord Tanner has on his mind is how soon he can bed you! Or has he already done so?"

In spite of the quietness of her mother's voice, Merry heard both her words and her tears. "I danced only one country dance with Lord Tanner. Do you want me to ignore my old friends? Mrs. Chomby had already gone to the card room to find a game of whist. Was I to ignore my other guests to accompany her? Robert, you didn't dance with me all evening. Was I to refuse all invitations simply in the hopes that you would?"

"If things work out as Father and I have planned, we will be expanding our trade in Italy. Mr. Chomby is one of the largest fabric merchants in England. His business alone will ensure our success." Her father's voice, which had begun to soften, took on a harsher note. "Besides, I told you that Lord Tanner was no longer welcome in my home. How dare you disobey me!" He crossed to the open door and entered the sitting room.

Merry shut her eyes, hoping he would think she was asleep. "Jayne, what is Miranda doing here? Can't you hire someone competent to care for her?" Gathering Merry into his arms, Robert returned her to her trembling nursemaid. That night, Miranda had her first nightmare.

As the years had passed, her nursemaids and governesses had tried to protect her from the explosive arguments that had raged between husband and wife. It had been worse when they were traveling by ship. Frequently her cabin had been beside her mother's. Through the thin walls she heard the thunderous accusations and the hysterical replies.

By the time she was twelve, she had lived in all the major trading ports of Europe. No matter where they lived, the family ritual was always the same. Three times a week at tea time she was called into her parents' presence. The scenes were always similar; the only difference was whether or not there were guests. Her father's commands to "Stand up straight," or "Speak up, girl," or her mother's comments that "Miranda certainly does not take after my side of the family—we're all beauties," only made her more insecure. At first she had tried to show her affection by running to them to give them a hug. These attempts usually ended with "Don't bother me now, I'm busy," from her father and "Don't muss my dress—I simply don't know how any daughter of mine could have so little beauty or grace," from her mother. More and more she retreated into herself.

As Merry grew older, her appearances at tea were fewer and fewer. Most of the time Robert forgot he had a daughter, and her mother did not care to be reminded of how old Merry was. In India, Merry had finally found an interest. She and her ayah had wandered through the marketplace almost at will. There she saw the excitement of magic and learned the harshness of poverty. Because her mother had not bothered to arrange a governess for her, her grandfather had requested one of the clerks in the company, a son of an old friend, to tutor her. It was then that she first became interested in the business. The numbers and the calculations fascinated her. When her mother discovered how she had been spending her time, a new governess appeared. But Merry refused to stay away from the offices. She learned French and Italian, music and needlework, but she also knew what goods to trade, where to get them, and how much profit she could make.

After her parents had died of the plague, Merry had been sent to her grandfather. Although she had loved him dearly, it had been almost a year before Merry had been able to talk freely even about the most trivial items. She remembered how hard he had worked to understand her. Perhaps her gift for mathematics and organization had given them their chance to know one another.

By the time she was nineteen, her mother's sister, Mathilda, was insisting that she be presented at Court. Only Grandfather had understood why she refused. The only concession he had insisted upon was that she visit her aunt in Bath for the last few summers. He had wanted her to have some idea of how to behave in society. Although she had never been a great success, being both too short and too plump to be considered a beauty, she had never been an antidote either. She had made some acquaintances and one close friend, Arabella. "Arabella will be here tomorrow," she murmured as she drifted off to sleep.

From the moment Pilgrim brought her a breakfast tray, Merry was caught up in the preparations for the day. Mrs. Barrow presented the final menu for her inspection. It was going to be a much more elaborate supper than she had thought necessary. Yet she did not want to disappoint the servants by altering it. If they wanted a part in the wedding, they should have it.

No sooner had Pilgrim washed her hair and dressed her in a morning sacque than Madame Camille was ushered in. For almost an hour Merry stood rather impatiently while the modiste made minute changes in the drape of the skirt or the fall of the lace and chattered both in French and in English. Finally satisfied, Madame Camille permitted Pilgrim to remove the gown. "The dressing gown and nightrobe are also here. The other dresses will be finished tomorrow. Send for me later and we will plan the rest of the wardrobe. And please accept my best wishes."

As the dressmaker swept out, Merry sank to the chaise, hoping for a chance to have a cup of tea. No sooner had she picked up her cup, than Barrow announced, "Lord and Lady Montrose have arrived. I have shown them to the small salon."

As Merry entered the cream and rose room, Arabella, her blond curls bouncing, ran to embrace her exclaiming, "Why haven't you mentioned Giles before? When did you decide to marry? Does your Aunt Mathilda know? How did you meet him?"

"Slow down, Arabella," Brandon said, laughing. "Merry will never be able to answer unless you stop talking."

Smiling at the quiet, blond man who was her friend's husband, Merry related the story she and Giles had planned. "Giles is a partner in the family business. Before Grandfather became ill, we had planned to announce our engagement and marry in the summer. As Grandfather realized he was dying, he made us promise to marry as soon as possible. He even arranged for the special license, but by the time it arrived, he had slipped away. Giles and I decided to respect his wishes and marry immediately. Do you think society will frown on us?"

"Nonsense, my dear," said Arabella. "Once people realize that your grandfather arranged it, everyone will accept the marriage. I suppose that I must wait until the ceremony to meet your groom. What are you wearing? Do let me see it."

Before Merry could answer, Brandon spoke, "If you will excuse me, my dears, I will take this opportunity to conduct some business of my own." With his wife's reminder not to be late for the wedding, he slipped away, hoping to wile away the time with his agent.

As soon as Brandon had disappeared, Arabella exclaimed, "Now tell me everything about Giles. Is he handsome? When did you meet? How long have you been engaged? Where are you going to live?"

"Come, let me show you my dress. We'll have Barrow bring us a luncheon tray in my sitting room.

Then I'll try to answer your questions." Merry knew
she would have to be careful so that she and Giles
would relate the same facts.

Trying to answer Arabella's queries without revealing the truth occupied most of Merry's time. With the
help of Pilgrim and with Arabella's distracting super-
vision, Merry finally was almost ready for the ceremony. Although she knew she would never be beautiful,
the soft lines of the dress that emphasized her bust
rather than her hips seemed to make her look taller,
less rounded. As Pilgrim put the last pin in place to
hold the wreath of roses in her curls, someone scratched
on the door.

"With Mr. Giles's compliments," stated the butler
proudly, handing Merry a lovely nosegay of creamy
roses and ivy. As she bent her head to breathe in their
scent, he cleared his throat. Looking up she saw that
he had extended a flat white velvet box. Her fingers
shook slightly as she opened the box, revealing a lovely
pearl necklace and matching earrings.

"Just the thing and very lovely," said Arabella. "They
will show to advantage with that gown. Let me help
you with them."

The pearls were lovely, but to Merry they seemed
almost a burden, a reminder that Giles would have
the right to order her life after today. Thinking of
Giles sent a shiver down Merry's spine. All day she
had caught herself remembering that kiss. Soon that
would be his right, too.

The chill and fog of the morning had burned away
by the time the bride's party arrived at the church.
Arabella kissed Merry on the cheek and slipped away
to join Brandon, who escorted her to their seats in the
first pew beside Mrs. Pettigrew. The few seconds'
wait allowed Merry to become accustomed to the quietness of the familiar church. The golden glow of
massed candles surrounded by greenery made the altar a focal point of color against the gray stone walls.
Merry smiled tremulously as Pilgrim patted one last
curl into place. The maid then slipped quietly to her

place beside the Barrows. Although there were fewer than a dozen people in the large church, it did not seem empty, but filled with a deep peace.

Mr. Pettigrew settled Merry's shaking hand on his arm, patted her encouragingly, and led her slowly to the altar where Giles, the minister, and a slender, brown-haired man waited. The opening question of the ceremony finished, the lawyer's voice trembled slightly as he answered, "As her grandfather's representative, I do." He lifted Merry's hand and placed it carefully in Giles's waiting one.

From the moment Giles took her hand and moved close to her side, Merry remembered only snatches of the ceremony. Wondering who had arranged the greenery, she heard herself say, ". . . for richer, for poorer . . ." Except for one quick glance at Giles as she neared the altar, Merry kept her eyes on the minister, whose white vestments seemed to glow golden in the candlelight. Then she heard Giles say, ". . . with my body I thee worship." The words startled her, and she looked up into Giles's clear, kind eyes.

He too had had a sense of unreality as he had watched Merry enter on the arm of Mr. Pettigrew. As they came closer, Giles took a deep breath and wondered why he had not noticed the translucent quality of Merry's skin before. It almost glowed. He repeated his vows clearly, firmly. As he listened to Merry's promises, he wondered if she knew what marriage to him would mean. As she looked up into his eyes, he made a silent promise that he would try to keep them as clear as they were at that moment, free of sadness and fear. After the benediction, he placed a deep, gentle kiss upon her lips.

Surrounded by well-wishers, Merry and Giles signed the register in the vestry. Giles noticed that Merry's hand was not as steady as usual, and when she had finished signing, he captured it in his own. As they entered their carriage, he saw once again the fear and doubt drift across her face. In the few minutes from the church to the Sommerby house, he tried to ease her fears, speaking of commonplace things.

Barrow met the couple at the door. "On behalf of the staff, we offer you our best wishes. There is champagne in the large salon, and supper will be served shortly."

The rest of the afternoon became a blur for Merry. She knew she had responded when she was addressed, but could only hope that what she had said had made sense.

At one point Arabella gushed, "My goodness, Merry! How could you keep quiet about such a handsome man? Why haven't I met him before? If I weren't so fond of Brandon, I'd make him one of my flirts. When you return from London, you must visit us immediately. We will not take part in the Season this year because of family obligations." Here she fluttered her eyelashes and blushed, reminding Merry of the news Arabella had given her earlier. She and Brandon were expecting their first child in August.

Babies, Merry thought. Giles and I may have babies. The idea caused her to gasp. Thinking that the last few days might have been too much for her, Giles led her to a sofa. There his friend Alex Ramsey joined them. "I wish you and Giles a long, happy marriage," he said. In spite of his words, Merry had the feeling that he had doubts the wish would come true.

"Supper is served," announced the butler. With Merry on his arm, Giles led the way, seating her beside him instead of in her usual place at the foot of the table. All of Merry's pride in her home was reflected in the gleaming plate and the sparkling china and crystal that graced the table. The low silver vases in the center of the table filled with the same creamy roses and ivy as in her nosegay gave off a sweet scent that rivalled the mouth-watering aromas of the meal. In a home that was known for its good food, the kitchen staff had surpassed all previous efforts. From the first course, a light clear soup, the success of the meal was assured. Although Giles and Brandon especially seemed to enjoy the lobster patties garnished with salsify and all succeeding removes, Merry did little more than taste hers. The capons stuffed with oyster dressing, the glazed parsnips, and the green peas she pushed from one side of the plate to the other. Even the beef in pastry served with spinach, usually a favorite of hers, she largely ignored. She ate only a few bites so that the chef and the housekeeper would not be hurt. With each course, new toasts were made. As the champagne continued to flow, these grew more and more ribald. Finally the wedding cake had been cut and everyone had finished. Merry signalled the women to leave the men to their port and cigars.

Almost before the women were settled, the men joined them. Soon everyone began to leave. Both Lord and Lady Montrose and Lord Ramsey had some way to travel. Promising Arabella that she would write soon, Merry said good-bye. Mr. Pettigrew's words as he left brought tears. He said, "How proud your grandfather would be of you. I know this is exactly what he wanted for you." How she longed for her grandfather's comforting presence.

—3—

The door closed behind Barrow and their guests and Merry was alone with her husband, a moment she had been dreading. As if aware of her distress, Giles suggested, "Why don't you rest for a while, and then we'll talk. I'll have Barrow arrange for a light meal to be served in our sitting room later."

"Our sitting room? What do you mean?"

"Today while you were preparing for the wedding, my valet and your maid moved our things into the master suite. I believe Pilgrim moved your remaining belongings during the supper tonight." Giles smiled brilliantly. "You know we agreed that everyone, especially the servants, must believe that our marriage is a normal one. If not, your cousin will never accept it." Giles, grasping her arm firmly, led her out of the room and up the stairs.

Merry, emotionally exhausted from the long weeks of her grandfather's illness and the pressures of the last few days, allowed him to escort her to their new suite without protesting. She knew she would have to come to terms with him, but at the moment she was too tired to care. At least, she thought, they were not using her grandfather's rooms. When she had redecorated last year, her grandfather had insisted that these rooms become the principal guest suite. Now the clear blues and soft golds welcomed her into a quiet, fresh world.

Seeing the pallor of her skin and realizing the strain

32

she was under, Giles again urged her to rest. Calling
her waiting maid, he said, "Take your mistress into
her room and see that she rests. We will have a light
meal in the sitting room later. She will need only a
dressing gown for that. Make her comfortable."

Resenting his organization of her life, Merry opened
her mouth, but Giles whispered in a voice just loud
enough for Pilgrim to hear, "Please rest, my dear. I
want our first night together to be perfect."

Blushing and wondering if he meant what he had
said, Merry quietly followed Pilgrim into her new
bedroom. In this room she had chosen to emphasize
the clear robin's egg blue and to use gold for accents.
She had draped the bed with blue muslin accented by
gold velvet, hoping to create an airy effect. The muslin was repeated at the windows under the rich gold
velvet drapes that were looped back to allow in the
late afternoon sun. Sinking onto the blue and gold
striped satin chaise, she allowed Pilgrim to remove
the flowers from her hair and the pearls from her
neck and ears.

"Come, Mrs. Merry, let me unfasten your dress and
slip you into this nightrobe and dressing gown. There
will be plenty of time to rest." Pilgrim coaxed Merry
toward the bed, helping her to climb the steps after
she had removed the coverlet. Settling her mistress,
she crossed to close the gold velvet drapes.

Merry lay quietly, but her mind was in turmoil. In
spite of her anxieties, she slowly drifted off to sleep.
At first her sleep was peaceful. Suddenly, though, she
was plunged into a nightmare, one that had occurred
often. It was late afternoon, and she was in the garden
in India. The French windows to the small salon were
open to allow the light breeze to drift through. Her
mother was entertaining a man, an officer in one of
the British regiments stationed nearby. She had no
idea that her daughter was where she could see and
hear whatever went on in the room.

As the couple sank to the sofa, arms wrapped tightly
around one another, burning lips pressed tightly

together, Merry stood transfixed. The officer, loosening her mother's lace fichu, began to caress her breasts. The door to the hall flew open. Robert Sommerby stood there, a riding crop in his hands. Striding into the room, he began striking the man, leaving welts on his face and hands.

Although the man had quickly escaped, running out through the open windows, her mother had not. Merry could still hear the blows. But her mother had not uttered a sound, had simply stood, glaring at her husband, refusing to allow him to see her pain. When Jayne Sommerby did speak, her voice was as cold as the wind crossing a glacier. Through clenched teeth she said, "If you ever strike me again, I will kill you." Listening to her, Merry had known that she spoke the truth. "Go back to your mistress and abuse her if you like. If you touch me again, I'll leave India on the next ship and take Miranda with me." She crossed to the bellpull.

"Before you call in the servants, my dear, remember this. I'll leave you alone. But if I can't have you, no one will. No, I won't kill you. But there are so many ways a man can die accidentally here. When word gets around that when a man makes love to you, he dies, how many lovers will you have?" Robert had laughed. The door slammed behind him. As soon as his footsteps had died away, her mother had broken into deep, body-wrenching sobs as if she had kept them in by force of will alone. Merry never remembered returning to the schoolroom. She had been crying so hard when her ayah found her that it was hours before she was calm.

"Merry, Merry! Wake up." Giles was shaking her. "What's wrong?" he asked, wrapping his arms around her. Waking up, she found herself held close against him, much as she had been held by her ayah. She drew back, and he loosened his arms.

"It was only a bad dream. I'll—I'll be fine now," she said, still sobbing slightly.

Picking her up, Giles carried her into the sitting

room. "Here, Barrow has just brought some meat, cakes, and wine. While we share them, you can tell me about the dream." He put her on the sofa and sat close beside her. Filling her plate, Giles urged, "Tell me the dream. It helps to talk about it." When she refused, he sighed and handed her a glass of champagne. He knew she needed a chance to compose herself and started to tell her of his travels. "When I was twenty, I decided that I had had enough of school and wanted to see the world. My mother's father suggested that I speak to your grandfather. That conversation resulted in my first trip to the West Indies. . . ."

As she listened to the deep, quiet tones of his voice rather than his words, Merry grew calmer. The stiffness that had been present was gone, and she sank back onto the pillows Giles had placed behind her. Suddenly she realized that her plate was empty. She had eaten every morsel Giles had given her.

". . . wanting a little fun, I decided to see if the rumors that the captain was afraid of snakes were really true. I arranged for one of the dock workers to find a harmless grass snake. While the captain was arranging for the last of the supplies and was out of his cabin, I sneaked in and hid the snake—it was about five inches long—in the desk drawer with his pens and paper. I waited in my cabin, which was next to his, for him to return. I heard him enter and open the drawer. After a while I grew worried because I could hear no other movements. I quietly opened his door and crept in. Before I knew what was happening, I had been grabbed by the collar and a wiggling creature dropped down the back of my neck! Fortunately for me the captain also enjoyed practical jokes," Giles concluded.

Laughing for the first time in several days, Merry captivated him with her happy sound. "How fast did you remove that snake? And how much wine did it take to forget it?" she gasped when she could control her laughter.

"Ah, Mrs. Lindsey has once again returned to her

usual plane of existence," he said. "I wondered if I were going to have to start making up my adventures. Someday I'll tell you the ones about being the only man allowed in a harem in Tangiers."

A blush spread from her neck to her face although she tried to control it. Before Merry could speak, Giles continued, "Seriously now, we must discuss our plans for the next few weeks. We must present a united front. Hugo Darryl will arrive soon. We must make definite plans for Charlotte's presentation. And with Napoleon's annexations on the continent, we must plan for some changes in the business."

"Grandfather had already begun making plans before his illness. Perhaps you've seen them?" At Giles's dissent, she explained. "Since his illness I've been working in the library. Would you like to go down now and see what has been done?"

"That can wait until tomorrow. Tonight, let us put our domestic affairs in order. In the next few days we can expect to see Hugo. Whatever we tell him, we must be absolutely certain he will hear the same story from us, from Mr. Pettigrew, and from the servants. Tomorrow we will put all the legal aspects in order. Mr. Pettigrew will ensure your cousin has no legal claims on you. From what I've heard of Hugo, he has an empty cockloft, but your grandfather said you were afraid of him. Why?"

Hesitating, as if afraid that putting her fears into words would make them more real, Merry shuddered and then breathed deeply. "For years Hugo had no interest in the business, preferring to take his share of the profits to further his gambling. Since my father's death he has seen himself as the heir, and he's been living on his expectations. About two years ago his debts grew so large that several merchants from London approached Grandfather. Grandfather called Hugo to Bristol. He paid all his debts but told Hugo that would be the only time he would bail him out of the River Tick.

"Hugo even had the audacity to ask my grandfather

father's allowance would go to him since he was the
new heir. Grandfather made it clear that the money
my father had received had been for his work, and if
Hugo wanted to work, he too could earn a salary.
Naturally Hugo refused." Once again the anger she
had felt when she had seen the letters for the first
time threatened to engulf her.

"Mr. Sommerby knew exactly the right approach to
take with that pretentious, social-climbing man-mil-
ner," said Giles.

"I don't know what else went on between them. But
I never saw any more letters from Hugo asking for
money. After he had the confrontation with Grandfather two years ago, I don't think he has visited Bristol
again," Merry said.

"Never? Then why did your grandfather fear for
your safety? He told me that Hugo was physically
dangerous." Giles was confused, thinking for a moment that the old man had trapped him.

"Perhaps *physically* was the wrong word. I could
have survived that, but mentally? No, I would have
died first!" Even her voice trembled.

Once again Giles saw the fear in her eyes. He said,
"Come, come. There is no need to disturb yourself
tonight. This also can wait until you feel more like
talking about it."

"No, you need to know the facts. Besides, I expect
Aunt Mathilda will arrive soon. And she is part of the
problem." Once again Merry had her emotions under
a tight rein; once again her logical mind took control.

"The aunt you visited in Bath? Isn't she your
mother's sister?"

Merry, nodding, continued, "After I had been in
England for a time, my aunt decided that I needed to
be presented to the *ton*. She felt my mother's social
connections would erase the odor of the shop. Even
though I refused a Season in London, my grandfather
finally insisted that I spend summers in Bath with
her. He thought I needed some younger friends, a
little town bronze. Therefore I went.

"Even though my aunt is the kindest person imagi[n]able, she has had one goal since the first day I set fo[ot] in Bath—my marriage."

"We solved that problem for her today," Giles sai[d] trying to relieve Merry's tension.

Merry frowned at him as she continued. "I enjoye[d] my visits in Bath at first. The first summer I wa[s] there I met Arabella, and despite the differences i[n] our temperaments and stations, we have become fa[st] friends. Even when she married Brandon, nothin[g] changed. The only difference is that now she live[s] on an estate outside the city instead of across th[e] square.

"We would accompany our chaperones to the Pum[p] Room, to the shops, to the library. In the afternoon[s] we drove in the countryside or took tea with friend[s.] Arabella knew everyone, and we went everywher[e] together. In the evenings the musicals and assembli[es] were delightful. Because Arabella was such a flirt, [I] never lacked partners. By dancing with me a gentle[-] man might meet my friend," laughed Merry. "T[o] Aunt Mathilda's chagrin, however, although I wen[t] along with all her other plans, I refused all her candi[-] dates for my hand. She had begun to grow desperate. [I] was already on the shelf.

"Two summers ago everything changed. Shortly af[-] ter Brandon and Arabella were married that summer Hugo and his wife and daughters arrived. He had hi[s] own candidate for my hand. After arranging an intro[-] duction to my aunt at the Pump Room, he set out t[o] charm her, and he can be very charming." She paused experiencing again the nausea she had felt when sh[e] had seen Hugo approaching that morning. At tha[t] time, though, she had not realized what a threat h[e] could be. "You understand about the will?" she asked

"Yes, in general. But what part do you play i[n] Hugo's plans?"

"The goal of Hugo's life since my father's death has been to gain and spend as much money as he could The company was to be his private cent-percenter. [He]

was the way he could have it all. If I married and had
a son before Grandfather died, that child could inherit everything. And Grandfather could appoint the
executor—definitely not Hugo.

"Grandfather knew of my plans to stay single, but
Hugo didn't. I don't know whether he learned that
Grandfather was trying to break the will or whether
he simply wished to solidify his own position. That
summer Hugo introduced his own candidate for my
hand, his younger brother Charles. I suppose if Hugo
had not already been married himself, he would have
proposed.

"Aunt Mathilda was elated. Charles is a handsome
man of medium build. Aunt Mathilda, who likes dark
men, liked his shock of dark brown hair, but all I
could see was the vacant look on his face. Oh, Hugo
was so clever. We only saw Charles in company, at
soirées, at musical evenings, or at the Pump Room.
He never said much but smiled often. In fact, when
he did begin to speak, his companion, a Mr. Grey,
would often interrupt."

Merry shivered as if remembering the pressure she
had felt. She continued, "I returned to Bristol early
that year after Hugo approached me as his brother's
spokesman. I refused his offer. Unlike my other
refusals, Aunt Mathilda absolutely would not consider my answer final. Whenever she gets an idea in
her head, she worries people until they give in and
accomplish it. Therefore I left. I felt that by the next
summer she would have forgotten Charles and forgiven me. How little did I know!"

Her aunt, a notoriously poor letter writer, had bom-
barded her with letters that winter. Even when
Mathilda had come to Bath for Christmas, she had
tried to convince Merry to accept Charles's suit.
Somehow, Hugo had been accepted by her aunt's set
and kept pleading with her to get Merry to change her
mind. Finally she had been forced to tell her grandfather. He tried to discover Hugo's motives. As far as
his sources knew, Charles was a pleasant young man,

very quiet and not very social, who spent most of hi
time in the country. He always seemed to be in th
company of Mr. Thomas Grey, a medical student. O
the surface it appeared that Hugo was simply tryin
to help his brother find a wife.

Giles, who had been waiting for her to finish th
story, grew worried as he saw her face. Usually quie
and peaceful, it was twisted by anger. He knew if sh
looked into his eyes he would see fear in hers. "Merry
I need to know everything. Go on."

Merry continued in a voice that seemed almos
lifeless. "After Aunt Mathilda's Christmas visit
Grandfather investigated but could find out little abou
Charles. Also, Aunt Mathilda seemed to have forgot
ten about the match. I thought she was resigned to m
decision or was thinking about someone else to pre
sent to me." Merry drew a shuddering breath before
she could go on.

"During the peace last year, Grandfather and I vis
ited Paris." Merry's voice was happy as she though
of the pleasure she and her grandfather had shared.

Giles smiled. "Mr. Sommerby told me how you res
cued Madame Camille and brought her home with
you. May I also expect you to bring home strays?"

Merry exploded indignantly, "I will have you know
that Madame Camille has proved a very wise invest
ment. She has already repaid what money it took to
establish her dressmaking business. And my share in
the business is not ha'pence."

"My dear, I did not mean to upset you." Giles
realized he would need to remember what a fiery
little thing she could be. He could envision some lively
arguments in the years ahead. "I can see that I must
watch my words until you become familiar with my
teasing ways. Continue, please."

Slightly ashamed of the way she had reacted, Merry
smiled her apology. "Because I was helping Madame
Camille set up her shop and working with Grandfa
ther on plans to circumvent Napoleon's encroachment
on our suppliers, I was late going to Bath."

"Isn't it strange. I left the West Indies later than usual last year. Otherwise, my dear, we might have met then." Giles's tone was ironic. "Why didn't you refuse to visit Bath?"

"Arabella and Brandon were going to be there. Because of their wedding journey and the Season, I had not seen them for a year. We had corresponded, but I missed the talks we had. Also, Aunt Mathilda convinced me that I had nothing to fear," Merry said.

"But Aunt Mathilda and Hugo had not given up. As soon as I arrived, Charles appeared for morning calls, for afternoon tea. On any occasion we were together, Aunt Mathilda reminded me that I was not growing any younger, that Charles might be my last chance, that all she wanted was for me to be happy. Hugo began visiting regularly, telling me that I was breaking his brother's heart.

"Finally, Arabella noticed what was happening. When she told Brandon, he was horrified." Merry put a hand over her mouth to hide its trembling. Shaking badly, she went on, "Brandon was familiar with the Darryls. One of his properties, the one where his mother lives, is in Yorkshire near Hugo's home."

At this point Merry was shaking so badly that Giles poured her a glass of wine. Her hands were trembling so she could not hold the glass without spilling it. Giles reached out and gathered her close to him, holding the glass to her lips. He soothed her gently. "He can't hurt you now. But I must know why you are so frightened." Feeling as though he were committing an outrage, he forced her to go on.

Still clasped tightly in Giles's arms, Merry said, "Charles Darryl was born years after his brother Hugo. In fact, most people thought Hugo to be Charles's uncle. No one knows what happened, but Charles grew into a man in everything but his mind. It was a fact that had been carefully hidden. Brandon had learned of it only when a maid Charles assaulted sought shelter with Brandon's mother. She died in childbirth a few months later along with the child.

After that, Hugo was appointed Charles's guardian and Thomas Grey became his constant companion. And Hugo wanted me to marry him," she sobbed.

"You're safe, Merry," Giles whispered as he held her. "I'll never let him come near you again. This afternoon you married me. I will keep you safe." Horrified at what he had heard, Giles picked her up and walked toward her bedroom. The thought of the torture that Hugo had been willing to inflict on his own cousin made the bile rise in his throat. Merry with her sharp mind condemned to life with an idiot. The idea was monstrous.

The bed had been straightened and the covers turned back. As she still sobbed, Merry was not aware that it was Giles who took off her dressing gown and tucked her into bed. In fact, in her distress she was not even aware that he had climbed into bed with her. All she wanted was to be held close and reassured that she was safe. She had been so afraid. Ever since her grandfather's death, she had been shaking with fear.

Her tears slackening, Merry snuggled her head into Giles's shoulder. Suddenly realizing that the object in which she had her face buried was hard, not like the down pillow she was used to, she jerked backward. But Giles's arms kept her close beside him, the warmth of his body radiating against her. She blushed and closed her eyes as she realized that she was alone in bed with this man and there were only two layers of clothing between them.

Before she could speak, Giles explained, "Merry, you became my wife today. The servants expect us to share a bed. Can you imagine what Hugo Darryl would do if he thought our marriage was not real?" The fear was back in her eyes. She nodded her agreement.

Giles said, "This must be a real marriage. Do you understand what I mean, Merry?"

Merry had been in India when her menses had begun. Although Jayne Sommerby had never bothered to interest herself in her daughter as she grew older, Merry's ayah had helped her understand what was happening. And although the woman had been protective of her charge, she had made certain Merry understood the role of sex in marriage. Several times she and her ayah had gone to see some temple carvings in a small out-of-the-way temple. Although Merry had been frightened at first and had not understood what they showed, her ayah had explained. For the first time, Merry had understood the demands of marriage, the idea of lovers. Unknown to her parents, she had also witnessed the birth of a child. It was shortly before the plague struck. Although her ayah had not allowed her to help in the delivery, Merry still remembered the wonder she had felt.

With Merry's whispered "yes" in his ears, Giles explained, "From what you say of Darryl, he would not be above forcing you to undergo a medical examination to determine if the marriage could be annulled." Merry gasped as she realized what he was saying, drawing away from him, her face paling to match the sheet. For a moment she thought she would never be able to speak again. Before she could say anything, Giles said, softly, reassuringly, "But it does not have to be tonight. Let me simply hold you, comfort you. The rest can come later."

Long moments seemed to drag by as he waited for her reply. When her whispered agreement came, it was so soft he almost missed it. He breathed a sigh of relief, his arms once more closing about her and bringing her close to his side. As she resolutely kept her eyes closed, he whispered, "Won't you look at me, my dear? I promise I will be gentle."

Merry's eyes opened. His face was close above hers, and his clear blue eyes reassured her. He bent his head and kissed her softly. As he lifted his head, her lips seemed to cling to his. His kiss this time was deeper, his tongue lightly touching her lips, trying to find an opening. When she drew back, startled, he settled her closely beside him. "Don't be afraid of me. I only want to touch you. Relax." Cautioning himself to patience, he held her soft rounded body in his arms until she seemed to lose her tension.

Then he began stroking her hair with one hand, the hand that kept her close to his side. Turning on his side toward her, he dropped light kisses on her forehead and eyelids. Gently, he allowed his free hand to wander to her shoulder, touching lightly, stroking. Smiling to himself as he realized she was not resisting him, he let his hand drift from her shoulder to her arm and to her breast. As she tensed against him once more, he soothed, "I can't resist touching you, Merry. Your breasts are so full, so lovely."

Merry tried to pull away, but Giles would not let her. He continued to hold her as his hand released the bow that held her nightrobe on her shoulders. She was frightened and yet excited at the same time. She kept her eyes closed tightly as if afraid to see what was happening. Her body seemed to tingle all over.

As he released the ribbon, Giles drew the fabric away from her breasts. His hands ached to hold the soft white flesh, and his mouth thirsted to taste the pink tips hardening in the cool air. Softly, as though his touch might frighten her, his hand delicately teased first one breast and then the other. Growing bolder as she permitted these caresses, he bent his head to kiss her throat where he could see the pulse beating. His kisses dropped lower until he was kissing one breast, teasing the nipple with his tongue. Suddenly he was aware of her hand trying to push him away, her voice saying, "No, no."

He drew back, releasing her slightly. She moved frantically trying to get away. "Merry, look at me," he commanded. "No, open your eyes. Look at me." Merry's eyes opened. "Tonight, all I want to do is touch you. I won't hurt you. Did you feel any pain?" As she shook her head, he retied the bow on her nightrobe, wondering if he would have the patience to wait until she was ready. As soon as she was covered again, he whispered in her ear, "You are very lovely. I've always appreciated beautiful, full breasts." When she blushed, he told her, "Now go to sleep. I promise that I will only hold you."

As she drifted off to sleep, Merry could feel his soft breath on her hair and his hand lightly stroking her hip. But it was a long time before Giles slept that evening.

—4—

The soft morning light crept under the gold drapes, creating variations in the blue of the room. When Merry opened her eyes, for a moment she was confused. Instead of the crispy white draperies she was used to, she saw blue ones. As she started to sit up, an arm snaked around her, holding her in place.

"Good morning, Mrs. Lindsey," said Giles. Looking at her startled hazel eyes and heaving breasts, he wondered how he had gotten any sleep the night before. He put his hands beside her head, holding it still, and bent to kiss her. At first his kiss was soft and tentative, but when she did not pull away, it deepened. Taking a breath, he said, "I think I'm going to enjoy waking up with you." As if to track the path of her blush, his lips drifted across her cheeks and down her throat. "Aren't you going to give me a good morning kiss?"

Merry's blush deepened. Her heart raced. He had said he would not make love to her last night, but what about this morning? Then she realized that he had already been up. His dark hair was damp as if he had dunked his face into the wash bowl. He was dressed in an elegant wine silk dressing gown trimmed in black velvet.

"Well, slugabed, is this how you plan to spend the morning?" Giles laughed. "If so . . ."

Merry sat up quickly, looking frantically for the dressing gown she had worn the night before. "Here,

my dear, is this what you are looking for?" Giles held
the garment just out of reach.

Merry reached for it, aware as she did so that his
eyes were fixed on her heaving bosom. She hastily
pulled it around her shoulders, buttoning it up as far
as she could. Moving to the edge of the high bed, she
cautiously stuck one foot out. Before she could put a
single toe on the steps, Giles grabbed her waist and
swung her to the floor. "Pilgrim is waiting in your
dressing room," he said in her ear as he gently nipped
the lobe.

Dashing quickly from the room, Merry wondered at
her own reactions. Whenever Giles touched her, she
seemed to grow limp and boneless. A tingling sensation ran along her spine; an ache filled her loins. She
shook her head, as if by doing so she could rid herself
of her traitorous emotions. The sight of Pilgrim and
the waiting bath brought her flight to a halt.

"Good morning, Mrs. Lindsey. Do you want a tea
tray while you dress or will you go down to breakfast?"
Pilgrim asked.

After Merry had left the room, Giles took a quick
look around. Merry had not noticed the blood on the
sheets or towel, but the servants would. He had taken
care of those the night before, making a small cut in
his finger with his pen knife.

Giles was a very experienced ladies' man. His good
looks alone would have won him the approbation of
many women of his set; his fortune brought him others.
But Giles had also gained the reputation of a man
who could create pleasure. As soon as he had seen
Merry's sweet face and rounded figure, he had known
he would enjoy her seduction. He had planned it
carefully. The only thing he had not planned on was
her response to him and his to her. It had surprised
him, and he knew if he were to maintain control, he
would have to proceed carefully. Whistling softly, he
crossed to his dressing room. Today he would make
certain Merry was aware of him every moment.

Shrugging out of his dressing gown, he allowed his

valet to adjust his cravat and donned the dark blue
coat he had chosen earlier. When he reentered the
bedroom, Pilgrim was laying out Merry's clothes, and
the bed had already been remade. He crossed to Merry's
dressing room, an impish look in his eyes as he thought
of Merry's reaction when she saw him.

As he opened the door, Merry said, "May I have the
towel? I'm ready to get out."

Giles enjoyed the sight of Merry, her hair piled on
top of her head with only a few tendrils escaping
down her creamy neck. As he picked up the towel
from a chair beside the door, he moved to have a
clearer view of the round white shoulders and rosy
tipped breasts. Merry had started to emerge from the
water when she heard him say, "Here it is, my dear.
Do you want me to help you?"

With a gasp she sank, trying to hide under the few
bubbles left on the top of the water. "What are you
doing here?"

"I just came to tell you I will wait for you in the
breakfast room. We can see Mr. Pettigrew this morning.
But I much prefer this view. Maybe we should stay
here." Giles came closer, and Merry tried to sink
further into a tub that now seemed too small. Placing
the towel on a small stool beside the tub, he bent,
once more caressing her lips with his and running his
finger across the tops of her breasts. "Don't keep me
waiting too long," he said with such seriousness that
she looked at him questioningly. The deviltry back in
his eyes, he kissed her lightly once more and left her
alone. For a few moments she sat there dazed and
tingling.

"Are you ready to get out, ma'am? Madame Camille
has finished the gray walking dress if you wish to
wear it this morning." As Pilgrim dressed her, telling
her of the party that Giles had arranged for the servants the evening before and of how pleased the household was for her, Merry made automatic replies. She
wondered what Giles had planned for her, she who
had always thought she could control her emotions.

"You must sit still, Miss Merry, if you want me to put your hair up smoothly." Holding her head still as she waited for Pilgrim to put the last ribbon in place, Merry wondered if these were normal emotions any married lady felt. If only I'd asked Arabella, she thought, and then blushed as she realized that not even with Arabella could she have discussed what had been happening.

Every hair in place, she determinedly arranged her face in its usual placid expression. As the footman opened the breakfast room door, Giles rose and seated her, brushing a kiss across the exposed nape of her neck. "Giles, the servants," she whispered.

"They know we were just married," he said. Then she understood. He had said that they must convince the servants if they were to convince Hugo. A slight chill ran down her spine, and she sat straighter in her chair.

"Of course, the servants," she said in a cold voice. Her parents had tried to fool their servants, too.

Puzzled by her cold tone when only moments before she had been blushing, Giles reviewed his actions. As Merry poured a cup of tea, he chose his breakfast from the sideboard, pleased that the servants had remembered his favorites—crisp muffins, sirloin of beef, eggs, and raspberry jam. Merry refused everything but the muffins. Trying to capture her attention, Giles reminded her of the actions they would take that morning. "I suppose we had best sign the settlements first, just in case Hugo arrives today. Be certain to read them carefully. I want you to understand exactly what your rights are." Before she could reply, he continued, "What do you plan to do with the business while we are in London? Do you have someone you can leave in charge?"

When she realized that he was leaving the decision to her, one fear inside Merry relaxed. He could not want to force her to give up all interest in the business. Maybe her grandfather had been right. She glanced at him, once again struck by the idea that she had seen him somewhere before. "I had not considered the problem. Although Grandfather had many able people under him, I am not personally acquainted with many of them. Most of my work was done here, in the library. Perhaps Mr. Pettigrew, you, and I should list those we think most qualified and our reasons. Some you know better than I. Didn't one of the men just return after a long stay in the West Indies?" Merry asked.

Delighted that she would ask his assistance, Giles related what he knew of the man. As the clock struck the hour, he rose and escorted her to the entrance hall where Pilgrim was waiting with her pelisse and bonnet. Quickly, Merry donned the dark gray velvet wrap and tied the matching bonnet under her chin.

As he handed her into the waiting carriage, Giles felt Merry shiver in the damp air from the sea. Seating himself beside her, he drew her close, pulling a fur robe over their laps. As soon as the coachman had sprung the team, he turned her face toward him. Leaning down, he kissed her deeply.

"But—but, there are no servants about now," she stammered.

His brow creased and then cleared. "Merry, my dear, a gentleman does not kiss a lady just because the servants are watching." He pulled her closer, teasing her lips with his tongue. "Blast this bonnet," he cursed as he hit his eye as he was trying to nibble her ear.

Merry twitted him gently. "But you just told me how lovely it was, sir. Are you that changeable?"

Before he could reply, the coach pulled to a stop. Releasing her, Giles moved to the door. "We'll discuss the bonnet later. Now, Mr. Pettigrew is waiting."

For hours the three of them checked documents, making certain every word was precise. Finally satisfied that there was no way Hugo Darryl could threaten Merry again, Giles and Merry signed their names. Although the papers gave Giles nominal control of the company, Merry now realized how insignificant that was in comparison with his other holdings. From his maternal grandfather he had already inherited his own shares in the company, three estates, thousands in Consuls, a plantation in the West Indies, and a house on Grosvenor Square. Not only was she guaranteed her income from her grandfather's estate, but Giles had also insisted on her taking a handsome jointure as well as dower rights to whatever estate she liked best. From his father, Sir Gregory Lindsey, Giles, an only son, would receive Linden Hall as well as several more estates including a hunting box in Scotland. No wonder that woman was after him, Merry thought.

As further protection, the settlements also included their wills. Since Giles's estates from his grandfather were not entailed, they were left to Merry, and Merry's property to him. Under Mr. Pettigrew's urging, the will also provided for any future children, much to Merry's embarrassment.

The problems with the business were not so easily solved. Whoever was left in charge would need to be absolutely trustworthy, and although they believed that the candidates all met that requirement, the three of them knew they must investigate. After selecting the four men they felt most suitable, Merry and Giles asked Mr. Pettigrew to carry out inquiries about their financial and moral integrity. Merry and Giles would be available for all major decisions, but the person chosen would need to have a keen grasp of the business to keep up with the day-to-day decisions.

It was long after the normal time for dinner when Giles and Merry returned to the mansion. As the footman took her pelisse and bonnet, Merry asked Barrow for a tea tray to be sent to her room, declaring she would rest for a time. Somehow, the decisions they had made that day had left her almost as drained of energy as she had been after her grandfather's death.

Giles stopped to add a few low-voiced comments to Barrow. Bounding up the stairs after Merry, he slipped his arm around her waist as if to carry her up the stairs. Her head almost on his shoulder, she let him help her to her room. The butler, pausing before carrying out his orders, smiled to think that there was someone on whom Miss Merry could depend.

"Slip into that rose thing," Giles suggested. "I told Barrow I would join you for dinner in the sitting room instead of going down. Do you want me to help you disrobe?"

"My maid will help me, thank you!" she snapped. She pulled from him. Resenting his right to arrange her life, she said, "I'm not certain I want anything." But she thought longingly of her tea.

"Merry, you're tired. Change into something more comfortable and come back." He pushed her toward her bedroom. "I'll keep your tea warm." Slowly she turned to look back at him, a slight smile crossing her lips as she realized that he was manipulating her much as she had her grandfather.

"A cup of tea would be nice," she said.

Giles, shutting the door behind her, stretched before rushing to his dressing room where he quickly whipped off his cravat and his coat. His boots took longer, but soon he was dressed simply in his shirt and the pantaloons that hugged his legs and hips. He returned to the sitting room in time to admit Barrow with a well-filled tea trolley.

After the door closed behind the butler, the bedroom door opened. He smiled at the picture she made. Pilgrim had brushed her hair until it shone, leaving it hanging down her back almost to her waist. Merry was dressed in a jonquil yellow dressing gown that dripped with lace. Taking her hand to lead her to the sofa, Giles drew her to him with his other. She was still wearing those damn stays. Well, he thought, those can be taken care of.

As she filled his cup, Merry thought about the previous evening. She handed him the cup filled with the plain tea he preferred, and their fingers touched. She drew back as though she had been stung, a tingling sensation flashing straight up her arm to her heart. As though he had not noticed her reaction,

Giles urged her to sample the delicacies the chef had included. Not only was there the paté she had learned to enjoy in France the previous year, but there was also creamy butter, cheddar cheese, hot bread, and slices of pheasant for Giles's heartier appetite, and some pastries. After filling her plate at Giles's urging, Merry stared at it for a time before she took a bite. For a while neither spoke, being too busy eliminating the hunger they had not realized they had until they had taken their first bites. Merry finished first and put her plate on the trolley. The resentment she had felt earlier had vanished.

As Giles put his plate down after finishing a cream cake, he flashed his smile at Merry. She sank back into the corner of the sofa and tried to stifle a yawn.

"Have you decided what you want to do with this house while we are in London?" he asked. "If possible, we need to leave within the fortnight."

"Is your house fully staffed or will we need further servants?" she questioned, her mind glad of the new problem.

"I've never really stayed there long. Perhaps you need to have a look and decide. The butler and housekeeper seem good sorts, but the chef leaves much to be desired. Why?"

"If we need more servants, I would prefer to use my own. In any case, Pilgrim will come with me. Perhaps you are right. We shall inspect the situation and then send for those we need." Merry mentally began to organize the situation. "Barrow and Mrs. Barrow I will leave in charge here with a small staff. For the rest, we shall see."

Giles regarded her carefully, thinking how society would react if they saw her in her outmoded clothes. They were certainly an effective disguise. "Do you wish to wait until we reach London before you purchase a new wardrobe? Charlotte has written that nothing she owns is in style and that she must be reoutfitted immediately."

Thinking of the new styles Madame Camille had

shown her, Merry agreed with Giles's sister. "For a young lady soon to be presented to the *ton*, a wardrobe is of the utmost importance. With the change in styles we shall both need complete wardrobes. I wonder . . .' She stopped, a faint frown creasing her forehead.

"What?"

"Madame Camille recently mentioned that custom has fallen off since many of her patrons have gone to London for the Season. Perhaps . . . Do you have an agent in London, sir?"

"What are you planning, Madame Wife?" Giles asked, his eyes narrowing as though to see the plans developing in her mind.

"We need a second location—in Bond Street. I believe London is ready for a new modiste. Between your sister and me, Madame Camille may make a profit the first season. I must write her immediately." Before Giles could answer or do more than stand up, Merry swept from the room. Giles, a slight smile on his face, followed.

He quickly walked to the desk in his room. As he pulled out the paper and sharpened the quill, Giles planned his letter to his agent carefully. He wanted to make certain Merry's surprise would be ready when they arrived in London.

Some time later, her letter finished and in the hands of a footman who would deliver it on the morrow, Merry sat before her dressing table, her maid braiding her long, wavy hair. Her eyes were closed as though she were asleep. She did not notice when another figure joined Pilgrim's in the mirror. Silently Giles waved Pilgrim out of the room. Being careful not to break the spell, Giles quickly unlaced the stays Merry wore over a soft chemise. Giles then carefully moved the braid to rest over one shoulder. He ran his hands under the loosened corset to clasp her breasts as he bent to kiss her neck.

"Dreaming of me or of the London shop, Merry?" he asked.

Startled, she tried to pull away, but he refused to

let her go. Instead, he lifted her and turned her to face him. His black hair glistened blue-black in the candlelight as he lowered his head toward hers. Fascinated, Merry watched his lips come closer and closer until they were pressing hotly against hers. With a sigh, she relaxed against his shoulder, her arms reaching to circle his neck. Carefully loosening first one arm and then the other, Giles freed her of the corset. Her chemise quickly followed.

Merry's breath caught in her throat. Her heart was beating so fast it seemed as though it would burst from her breast. Giles, recognizing her fear, slowed his wandering hands. For a time he simply held her close, his emotions kept in check by a tight control.

Her breathing slowed. Giles cautiously renewed his slow explorations of her body. At first his hands drifted over her back, soothing her fears yet enflaming the desire she had not known she possessed. As his hands pressed her close against him, Merry's eyes opened wide. His lips captured hers for a kiss so deep that it left Merry breathless and shaking. Giles's lips caressed her earlobes and nuzzled her neck as his hands released her hair from its braid. Shaking her hair loose over her shoulders, he held her away from him slightly. "I knew it would be glorious loose," he said.

Merry's eyes opened lazily and then shut again quickly before the passionate blaze in his. She turned as if trying to pull away from him, yet not wanting to escape the feelings his fingers were creating.

Giles caught her close against him again, once more letting his fingers continue their exploration. One hand drifted lower to her hips while the other circled her to stroke the side of a breast.

"Oh, Merry, you are so soft, so sweet," he breathed in her ear. Shivering as though from the cold, Merry trembled against him. What she was feeling couldn't be normal. For a moment Giles drew back, releasing her momentarily so that he could sweep her up into his arms. Picking her up, he carried her to the bed, his lips forging new trails down her neck.

Settling her carefully on the cool sheets, Giles le
his fingers discover new territory while his lips made
hers pay a toll. As his hand reached for the top of her
thigh, a soft "no" broke from her. Her startled eyes
stared into his.

"Shh, it will be all right," Giles reassured her as he
held her close against him. Once more his hands re
turned to the already explored regions of her back and
sides. While he caressed her, he whispered his plea
sure in her softness, her fragrance.

As he felt her arms creep up around his neck, Giles
breathed a sigh of relief. A few minutes later, his
hands were uncovering the unexplored territories of
her soft white legs.

Merry was caught up in a world of sensations new
to her. Slowly one hand crept into Giles's black hair,
ruffling the curls she found there. The other slipped
beneath the collar of his dressing gown to stroke the
muscles of his back.

For a moment, Giles's careful control slipped. He
pulled her hard against him and kissed her deeply,
tongue probing her softly closed lips. Startled, she
drew back.

Once more Giles regained control. Slowly, he forced
his breathing to slow. He nestled Merry's head against
his shoulder. "You are so warm, so sweet," he whis
pered. "You are more intoxicating than the rarest
wine."

Merry, embarrassed by her reactions, turned from
him, burrowing her head into the pillow next to her.
Giles took advantage of the moment to shrug out of
his dressing gown and then moved close to her again.
"Tell me what you are feeling, Merry," he commanded.

Slowly she shook her head, too afraid of the new
sensations running through her to give them voice.

"Do you like this?" Giles asked as he pulled her
back against him and cupped her breasts in his hands,
his fingers teasing her nipples.

"Oh, Giles, oh," she breathed as she turned on her
back and looked up at him. His shoulders and the hair

on his chest gleamed in the candlelight as he bent over to run his tongue lightly around her slightly open lips while his hands returned to her breasts.

Startled, she drew back. "Giles, where are your clothes?" Merry asked, puzzled. His assault on her senses had dulled her sense of shock but not her curiosity.

Laughing, Giles drew one of her hands to his mouth, kissed it, and then guided it to the curls on his chest. "Where the rest of yours will be soon, I hope. On the floor," he told her.

"You mean, you're ... Oh!" Merry's eyes widened and then snapped tightly shut. Before she could pull away from him, Giles had captured her open lips with his and was teasing them with his tongue. Her hand on his chest closed and then opened to stroke him. Her other soon joined it.

With her hands occupied, Giles sent his on a mission of their own. Slowly but surely they eased her chemise up over her head, stealing it from her so cautiously that only at the last minute was she aware of what he was doing. And then it was too late.

"No, Giles, no," she tried to protest as his hands drifted from her breasts to her stomach, creating new paths of fire wherever they went.

"Just let yourself feel. Don't you like this?" he asked as his lips closed on one rosy nipple, pulling it taut.

"No, no, ohh ..." she cried.

His hands and lips drifted lower. Merry felt a sensation deep inside, one that seemed to build, to pulse, to cry out for something more. Her soft moans delighted Giles. Finally his hand drifted across her stomach to the dark patch of hair below. His other hand stroked her upper thighs until she relaxed, giving him access to her. Giles fought for control, reminding himself of his goal—to teach Merry the delights of her own body. His fingers teased her. Merry writhed in exquisite agony as he brought her to release, her moans enflam-

ing him with more desire than he had ever before
experienced.

Before her shudders of pleasure had completely
died away, Giles slid his legs between her now relaxed ones. Still caressing her, he found her moist and
ready. He kissed her again, allowing his tongue full
play of her mouth as he parted her thighs. Slowly, he
filled her until he reached the barrier that protected
her secret warmth. Once more, Giles captured her
mouth. He thrust deeper.

Counting to one hundred slowly, Giles held Merry
close, covering her face, neck, and breasts with soft
kisses. One hand returned to the dark curls below her
stomach. After the first sharp pain, Merry had tensed
and tried to pull away. But he kept her firmly beneath him. As his kisses and caresses soothed her,
Merry felt the pain disappear, to be replaced by the
yearning sensation she had felt earlier, now made
worse by the throbbing within her. Her hands crept to
Giles's shoulders and pulled him closer. He gasped,
his control slipping, and reached beneath her, lifting
her hips to meet his thrusts. The rhythm of his movements echoed the ebb and fall of the waves, growing
wilder by the moment. Finally he shuddered and
exploded, filling her with warmth. Her own explosion
echoed his. As his breathing slowed, Giles pulled away,
reaching out after a moment to draw her close again.

"I'm sorry I had to hurt you. The first time is
painful for a woman," he explained as his hand stroked
her back and hips. With a sigh Merry moved close
beside him.

After a few minutes, he pulled away and crossed
the room. To her great embarrassment, he returned a
short time later with a soft, damp towel to care for
her. Keeping her eyes tightly closed, she tried to deny
the presence of the naked man beside her. As he
finished, he bent and placed a kiss on her soft breast.
Startled, she opened her eyes to see him climbing
back into bed. Hastily she shut her eyes. Grabbing her
hand, he placed a kiss in her palm and drew it over

his chest. When she resisted any further advances, he dropped her hand and blew out the candles. Drawing their moist bodies close to one another, he whispered, "You are a very sweet lover, Merry. Thank you."

Merry lay rigid for a time. Then she heard his breathing become regular, and she relaxed. Her thoughts as she drifted into sleep were that she now understood one of those carvings she had seen in India.

—5—

The moment she opened her eyes, Merry had retreated behind the wall of calm that had kept the
world away for so many years. Because her sleep had
been restless, she was awake before Giles. She slipped
into her dressing room, choosing to dress herself rather
than call her maid. The door to the hall closed behind
her.

For the rest of the day Merry managed to avoid
Giles. An appointment with Madame Camille extended
into luncheon, and she ordered a tray for them both in
her sitting room. Madame was enchanted with the
idea that she could open a shop in London. "Just
think, little one," Madame Camille said. "We will be
famous. Our dresses the best! Our laces and trims the
finest! Such excitement!"

Finally Madame Camille left, still exclaiming over
her good fortune. Together they had not only planned
most of the gowns Merry would need for the Season
but also chosen which one of the assistants to leave
behind to run the shop in Bristol. Madame, ever a
wise businesswoman, said, "We must honor our commitments here. We must not forget out first customers."
In both their minds was the thought that the shop in
Bristol was insurance against the failure of the shop
in London.

By the time Giles found her that afternoon, Merry
had a pounding headache. She was white with pain.
Only in India had she ever had a headache as bad as

this. As he tried to put his arm around her to help her to her room, she flinched and grew paler. With a silent curse, Giles led her to her bedroom.

As soon as her maid had reached her mistress, she knew what was wrong. "Just leave her to me, Mr. Lindsey. She only needs to rest," she assured him. Swiftly she began to loose the thick hair from its knot and undress Merry. As he stood unnoticed in the doorway, Giles's mouth tightened. The laughter had left his eyes long before. How was he ever to break through the defenses that she put up, he wondered. And if he couldn't, what kind of marriage would they have?

While Merry drifted off to sleep, he stood there watching the softness and sweetness that her face showed in repose. As he continued to watch, she began to move restlessly, and once again she began to weep. Before he could cross the room to her side, Pilgrim was beside her mistress, shaking her. "That's all right, Miss Merry. It's only a dream." Seeing how quickly Merry grew calm, Giles left the room, allowing the maid to finish the task. When Merry was sleeping again, Pilgrim entered the sitting room where he waited. "I had to give her some laudanum. When she has these bad dreams, that's all that will calm her," Pilgrim said.

Remembering how he had held Merry a few nights before, Giles knew she was wrong, but it was too late to avoid the sedative this time. He asked, "How long has she had these dreams? Since her grandfather became ill?"

"Oh no, sir! The first night here from India was the first I knew of them, but she has said it is something from her childhood. She has them only seldom now." Seldom, two nights within one week, he thought as he gritted his teeth. "She will sleep until morning, sir," she added.

As he walked up the stairs after his lonely dinner, Giles reviewed his plans. He had been looking forward to holding those full curves in his arms again

ever since the moment he had awakened and found
her gone. She was as lush as any bit of muslin he had
ever had in keeping. From being an obligation, this
marriage had become interesting.

He slipped into bed with her and drew her into his
arms. Even in her drugged sleep, he could feel her
stiffen and try to pull away, but he simply held her
close. Gradually her body relaxed once more and her
breathing deepened. As he drifted off to sleep, Giles
wondered if he would ever find again the warm, excited woman he had held in his arms only the evening
before.

Merry opened her eyes the next morning, still rather
groggy from the drug. She could feel Giles's warm
body at her back, his arm resting casually over her
hip. She tried to draw away from him, but his arm
tightened. He was awake. She quickly shut her eyes.
Turning her over on her back, Giles looked at the
tightly closed eyelids, but his usual smile was missing.
His quiet voice seemed to echo in the room. "I know
you are awake, Merry. Open your eyes."

Cautiously she opened first one eye and then the
other. He was sitting beside her instead of leaning
over her as she expected him to be. Relaxing a little,
she sat up too, her back against the soft pillows.

"Merry, I will try not to rush you more than I
already have," Giles promised. "But no more hiding
from me, either. We certainly will never have a successful marriage if we never talk to each other. What
will your cousin think? We're so much in love that we
never talk to one another and you rush from any room
I enter to avoid seeing me." His irony slapped Merry
hard. She drew away from him. "Promise to rest
today. There is much to do before we leave for London,
and if you are exhausted, it will be more difficult for
you."

Merry nodded. But she doubted she would ever rest
easily again. How could she have allowed her emotions to get out of hand? She thought of the way her
body had been curled up against Giles. Was she no

better than her mother and father? Would her passion make her cruel? She cringed at the thought.

Noting the dazed and frightened look in her eyes, Giles rose. As he picked up his dressing gown, he said, "We must spend more time together today. And, Merry, wear that pretty blue in your clothes press."

Startled, she looked at him and then gasped and turned bright red. He was naked. She averted her eyes, but his beautiful body with its rippling muscles was firmly painted on her memory. His soft laugh seemed to mock her embarrassment. "I will meet you presently for breakfast, Madame Wife," he promised.

As she poured his tea and handed it across the table to him an hour later, Merry blushed again. Even though Giles was now dressed in a dark green coat with buff pantaloons, she could still see him as he had stood there, his long lean lines silhouetted against the blue curtains. When he had taken his cup, she lowered her eyes to her plate. The poached egg and ham seemed less appealing than a few minutes earlier. She took a small bite of the meat and concentrated on chewing and swallowing. Giles had said they must spend time together. To do so, she must be in control. Carefully, she built her wall of calm with deep breaths. Giles could almost see the changes she made inside as her face resumed its calm mask.

The sound of voices in the hallway halted Giles's comments before they even began. With a frown, he looked toward the door. Merry breathed a sigh of relief, which swiftly changed to dismay when Barrow announced, "Mr. Hugo Darryl." Before Merry could utter a word or Giles do more than rise from his chair, Hugo pranced into the room.

"My dearest cousin, I'm so sorry that I could not be here sooner. You should have sent for me so that I could handle all those wearisome details. I'm certain Uncle Julian would have wanted me to assist you," he stated in an affected tone.

Giles quickly swallowed his snort of disgust. Hugo

would never convince Merry that he knew more about Sommerby's affairs than she did. He regarded the short, fat man in the dark brown peruke with interest. Hugo certainly looked harmless enough. In spite of the fact that he looked ridiculous in them, Darryl had on the latest fashions—a dark blue cutaway coat with huge silver buttons and padded shoulders, high shirt points, a crisp cravat, and the latest in yellow knitted pantaloons that clung to every ripple of fat in his hips and thighs. A lace handkerchief and an enameled snuffbox completed the outfit.

To Merry, the contrast between the two men was almost comical. Giles towered over Hugo, and his understated elegance made Hugo look ridiculous. Trying to hide her amusement, she glanced at Giles and almost laughed as she saw the disbelief in his eyes. He moved to stand beside her, his hand resting on her shoulder.

Finally Hugo deigned to notice Giles. "And who is this?" he asked. "The husband of a friend? Really, my dear, you must be more careful of your reputation. It would never do for it to become known that you breakfasted alone with a man, even if he is the husband of a friend who is staying with you. You would have done better to have taken breakfast in bed." His voice dripped concern.

"There, you see, Merry! I was right. We should have had breakfast in bed," Giles agreed, his love of the absurd taking control.

Hugo gasped, his face turning an unbecoming shade of purple. "How dare you insult my cousin so, sir! I must demand satisfaction." He raised his hand as if to strike Giles, but Merry intervened.

"Giles, your wicked sense of humor will land us in the suds someday," she said. "Hugo, may I present my husband, Giles Lindsey."

The words *my husband* caused Hugo's face to darken. He scowled. His body trembled with anger. He was not pleased to have his plans fail. But a sudden thought crossed his mind. He changed what he was going to say. His voice simply oozed honey. "How enchanting, I'm sure. Have you known each other long? When I last corresponded with Uncle Julian, he did not mention that you were engaged, Merry. May I be the first to welcome you to the family?" He paused. "But how strange that you did not mention marriage when you wrote of Uncle Julian's death." Hugo's smile glittered like the gold he could see piling into his hands.

Behind her wall of calm, Merry was shaking. Giles watched as the knuckles on the hand on the edge of the table turned white. Dropping his other arm lightly on Merry's shoulders, Giles encircled her protectively. He said, "Mr. Sommerby introduced us, sir." He paused, considering his next words. He was going to enjoy making Hugo uncomfortable. He would wait a while before he revealed his identity.

Hugo's smile grew. He was now master of the house, he thought. He turned to Barrow, who was waiting for directions from Merry, and shouted, "Bring me some fresh tea and be quick about it. Some hot bread, too." His high squeaky voice broke as he uttered the last word, as it always did when he was excited. The business, the money, the power—it would all be his. His gloating smile was all too evident as he took Giles's place at the head of the table, ordering the footman to bring him clean dishes.

Merry was indignant. As she opened her mouth to protest, Giles pushed against her shoulders, settling her deep into her chair and squeezing her shoulders to indicate that she should be silent. He picked up his tea cup and took a seat on her right. He quietly reached out and took her hand in his. He smiled at her as if to remind her that their plans were already made. They had arranged earlier that a messenger would be sent to Mr. Pettigrew as soon as Hugo Darryl arrived. He wanted to wait to reveal the truth until they had legal counsel at hand. As Darryl complained about the cold tea, the less than perfect bread, and the tough sirloin of beef, Merry bit the inside of her cheeks to stay quiet. Her grip on Giles's hand grew stronger. As if to whisper sweet love words in her ear, Giles bent his head and whispered, "He cannot hurt you. I'm here. Soon it will be settled, but let's not act rashly now."

After Hugo had finished the tea, consumed the last muffin, and demolished the sirloin, he leaned back in his chair and considered Merry and Giles. "I simply will have to install a new chef. The one you have now will never do. But enough of that. My rooms should be ready now. I told Barrow I would occupy Uncle Julian's rooms. We can discuss the arrangements that must be made for your removal after luncheon," he said.

Merry's gasp of outrage was cut short as Giles quickly leaned over to her. "See dearest, I told you your cousin would understand." Before she could answer, Darryl had left the room and was shouting once again for Barrow.

Her wall of calm crumbled. "How dare you allow that man to occupy my grandfather's suite! He is repulsive," she cried. "All he wants is a chance to snoop through Grandfather's belongings."

"And most of those you have already removed," Giles reminded her. "Let's see what he has planned before we confront him. It will be this afternoon before Mr. Pettigrew can have all the documents ready and here."

Merry realized the wisdom of what he was saying, but every element of her spirit wanted to reject it. Only her grandfather's insistence that she consider all her options made her agree. Marshaling her thoughts, she suggested, "Let's go to the library."

"That's my girl." He drew her up from her chair. "I'm going to enjoy baiting him." He kept his arm around her waist even as they walked down the hall. As they entered the library, he said, "As much as I will enjoy disappointing him, I would much rather please you. Perhaps the library is too public. Maybe we should adjourn to your bedroom." His leer and caressing hands helped distract her from Hugo, as Giles had meant for them to.

She hastily drew away from him, a blush staining her cheeks. "Stop that!" She batted at his hand as he ran it down her side. "We need to decide how to tell him." Giles laughed and stopped. Merry was confused. He had done as she had asked, yet she felt disappointed. She said, "We can't afford to wait very long. As you can see, Hugo has a way of alienating all the servants."

"Let him enjoy his moment of glory. It will be brief. As soon as Mr. Pettigrew arrives, he will have to accept the situation. I don't expect that he will stay long after that."

"I hope you're right." Merry's voice implied her doubts. Sinking into the only chair behind the desk, she quickly put the immense piece of furniture between herself and her husband as soon as she realized he was advancing toward her. "Have you seen the report Mr. Pettigrew sent over? It seems to eliminate at least one of our candidates."

Recognizing that he could get no further with a personal discussion, Giles eagerly entered into an analysis of the men. He crossed behind the desk and leaned over her shoulder to look at the closely written report. "From what your grandfather said, I imagine you have made a chart with all these facts included," he teased. Merry hesitantly pulled a roll of paper from the desk. "I knew it," Giles crowed. She flashed her eyes as though she would like to wipe his smile away with a slap. "Come, let me see what you've done." Reaching over her shoulder he unrolled the chart. "Merry, this is outstanding. You've done an excellent job."

As she looked up into his smiling face, her lips slightly parted in a smile, Giles was tempted. He bent down and kissed her. She pulled away hastily as if she had touched a hot coal, and escaped from Giles's arms. She had begun to respond to him.

He said, "No, Merry. Please stay. I promise to keep my distance."

Without a word, Merry resumed her seat. She fastened her eyes on the chart she had made, trying to suppress the emotions that were raging inside her. Giles sank to a chair beside her, careful to allow her plenty of room.

The rest of the morning they spent on business. Merry's grasp of the complexities of supply and demand amazed Giles. Merry was impressed with his understanding of the personalities involved. For a few hours, thoughts of Hugo as well as their own feelings were suppressed.

All too soon the chimes of the clock on the mantle reminded them they must once again face Hugo. Retiring to her room to prepare for the meal, Merry felt her worries begin to build. Her cousin would do anything for money. Giles might believe he could protect her, but Merry was not so certain. She knew Hugo too well.

As they were finishing their meal, Barrow approached Giles with a whispered message. Hugo exploded, "Barrow, I'm the master of the house now. Any problem that arises should be brought to me, not to some outsider."

After receiving Giles's silent permission, Barrow answered him. "Mr. Pettigrew is in the small salon and wished to see Mr. and Mrs. Lindsey as well as you, Mr. Darryl." From the butler's frosty tone, Merry recognized that even his patience was wearing thin.

"Pettigrew—ah, yes, Uncle Julian's lawyer. Good, maybe now we can finally settle some things."

"We certainly can," whispered Giles to Merry. Unconsciously, she straightened her shoulders, tensing her neck and back. Following Hugo, Merry and Giles entered the salon. Instinctively, Merry chose a chair as far as possible from Hugo. Giles stood behind her.

Spread out on a table before the lawyer were several documents. He too knew Darryl. Mr. Pettigrew straightened his lace cuffs and lined the edges of each sheet of paper neatly.

"Well, how much did Uncle Julian leave me?" asked Hugo.

Mr. Pettigrew had not expected such a direct question so early in the session. He cleared his throat. "According to the will of the founder of the company, all shares must be voted by a male shareholder. A woman may hold shares only if . . ."

"Yes, yes. We all know about that. And Merry is married to Mr. Lindsey. Therefore she cannot hold any shares." Hugo was almost jumping with excitement.

Hesitantly, the lawyer disagreed. "Your assessment is not totally accurate."

Hugo looked at him sharply and then back at Merry and Giles. Merry grabbed Giles's hand, holding it so tightly he winced. In a voice that had grown icily cold, Hugo asked, "And what do you mean, I am not totally accurate?" His face was so dark with color it resembled a damson plum.

Giles's nod urged the lawyer on. "Mr. Sommerby left all his shares to his granddaughter Miranda under the control of her husband, another shareholder, Mr. Giles Lindsey."

The words struck like blows on the ears and the mind of Hugo Darryl. Then his scream of rage echoed around the small salon. Merry, turning whiter than before, sank further into her chair, as if to hide from the anger in front of her. Giles crossed to the raging man, shaking him briskly. "Hysterics will not change anything," he said.

"You're trying to cheat me. My only brother is the sole unmarried shareholder in the company. What do you think I am, a fool?" Hugo's voice grew higher and more squeaky.

"Come man, pull yourself together," Mr. Pettigrew urged. "Look at these documents. I've prepared copies for you to study at your leisure or to show to your man of business." He waved a document in front of Hugo's face. Shaking off Giles's restraining arms, Hugo grabbed it. It was a chart of the relationship between Giles, Hugo, and Merry. After glancing at it and recog-

nizing the truth of the lawyer's claim, Hugo crumpled
it in his fist. For a moment he seemed frozen. Giles
stepped hastily toward Mr. Pettigrew as if to protect
him. Whirling rapidly and moving across the room
much faster than anyone would have expected, Hugo
stood in front of Merry before Giles could move. His
hands circled her neck, and he shook her, screaming,
"You viper! How dare you spoil my plans!"

Giles raced silently across the room and floored
Hugo with one punch. As he fell, Hugo hit his head on
the edge of a table. Giles ignored him. Kneeling in
front of his shaken wife, he took her in his arms. "Can
you talk? Did he hurt you seriously?" he asked
passionately. "I'll kill him if ever he touches you
again." As he lifted Merry in his arms to carry her to
her room, Giles shouted for a servant. When Barrow
appeared, Giles ordered, "Fetch my wife's doctor
immediately. We'll be in her room waiting for him."

"Giles, wait," the lawyer called. "I think Darryl's
hurt."

Giles did not slow his steps. "Good." He then paused.
"Call a footman and have him taken to his room.
When the doctor has finished with Merry, he can take
a look at that maniac." He almost ran up the stairs to
their suite, shouting for Pilgrim as he went.

The lawyer, sighing, returned to the unconscious
figure of Hugo Darryl. After checking to make certain
the man was still breathing, Mr. Pettigrew crossed to
the bellpull. When a footman appeared, the lawyer
instructed, "Get him to bed and call his valet. The
doctor will see him shortly." Once again alone in the
room, he mopped his brow and breathed a sigh of
relief. He gathered the copies for Darryl into one
pile and began to put the rest away in his portfolio.
He would stay until the doctor gave his report.

Some time later, Giles entered the room slowly.
"They won't let me stay with Merry. The doctor said
I disturbed her. I need a drink." He crossed to the
bellpull, but before he could ring, Barrow entered
with a tray of glasses and a bottle.

"I thought you might need this, sir," he said, setting the tray on the table. "I do hope Miss Merry will be all right."

Eagerly, Giles poured the brandy into the glasses, spilling some because his hand was shaking. "We won't know for certain until the doctor comes down, but I don't think she's badly hurt," he told the butler as he handed the lawyer his drink. With a sigh of relief, Barrow left the room, hurrying to reassure his wife.

As they waited, time seemed to inch by. Although Giles had at first sunk into a chair to nurse his brandy, by the time the doctor entered the room he was pacing wildly, ranting, "Why doesn't he let us know something?" Poor Mr. Pettigrew, convinced Hugo Darryl must be dead, grew more nervous by the minute as he thought about his testimony at a murder trial.

"Brandy, yes, thank you." The doctor took a sip before continuing. "They both will be fine." Mr. Pettigrew's sigh of relief and Giles's dash for the door occurred simultaneously. "Mr. Lindsey," the doctor said. Giles turned. "Your wife is sleeping and will probably not awaken until the morrow." Giles closed the door and crossed to sit down. The doctor continued, "Mr. Darryl will have a headache when he awakens. I have given his man some powders that should relieve it. He should remain in bed for the rest of today and tomorrow. I'll check on my patients again tomorrow morning. Send a footman if you need me tonight." Replacing his glass on the tray, the doctor left.

"I also must be leaving," the lawyer said. "Send for me tomorrow if Darryl wants to discuss these papers." He handed them to Giles.

Left alone, Giles refilled his glass and sank into the chair Merry had occupied. "I'll protect you. He can't hurt you." His own words were like daggers in his brain. It was late when he stumbled up the steps to his room, a watchful footman following anxiously.

Breakfast the next morning was late. But Giles had finished and was crossing to the large salon when he saw Merry coming down the stairs. He drew her into the room. "Should you be up? The doctor has not yet been here this morning." His voice roughened with emotion, he said, "Oh Merry, I was so worried that he had hurt you." Giles took her into his arms, oblivious of the servants and to the noise behind him.

"From the way you are holding my niece, sir, I hope you are Giles Lindsey," said Merry's Aunt Mathilda in a slightly ironic tone. Startled, Giles dropped his arms, and both he and Merry turned toward her aunt. Like Merry, her first glance of Giles caused Lady Mathilda Evans to catch her breath. She wondered why all the young men were so handsome these days. Quickly regaining her composure, Lady Mathilda chided the pair. "Why didn't you wait for me?" She settled herself and her fashionable skirts into the most comfortable chair in the room. "I would dearly have loved to see my only niece's wedding." Affecting a sigh, she raised a hand to her forehead as if in pain, but actually to check to see if her turban were still in place. She learned the art of combining two gestures long ago. "Why you had to be in such a hurry, I simply do not understand. Of course, Merry, had I been in your position I might have made the same choice." Her coy smile at Giles was a duplicate of one she had used as a debutante. Part of Lady Mathilda's charm had always been her beauty, now faded, and her knowledge of how to use it. She continued, "What the *ton* will say, however, I simply do not know. A marriage while in mourning. Really, you should have waited at least six months."

When Giles could interrupt her without being rude, he tried to explain. "Mr. Sommerby tried to arrange the marriage before his death, but the license failed to arrive in time. His instructions were to marry as soon as it arrived. We felt bound to follow his wishes."

Lady Mathilda raised one eyebrow as if to question the story but did not comment. She looked pointedly at Merry, who quickly added, "Giles is a distant cousin whom Grandfather sponsored in the company. Until recently he has been abroad. When we met, our marriage seemed fated. We really had no choice but to marry," she continued bravely. Merry hesitated, slightly out of countenance at the laughter in Giles's eyes.

"Well, what's done cannot be undone, as that playwright said. I must say, Merry, that when you made your choice, you certainly had an eye." Lady Mathilda's eyes roved over Giles, lingering on his wide shoulders and narrow hips. Not for anything would she give up her flirtations and appreciation of the masculine form. The modern fancy for knitted pantaloons allowed her to ogle to her heart's content. Merry blushed as she often did in her aunt's company. "Your taste is exquisite, my dear," Mathilda said.

Before her aunt could continue, Merry hastily asked, "Aunt Mathilda, will you visit us in London and help me arrange Giles's sister's presentation? He insists it must be this season."

"London so soon after grandfather's death? Why, how could you think it? Society will be outraged," her aunt exploded. "You must remain in black gloves for at least a year."

Giles interrupted. "Mr. Sommerby's will expressly forbids formal mourning. And my parents have begged us to rescue my sister from our cousin, Honoria Coverly."

"Your cousin is Honoria Coverly?" Mathilda repeated. "Any child left under her care must be rescued immediately. What were your parents thinking of? Everyone knows that Honoria and Lady Farrell, a rather fast widow, are pursuing more mature game this Season. Lady Farrell plans to snare her lover, Giles someone—my correspondent forgot his name—as a husband before the year is out. Honoria is supposed to be helping her by chaperoning Lady Farrell's lover's sister as a favor to her friend. Together they could ruin any young girl. Perhaps we should rescue both of the young ladies."

"Charlotte is the only one in my cousin's care," said Giles in an icy voice.

Her mouth forming an O, Lady Mathilda put a hand over it as if to stop the words she had just uttered. Giles's frown was enough to tell her she had erred. Merry turned to look at Giles, but he refused to meet her eyes.

"Well, my dear, I'm truly exhausted. Perhaps my room will be ready now. Could you have someone escort me to my room?" asked Lady Mathilda. She wanted to avoid the questions she could see in Merry's eyes.

Before Giles could cross to the bellpull, the butler scratched on the door and announced, "Doctor Jones has arrived. Shall I show him up?" Giles took advantage of the opportunity he was given.

"You show Lady Mathilda to her room, Barrow. I'll take the doctor to Mr. Darryl," Giles said.

"Hugo here? How delightful. And ill? How terrible. I can hardly wait to see him again. He is such a charming man. We will have so much to discuss." Her comments grew fainter as she trailed Barrow up the stairs.

Merry blanched when she remembered Hugo's rage. In spite of Giles's best efforts, Hugo had proved dangerous. At her thought of Giles, her face grew stormy. Before long she and Giles would have a discussion. No wonder his cousin had refused to present Charlotte, with Giles spurning her friend.

As Merry neared the head of the stairs, she heard Hugo's querulous voice declaring, "But I must see my cousin." She entered his room. "How can I ever apologize enough for my actions? I want to die." His melodramatic voice continued, "How could I treat my own dear cousin so? I'm extremely ashamed." Merry and Giles exchanged a skeptical look as he said, "The disappointment must have affected my brain momentarily. I simply do not understand how I could have been so violent. Poor Mr. Pettigrew, I must see him and apologize to him also." Turning to the doctor, he asked, "How soon can I relieve my cousins of my distasteful presence?" The answer was not one he was expecting.

"I believe you will be able to travel tomorrow if you wish."

A frown crossed Hugo's face, but he quickly erased it. "Perhaps I could see Mr. Pettigrew later today—to apologize?" he asked Giles. "I won't inflict my presence on you a moment longer than necessary."

Seeing the questions in Merry's eyes, Giles once more made good his escape. "I will see Mr. Pettigrew immediately. I'm certain he will see you this afternoon." He crossed the room and was out the door before Merry had a chance to comment.

"And now I would like to check my other patient. May we adjourn to your room?" the doctor asked Merry. Relieved to have an excuse to leave her cousin, she agreed.

For the rest of the day Merry saw little of Giles. She spent the afternoon with her aunt discussing the plans for opening a shop in London and showing her the new fashion plates from France. In spite of her objections to having a niece in trade, Mathilda enjoyed the idea of having a shop where she would be more important than one of the patronesses of Almack's. Although Giles joined them for dinner, he remained over his port in the dining room and then retired. For the second night in a row he slept alone.

Almost as soon as Giles and Merry descended the next morning, Hugo departed. Once again he apologized to Merry, assuring her that he regretted his actions intensely. Trying to erase their suspicions, he held out his hands to them. When they took them rather reluctantly, he joined their two very solemnly and said, as if giving a blessing, "May you always have what you deserve. I wish you the very best." He released their hands. "I must rush back to London— some important business affairs," he gushed. Merry knew that the business affairs meant staying ahead of the bailiffs, but if he were willing to make peace, she would accept it. Giles, however, had reservations.

Hugo had begun to plan ahead. He knew his creditors would be a problem for a time, but he would solve the problem. London, with its slums and villains, would provide just what he needed. Before the clock had finished striking nine, his coach and four were at the door, and he left in as much of a flurry as he had arrived.

—6—

No sooner had the carriage drawn away than Merry turned to Giles. "Perhaps now you can explain what my aunt meant yesterday," she commented. Giles caught his breath. He had known that the moment had to be faced, but he had hoped to postpone it a little longer.

He hesitated as he opened the door into the breakfast room. Seating her, he began, "Merry, remember when——" The door opened and in bounced Lady Mathilda.

"I can hardly wait to see Hugo. He's so amusing," she gushed.

Exchanging glances, Merry and Giles sighed. "Aunt Mathilda, Hugo had to leave for London; he had some urgent business to take care of," Merry explained.

"How rude. At least he could have waited and said hello to me. And to travel on Sunday, too."

"I'm certain that he would have been happy to see you if an emergency had not arisen, Lady Mathilda," Giles reassured her. "I understand it was quite a blow to him as well." The pun was almost the undoing of Merry, who sputtered and then coughed. Really, it was too bad of Giles to make her want to laugh when she was so angry with him. "Now, Lady Mathilda, what would you like for breakfast? Barrow and our chef are yours to command."

"Call me Aunt Mathilda, Giles." She smiled at him. What a handsome addition he made to their family, she thought. "Just a cup of tea for me. I had the most delicious rolls in my room. What a wonderful chef you have. Do you plan to take him to London?" Before Merry could answer, Mathilda continued, "If you are not, may I borrow him? I have the most annoying problem. The week after I went to London, I received a letter from my housekeeper saying that my chef had left. I have company coming, and I haven't been able to find a suitable replacement."

Laughing softly for the first time in days as she thought of Hugo's complaints about the chef, Merry said, "Giles has a house in London. As he has not lived there recently, he is not certain about the servants. It is possible that we will use some of the ones from here. If not, you may certainly borrow our chef. I'm happy his food pleases you."

Giles relaxed at the sound of her laughter. He offered a suggestion. "If your aunt needs our chef, let her borrow him. We can use my parents' chef. I'm certain he remained behind when they went to Russia."

"Robbing Peter to pay Paul? Well, I suppose it is one solution," Merry agreed. Her aunt smiled benevolently, as she always did when she got her own way.

"Are morning services at the same time as when I was here last, my dear? If so, I'll have to hurry. Such an interesting minister. Did I mention that I met his cousin, the Earl of Lyster, recently in London? I can hardly wait to give the vicar his regards. Such a wealthy family, and so entertaining. I'll only be a moment." As she swept up the stairs, Mathilda continued as if Merry were beside her, "You must see my newest bonnet. The most exquisite feathers. I rather wondered about them, but my milliner assured me they were the latest thing. Such a becoming blue. I do hope the vicar is giving the sermon himself this morning. The last time I was here the verger gave it. He really does not have quite as resounding a voice as the vicar." Only when the door closed behind her did her voice cease.

Giles followed her progress with amazement and then turned to Merry. "Is she always like this? My

ister is a chatterbox, but your aunt is beyond descrip-
ion. And you spent several months each year with
er?"

Merry laughed once more. "She means well and has
a good heart. I suppose living alone as she does makes
her rely on her own voice for company. When I am
with her, I have found it is sometimes better to nod
and allow her to continue. If she is interrupted, she
sometimes begins again at the beginning."

Giles raised his eyebrows. "I feel sorry for the poor
vicar. Perhaps I'll come, if only to rescue him."

"Even if you divert her momentarily, she will in-
vite the man back to dinner, and he will have to
endure several hours of her conversation about his
noble relative. But I did remind him Aunt Mathilda
would be arriving this week. Perhaps he has had time
to make arrangements to dine elsewhere."

"Miranda Sommerby Lindsey, what an undutiful
niece you are, depriving your dear, sweet aunt of her
prey." Giles's laughter exploded from him, and Merry
joined in. "Now we had better prepare for church
ourselves or that kind man will have to face her alone."

From the moment they entered the carriage until
they entered the church, Mathilda gave a running
account of her pleasures in the city. Afraid to look at
each other for fear of bursting into laughter, Giles and
Merry kept their eyes piously lowered. Only when
they were seated in the Sommerby pew did they exchange glances, but by then the memories they shared
were of their wedding a few days before. The readings,
the sermon, and the hymns sped by. As they left the
church, both Merry and Giles stopped for a quiet
word and a handshake with the vicar who had married them. Mathilda, of course, had reached the limit
of her quietness. Her voice bubbled forth, "My dear
sir, your sermon was so intriguing." Puzzled by her
choice of words, the vicar waited for her to explain,
but she didn't. "How your cousin, the Earl of Lyster,
will enjoy hearing about it. Did I mention that I met
him in London recently? You must come home to

dinner with us, mustn't he, Merry? I have so much
to tell you. So many messages to relate."

Even though both Merry and Giles added their
invitations, the vicar pleaded other commitments. As
soon as they could gracefully pull her away, Giles and
Merry urged Mathilda into the carriage. There she
sulked quietly in one corner. Mathilda hated to have
her plans go awry. With Giles and Merry once again
avoiding each other's eyes for fear of shocking Mathilda
with their laughter, the ride to the Sommerby house
was a quiet one. Sweeping up the stairs to her room,
Mathilda declared her intention of having dinner in
her suite.

Before Merry could even give the footman her cloak
and bonnet, Giles pulled her into the library. The
heavy door swung shut behind them. Their suppressed
laughter echoed in its corners. Laughing so hard he
could hardly get his breath, Giles urged, "Go on. Say
it. 'I told you so.' You deserve the pleasure. Did you
see the look of relief on that poor man's face when he
said he had another commitment?"

"Oh, I haven't laughed so much in weeks. But I feel
so guilty. Aunt Mathilda can be so sweet and helpful
sometimes. But she can also drive me to distraction.
You should see her in Bath surrounded by friends,
who are much like her," Merry said.

"You mean there are more like her? Lord, help us! I
think she rivals Lady Jersey for the nickname 'Silence.'
How did you ever manage?"

"Well, Arabella helped, and there are so many things
to do in Bath. With all her friends there, Aunt Mathilda
didn't spend all her time alone with me. Also, I found
it easier to go along with her plans usually. It was so
much more comfortable."

"I imagine she and the other magpies kept all the
local scandals in everyone's minds. Oh, my sides hurt.
But how am I to face her calmly again?"

"But, Giles, you will have several hours to compose
yourself. Simply do as I do. Think of doing some task
you dislike. I find it works marvelously." Still giggling,

she took the arm he extended to her and entered the
dining room. Although they periodically burst into
laughter during the meal, often startling the servants
who were serving them, by the end of the last course
they had gained control of themselves. For once, Merry
felt completely at ease with her husband; his sense of
the ridiculous so closely paralleled her own. For once,
she did not try to kill the thought that had begun to
slip upon her at the most unexpected times—the
thought that she might be in love with him. Giles, too,
was relaxed. Merry's laughter and giggles delighted
him. When she laughed, she became a warm, happy
person instead of the emotionless woman she tried to
imitate. If only he could keep her laughing.

As soon as the meal ended, Merry visited her aunt.
As usual, a few hours in her own company had caused
Mathilda to forget her irritations, and to long for
visitors. The rest of the afternoon she and Merry
spent in deciding what had to be done before the
Lindseys left for London. Before the day was over,
Merry had completed her lists—lists of household
problems she had to solve, of clothes to be completed
and ordered, of hostesses who owed her aunt favors,
and of merchants to trade with. Her aunt had even
given her a possible location for Madame Camille's
shop. Mathilda had also promised to dash off notes to
her closest friends telling them of the good fortune
that was soon to be theirs. Madame Camille would be
the latest rage in London if Mathilda could arrange it,
and she had great faith in herself. If anyone could
turn Merry into a fashion plate like Lady Farrell, she
assured her, it was Madame Camille. Merry froze for
a moment, but her aunt refused to allow her to dwell
on any one thought. Merry allowed herself to be
diverted, but she promised herself to approach Giles
about that situation as soon as possible. To think she
had allowed herself to relax with him!

From the moment the two women entered the room
before dinner, Giles recognized the change in Merry.
The businesswoman who was in control of her emo-

tions and her life was back. As hard as he tried, he could not break through the shell surrounding her. In fact, the harder he tried, the more calm she grew. Even later that evening when he entered her bedroom and climbed into bed with her, she showed no emotion. As he bent over her to kiss her good-night, she twisted her head away. Almost emotionlessly, she asked, "Was my aunt right about your cousin Honoria and Lady Farrell?"

With a sigh, Giles settled himself against the pillows beside her. So that was what had been wrong this evening, he thought. His postponement had been a short one. "Yes, but remember I told you about Lady Farrell when we first met."

"You did not mention that she was the choice of your family."

"She isn't. In fact, my father threatened to cut me out of his will if I even thought of marrying her." The minute the words had left his mouth, Giles regretted them.

"So you found someone else instead. Someone with a business you were interested in as a dowry." Merry turned on her side away from him, hiding the hurt that was in her face.

"That wasn't the way it was at all." His voice dropped off as he looked at the rigid back in front of him. They had been so close that afternoon. Damn that aunt of hers. But how could he have known that she would know his cousin? Giving up any ideas of trying to explain to Merry but refusing to sleep alone another night, he made himself comfortable.

After a while his breathing slowed. Merry realized he was asleep. Asleep, and she knew as little as she had known before. She could imagine what a reception she was going to get when they arrived to escort Charlotte to town. The anger she had been holding inside her boiled over. Climbing out of bed, she went to the sitting room and lit the branch of candles that stood ready there. Knowing it would be hours before she could sleep, Merry sat at the desk, pulled a sheet of paper from the drawer, sharpened a pen, and began: "Things to do on Monday . . ."

In spite of the fact that she had gotten little sleep the night before, Merry was up early the next morning. By the time Giles was up and dressed, she and Mrs. Barrow had already arranged for holland covers for the unoccupied bedrooms and the large salon, had inspected the pantry for preserves and other items to be shipped in advance to London, and had decided to send only a minimum of linens and then order more with their own monogram.

By the time Giles had finished his breakfast and begun looking for Merry, she, her aunt, and Madame Camille were safely in the sitting room surrounded by dresses in several stages of completion and by fabric and trims of every shade and hue. "Did you need me for something, Giles?" Merry asked, her voice as calm as if there were no problems between them. Recognizing the futility of any discussion while she was in her present mood, he made good his escape, reminding her that they were scheduled to meet Mr. Pettigrew after luncheon that afternoon.

Filled with anger once again as she thought of the way he had manipulated her, Merry nonetheless returned to the all-important question of fashion. Fortunately, most of the garments she had chosen after her marriage were almost finished. They would see her through the visit to Honoria in the country to pick up Charlotte. She turned to her aunt. "Will I need a ball gown, do you think? I know, Aunt Mathilda, I must not dance while I should be in black gloves. But what if Giles's cousin wishes to introduce me to the family at a ball when we go to Kent to rescue Charlotte?"

"You wrong me, Merry. Really you do. I was simply going to suggest that you confine your dancing partners to one person—Giles. No one should object to that." With effort, Merry controlled the dismay she felt from showing on her face. Mathilda continued, "One ball gown may not be enough. Could you finish two, madame?"

Madame Camille wrinkled her forehead as if mentally inspecting her work calendar. "*Mais oui.* But it will mean the packing must be delayed. Simple designs—exquisite fabrics. *Oui,* I will make her shine. The turquoise silk with silver ribbons." Merry remembered the fabric. It looked like Giles's eyes. "For the other, the rose silk gauze with rosebuds." Madame smiled as though she could see the masterpieces she would create. As usual, thoughts of gowns spun her into action. She gathered up the unfinished dresses and the lists of clothes for both Merry and Lady Mathilda and swept from the room.

Her aunt, excited by the glamor of the new styles, insisted on recommending the garments for each occasion. As she said, "Wearing the wrong gown to a party is so countrified. I know you have excellent taste, but even in Bath our activities were not as varied as yours will be in London. With Giles's father in the government, you may even visit the prime minister. Perhaps even His Majesty. No, his health has not been good this year, and he sees so few people these days. Why . . ."

Merry ignored her aunt's monologue. Would Giles turn to Lady Farrell again, she wondered. Even though their marriage was an alliance rather than a love match, it seemed they should be able to make it work. And more than she had ever wanted anything before, Merry wanted her marriage to succeed.

"Merry, Merry? Are you listening to me? I was just saying that I must return to Bath tomorrow. Commitments I had made before I knew of your and Giles's plans. Also, I have invited house guests for a month's stay. But I could put them off." Mathilda sounded rather hesitant, and Merry was quick to reassure her that they would not want her to change her plans. "By the end of the next month, I will come to London to lend you my support. Remember, the important thing in chaperoning a debutante, especially one as personable as I am sure Charlotte is, is maintaining her reputation. You must guard her carefully. Also, as a new bride, your own actions will be carefully scrutinized. But I can rely on your good judgment."

"Why me?" Merry felt like screaming. The thought of being the focus of attention appalled her. One thing she had liked so much about going to parties with Arabella was that her friend captured the center of attention and Merry could relax and enjoy herself. It was my own choice, she reminded herself. I know that will be part of what Giles expects of me.

Just then they were called to luncheon. Mathilda entered the dining room blithely. Merry's fears and the anger she felt over the possible confrontation with his family gave an edge to her voice as she greeted her husband. Even her favorite foods did little to soothe her. The rich chicken soup was excellent, the omelette as fluffy as a cloud, the mushroom fritters hot and delicious, and the *crème brûlé* delightful. Merry ate her way through the courses, answering any questions addressed to her in as few words as possible. Once again Giles regretted his hasty words of the evening before. He consoled himself with the thought that she would have to spend the afternoon with him.

After Mathilda retreated to her bedroom, planning a comfortable afternoon finishing the last volume of the latest novel from London, Giles and Merry entered the library. In spite of the warmth of the room, Giles had begun to dislike it. It brought out everything he would like to forget about Merry. Here the wall between them usually grew thicker. Afraid of saying the wrong thing again, he stayed quiet. The silence between them was almost tangible.

As time passed, Merry grew more and more uncomfortable. Finally she burst out, "Why didn't you tell the whole truth? Did you think I wouldn't find out? Ladies of the *ton* are not exactly kind, you know. What a fool I must have looked to them if I had not known." She turned away from him.

"Merry, I felt the situation in no way could alter your decision. I was a way out for you, and you would save me from Honoria's and Lady Farrell's plans. De-

nise was amusing for a time, but she had begun to
bore me."

"As I will bore you before long? And what then?"

Giles frowned deeply and said, "The situation is
far different between us. Neither of us feels a grand
passion for the other. And we both have what we
want."

"What I wanted was freedom to do as I please, not a
husband who forces himself on me," Merry cried,
striking back at him to suppress the pain she felt
when Giles reminded her of their loveless marriage.
And just when she had begun to love him!

Before Giles could reach her side, Barrow, who had
been told to show Mr. Pettigrew up as soon as he
arrived, opened the door and announced the lawyer.

Hastily, husband and wife hid their anger. But
Giles's eyes promised that Merry would not escape
retribution forever. For a moment, Merry was struck
with a sense of uneasiness. Where had she seen that
look before?

As usual Mr. Pettigrew settled himself quickly to
work. As soon as the pleasantries had been exchanged,
he reminded them of their need to make a choice.
With the aid of Merry's chart and new information
the lawyer had just received, they narrowed their
search to one man—Martin Danby. Merry breathed a
sigh of relief. With Danby in charge and Mr. Pettigrew
to help him, the business should be safe for a time.
The most pressing business finished, Mr. Pettigrew
turned to Merry and asked, "Do you wish to clean out
your grandfather's desk at the office, or shall I? I
believe your grandfather kept a few family mementoes
there."

"Grandmother's miniature. He had a portrait in his
bedroom but kept the miniature in the office." Merry
paused. "And the file of letters from India. I would
like to store them here for safekeeping."

Seeing the look on her face, Giles assured the lawyer they would visit the office that very afternoon,
using the visit as an opportunity to inform Danby of

his good fortune. "Would you care to accompany us, sir?" he asked.

A short time later the three of them entered the office. Startled and afraid of the changes they believed must happen, the clerks looked up. Merry and Giles simply smiled and entered her grandfather's office. Mr. Pettigrew promised to seek out Danby to bring him to them.

As she seated herself behind the desk her grandfather had occupied for so long, Merry raised her eyes and gasped. The bright blue-green eyes of her great-grandfather stared back at her. Perhaps that was why Giles seemed so familiar. Although he and Giles looked little alike in other ways, they resembled each other around the eyes. It was only just, she thought bitterly, that those eyes belonged to men who took advantage of women. She grimaced in disgust and opened the desk drawer, carefully sorting out the personal documents.

As she searched through the papers, she scarcely noticed when Giles left to cross the street to the warehouse and docks. As the pile of private papers grew, she put them in a small tea box that was conveniently at hand—a letter from her grandmother to her grandfather, a note in her father's hand, a report from India on her progress in mathematics and business, and finally a rather stained and crumpled letter in a girlish hand relating her father's and mother's deaths. She stared at it for a long time. She had refused to let anyone else write it for her. Even now, she remembered her feeling of desolation. Well, she was alone again. Carefully, she put the letter on top of the others in the box.

As if to prove her thought false, Giles, Mr. Pettigrew, and Martin Danby, his face reflecting his surprise and good fortune, entered the room. The meeting that followed was short and to the point. Giles encouraged Merry to explain Danby's new responsibilities, and both the Lindseys promised they would provide the new manager detailed instructions on the course of the company. Promising to see him again before they left for London, Giles and Merry took their leave. Although they offered him a ride, Mr. Pettigrew declined, preferring to walk down the street to his office. With his promise to bring his wife to dine with them on Tuesday evening, Merry and Giles entered their carriage.

The next two days seemed to fly by. After waving off her aunt, both Merry and Giles turned to the serious business of the removal to London. By late Tuesday afternoon, Giles had sent an express to his London staff and the fourgon with the linens and other necessities was on its way.

While Merry was drawing up pages of instructions for the Barrows and Danby, Giles insured their comfort on the road, sending grooms with fresh horses ahead in easy stages. With them went his instructions for securing places at the best inns along the road. With the weather as unpredictable as it could be, he knew the roads might be treacherous. The snow had fallen late into the year and was still heavy along some roads. As he included the ingredients for his special punch recipe for the host of the inn where they would stop for the evening, he thought of a brisk cold wind and of the two of them snuggled cosily under a fur lap robe.

Their promised visit to Danby completed and their farewells to the Pettigrews made, early the next morning Giles and Merry left. Hours earlier, their valet and maid had left with the luggage in Giles's coach. As always when she was going away, the Barrows were present to hand Merry into the large, comfortable carriage her grandfather had enjoyed. Before the footman put up the steps and closed the door, Mrs. Barrow said, "Remember to write, Miss Merry, and let us know when you will be returning." Merry wondered if she would ever live in Bristol again.

The door closed at last, the flaps over the windows tied down to prevent draughts, the coach plunged forward with a jolt. In spite of the latest in springs, the ride was somewhat bumpy at first, the traffic in the town having worn ruts and holes in the roads. Gradually Merry grew accustomed to the jolting. Because she had not slept well for several nights, after a time in the silence in the coach Merry drifted off to sleep, twisting and turning, trying to find a comfortable spot. Giles smiled ruefully as she angled herself carefully into a corner so that she would not bother him. After she had been asleep for a time, Giles pulled her out of the corner and close against him, tucking her head against his shoulder. Pulling the fur robe close about them both, he too slept.

Several hours later the coach pulled into the inn where they would make their first change of horses. Giles awoke feeling slightly stiff. As he lifted his arms to stretch, he felt Merry beside him. Reluctant to disturb her, he hesitated. But the noise outside had already awakened her. Realizing where she was resting, she pulled away.

"Shall we descend, my dear? I believe the innkeeper has nuncheon prepared for us. And the coachman and groom need some time to rest," he said.

As he stepped down, he turned to help her. Slightly stiff from her unaccustomed sleeping position, Merry stumbled. Only Giles's arms saved her from falling into one of the smelly puddles in the innyard. In spite of her protests and the raised eyebrows of the hostlers in the yard, Giles carried her into the inn, putting her down only at the door of the private parlor he had ordered. Slipping out of her cloak, Merry excused herself for a few minutes. While she was gone, the meal arrived. Though at first she tried to hurry, Giles encouraged her to relax and enjoy the hearty soup, meat, bread, and hot tea the cook had provided. As her body warmed, so did her spirits. Grimacing at a piece of stringy mutton, she said, "Why is it that English cooks tend to undercook the worst cuts of meat? But at least the soup is good."

"Yes, but you've never tasted stringy meat until you've been to the Americas. Indians there have a dish they refer to as jerky. And jerk is what you do when you try to bite into it. It is travel food, sun-dried meat with an excellent flavor. The first time I tried it, though, I thought my teeth would fall out. Maybe someday we can visit Canada, and you can taste some for yourself."

For the rest of the meal, Giles entertained her with stories of memorable or infamous travel meals. As they entered the carriage once more, Merry was trying to explain the variety of curries that India provided. As she sank into her corner and Giles into his, the coach rumbled forward, hitting a particularly nasty rut just as they left the inn. Merry, who had not yet taken hold of the strap beside her, was thrown almost into Giles's lap. Struggling away from him, she tried to resettle herself in her corner, but Giles held on to her. He said, "Perhaps if we sit together we can prevent some of the jolting and stay warmer too. In spite of the nuncheon we just had, I wish I had some of that curry if it is as hot as you say."

Cautiously, Merry relaxed slightly beside him, not even struggling as she was thrown against him again when they hit another bump. He continued, "This reminds me of traveling in the colonies. In some places the roads are so marshy and swampy that the people in the area have built corduroy roads. Have you ever traveled on one? It would make the bumps on this road appear mild."

The rest of the afternoon they exchanged travel stories. But by the time they reached the George and the Dragon where they were to spend the night, Giles had to admit that Merry had bested him. Riding an elephant certainly put his corduroy road to shame.

Letting the innkeeper's wife show Merry to the rooms where her maid waited, Giles checked on the accommodations for the servants, arranging for extra rations of ale to compensate for the chill in the air. As the door closed behind the woman, Merry stretched, smiling at her maid who stood ready with hot water and fresh clothes. "Was your trip comfortable, Pilgrim?" she asked, smiling again as she remembered the way she and Giles had squabbled over the importance of their adventures.

"Very pleasant, ma'am. Mr. Giles certainly knows how to travel well. There was luncheon waiting as though we were somebody. I've even got my own private room here tonight." At this Merry looked up sharply, realizing that unlike other journeys, Pilgrim no longer had to share her room because now it was Giles's responsibility to protect her. "It is just down the hall across from Mr. Giles's valet, Petersham. A very quiet man, Mr. Petersham, but very knowledgeable. It is a pleasure to work with him. But now perhaps you want to refresh yourself. Mr. Giles suggested that you would not need to dress for the evening as he had ordered supper to be served in the sitting room. Perhaps this nightrobe and dressing gown?"

Freshly attired in comfortable clothes, Merry was in the sitting room on the settee when Giles entered the suite. Bending her head over her needlework, she simply nodded when he announced he wished to change before supper arrived.

"And I have a surprise for you," he promised. No sooner had he emerged in his elegant dressing gown than a scratching sounded at the door. "The surprise," he exclaimed, throwing open the door before Merry could retreat to the bedroom. The inkeeper entered carrying a punch bowl, which he set carefully in the middle of the table. His wife, who followed, brought oranges, lemons, spices, lumps of sugar, champagne, brandy, and a sharp knife. "We'll ring for supper later," Giles promised as the pair left the room.

"Now let me see." He pushed up his sleeves and mixed the punch. In a few minutes he plunged a hot poker into the mixture, stirred, and poured her a mug and picked up one of his own. "To my Wife . . ." He raised his mug and downed the little he had put in it, urging her to empty hers as well. Although the mixture seemed a trifle sweet to her, Merry exclaimed over the taste. Refilling her cup, Giles smiled to himself. With any luck, she would soon be very relaxed. As she finished her second serving, Giles rang for supper, which appeared almost instantly. The roasted capons and hot apple tart topped with sharp cheddar cheese went well with the spicy punch. Giles made certain that Merry's mug was never empty, but slowed his own drinking. He wanted to savor this evening.

As they ate, Giles began to talk about what he wanted from life, what he hoped to accomplish. Like his father he wanted to serve his country, not as a soldier but as a businessman. "I've seen too many of the men I went to school with end up with useless lives, going from gambling to drinking and back again until they've ruined their fortunes and their health. As long as Father is gone, I suppose I must stay in England, but I promise someday we will travel again."

Merry smiled understandingly. She was feeling more in charity with Giles than she had in several days, and not just because of the punch. "India. That's where I want to go again," she said. "And Greece. Can we go to Greece?"

"As soon as Napoleon is no longer a threat. Now let's go to bed." He pulled her up from the corner of the settee. Putting his arm around her waist, he led her into the bedroom. Without a protest she allowed him to remove her dressing gown. He pulled her close against him and kissed her. His lips were gentle, persuasive.

For the first time since their marriage, Merry's protective armor completely disappeared. She glanced up at him, the love that she was still unwilling to completely admit even to herself shining in her eyes. Her fears of marriage were forgotten as she reveled in the feelings he was creating in her. He made her feel desirable, loved.

As Giles's hands ran down her shoulders and sides, his kisses grew deeper, his tongue teasing her lips and exploring her mouth. To his surprise and pleasure, Merry returned his kisses. She lifted her arms around is neck, pulling him closer. As his hands and mouth roamed her body, he slipped her nightrobe from her, enjoying once again the sight of her rounded figure and clear, glowing skin. For a moment he pulled away to enjoy the sight. Impatient, Merry reached for him once again. As she did, her hand caught the belt of his dressing gown and pulled it free. The garment swung open. Instead of lowering her eyes at the sight of a nude man as she once would have done, Merry ran her hands through the hair on his chest to his waist and beyond. Gasping with pleasure, Giles dropped the robe on the floor and pulled her close, letting her feel his arousal. As she wiggled against him, trying to let her body melt into his, he picked her up and carried her to the bed. The once light caresses became burning. His lips circled one nipple, pulling at it while one hand explored her womanhood, finding her ready for him. As he lifted himself above her, she opened her legs instinctively. Her gasps of pleasure echoed throughout the room as he plunged into her, careful at first not to go too deeply. Soon, however, their motions complemented each other and her hands pressed against him, bringing him closer. Her hips lifted upward as he plunged down. Soon her moans had become cries as she exploded with pleasure. As the vibrations rippled through her body, Giles too shuddered with pleasure and whispered her name before sinking beside her, still half covering her with his body. His voice made a song of her name as she sank into sleep.

—7—

Even though the church bells were pealing five, the sun had almost set when the fashionable traveling coach pulled into Grosvenor Square. As soon as the steps were let down, Giles jumped out. He turned to give his hand to Merry. By holding tightly to the door, she managed to descend without his help. His mouth tight, Giles led her into the hall where the servants stood waiting to greet her.

"Here is my butler, Johnson. He will present the others." Giles stood back, wondering as he had done all day if he would ever understand his wife. From the moment she had awakened, still held close in his arms, he had wondered about her reaction. She had opened her eyes. He could see her shock at their closeness. Then she broke into violent tears. If he'd had the choice, he would have preferred the tears to the person she had become for the rest of the day. As she completed the line and came to join him, he could see that her self-possession was as usual a pose. What had given her the need to hide her emotions, he wondered.

"Now, let me show you to our suite," Giles said, leading her up the stairs. "I just had it redecorated, but if you want to change it, or the rest of the house, please tell me." No sense in mentioning that it had been done as a surprise for her.

For a moment Merry's face lit up as she saw the ivory, gold, and green room. He had used the colors from her former bedroom. The walls were ivory. The curtains and sofa were soft green trimmed in light gold. The carpet was like a carpet of grass dotted with ivory, pink and gold flowers. Giles opened the door on the right. "Our bedroom and your dressing room." Her face froze into an expressionless mask again. Closing the door on the soft green walls and ivory curtains and bed hangings, Giles led her through a doorway on the left. Perhaps this would please her. "I hope you will be able to work here," he said. He led her to a rich, dark pigeonhole desk already equipped with paper, ink, pens, and a pen knife. "I had a chandler send over a ship's chart rack for you also." He smiled gently. "My dressing room is beside this. There is a door from the sitting room and the bathing room is beside it."

Merry looked around her in amazement. Never had she seen such a perfect place for her to work. The desk, although large, was the right height for her as was the chair she settled herself in. Fingering the feathers of the pens, she turned to him shyly. Her fears at her reactions to him seemed less important than his consideration. Her quiet thanks softened the severity of her expression. "I have never seen such a peaceful place to work. I will enjoy it," she said, turning once more to the desk. This room had so obviously been redecorated just for her. Appreciating the gift yet still hesitant, she said, "Perhaps I should write a note to Mr. Pettigrew to let him know we arrived safely."

"Please yourself," Giles said. He continued, "After the journey I have a need of a bath. Why don't you ring for Pilgrim and have her arrange for one for you, too?" Her gasp was quickly swallowed. "Your bathing chamber is beside your dressing room. Don't rush. We keep town hours. Dinner is at eight." He disappeared into the sitting room.

For the first time during the long day, Merry let her tension flow from her. Perhaps a bath would help. Sitting in the warm water, Merry allowed the memo-

ries to come drifting back across her mind. She felt
betrayed, but not by Giles. He was only a man with a
man's passions. She had betrayed herself. Her memories of the previous evening were blurry. But she
could remember the eager way she had reached for
Giles not once but several times during the night. Her
pleasure and excitement accused her now. She was as
wanton as her mother. The tears ran down her face
unchecked. She was afraid her body would betray her
again. Gradually she gained control.

Dressed for the evening, Merry had once again become the small, serene, individual she was used to
seeing in her mirror. Taking a deep breath, she followed the footman to the drawing room where Giles
waited. Although dinner seemed interminable, she
dreaded its end, but Giles once again surprised her.

"You go on to bed, Merry. I am going to visit my
club to see who's in town. Have to get our names on
the invitation lists. I will send an announcement of
our marriage to the papers in the morning. Private
ceremony and all that. By tomorrow, we'll be ready to
look for that shop. I want to make the trip to rescue
Charlotte soon." He bent over her hand gallantly and
left.

For the next few days they visited shop after shop,
checking each for showroom, dressing rooms, and work
room areas. Finally they settled on the building Lady
Mathilda had suggested. Located on a corner, it had
both ample working space and a place for Madame
Camille to live. After Giles signed the papers, assuring her that her wishes were his, Merry dashed off an
express to the modiste. With luck, she thought, Madame Camille would be in London before the next
week was out. Already, painters, carpenters, and cabi-
netmakers were busy creating a magnificent showroom with beautiful bay windows.

The problem of the shop solved, Merry turned to
the house. It needed little but extra polish to keep it
sparkling. Two footmen, a new upstairs maid, and
another tweeny would arrive from Bristol soon. After

he had inspected the house, Merry made few changes,
ut she insisted on having the walls of all the servants'
uarters whitewashed and lighting the fires in their
uarters to get the damp out. Ordering new linens
nd new household livery took only a day. Installing
he new closed stove that Andre, Giles's parents' chef,
equired would be done during the Lindseys' trip to
he country.

By Monday, they were ready to set off. When their
oach pulled away from the steps, Merry was happy
o see the last of the city for a while yet dreaded the
rdeal ahead. "Does your cousin expect us today?"
he asked, her face slightly shadowed with fear as she
hought of facing Giles's sister and cousin.

"I wrote Honoria as soon as we arrived. Charlotte
hould be ready. I don't plan to stay longer than one
ight or maybe two," he reassured her. "When my
arents get home, then we'll really go into the country.
think you'll like my property in the Lake District."

"I can hardly wait to see the area Wordsworth has
made famous."

"Wordsworth, that radical! Your grandfather let you
ead him?"

"I will have you know that I have long been the
rbitrator of my own taste. I need no one's permission
o read what I like." Merry's voice was cold.

Laughing at her indignation, Giles asked, "Have
ou read this?

> For oft, when on my couch I lie
> In vacant or in pensive mood,
> They flash upon that inward eye
> Which is the bliss of solitude;
> And then my heart with pleasure fills,
> And dances with the daffodils."

His voice seemed to swell as he finished the last line.
For a moment Merry was mesmerized.

"What is it called? Do you have a copy?" she asked.
"The poem is 'I Wandered Lonely As a Cloud,' and

as soon as we return to London I'll show you my copy
in his own hand," he assured her.

"You've met him. Tell me about him," she demanded.

A few hours later, the coach stopped. Startled, Merry
and Giles glanced out. "We're here already?" he
wondered. They had been lost in the beauties of nature and literature, and the hours had passed swiftly.
Merry took a deep breath. The ordeal was at hand.

A very stiff and upright butler showed them into
the formal drawing room where three women waited.
The older woman with graying hair rose. "Giles, what
a surprise you gave us. And this must be your bride."
Like her eyes, her voice was cold.

"This is Merry, Cousin Honoria. Merry, this is my
cousin, Honoria Coverly." Merry tentatively stepped
forward, and Honoria retreated as though close contact with Merry might contaminate her. With effort,
Merry controlled her face so that her dismay was not
apparent. But her eyes brimmed with tears. Giles
flashed an angry glance at his cousin before leading
Merry to where a beautiful dark-haired girl with eyes
like his own sat quietly on the sofa. Her face was alive
with excitement.

"And this troublesome brat is my sister, Charlotte.""

"Giles, how could you? What will your wife think
of me?" Charlotte exclaimed, rising to embrace him.
Although her handshake for Merry was not a warm
greeting, it was not a rejection either. Merry smiled,
and Charlotte smiled back. Charlotte was rather surprised by Merry. Although Merry was not the dasher
that Charlotte expected, she liked Merry and was
willing to accept Giles's choice.

"Have you forgotten me, Giles?" drawled a lazy
voice. Giles turned toward the chair in which the
third woman, an elegant blonde with beautiful but
cold eyes, was seated.

"Merry, Lady Farrell. She is Honoria's godchild."
His introduction was brief. This time, Merry did not
make the mistake of expecting a conventional greeting.

Denise's eyes seemed to be inspecting her from the top of her head to the tip of her toes.

Turning back to Giles, she seemed to suggest that Merry had been evaluated and dismissed. "When you left London in such a hurry, I little thought that the next time we met you would have married someone else. And without even a note to your family or me." Her purring tones suggested the claws Merry was sure she possessed.

"Oh, my parents and my sister knew my plans. I had an obligation to them, you know." The coldness of his voice startled Merry. Even Lady Farrell drew back from him. She knew well the anger he could display.

Sensing the tension in the room even though she was not certain of all the reasons for it, Charlotte said, "I can hardly wait to return to London. How I long to dance and to attend the theater. And shopping. Oh, how I miss shopping." Her voice was very wistful.

Merry smiled at her while Giles said, "Now, Charlotte, you sound as though you've been away for years instead of only three months. When we return, you may shop as much as your allowance will bear." He glanced at Merry. "Honoria, my wife and I would like to freshen up. Will you have someone show us to our room?"

As Giles, Merry, and Charlotte went up the curving stairs, Merry had a view of the scene they had just left. Honoria, her figure spare in its purple silk gown, was lecturing Lady Farrell, who had moved to the blue settee in front of the gold-framed mirror that reflected her dark blond hair and voluptuous figure. How Merry wished she could hear what they were saying. She knew, though, that they were not complimenting her.

Even though both Giles and Merry wanted to return to London promptly, Honoria insisted they spend at least two evenings with her. She had, as she told Giles, arranged to introduce Merry to her neighbors, first at a hunt and later that evening at a dinner and a ball. "Everyone of any importance will be here," she said. Her cold tone hinted that Merry would be out of place, but she was careful to stay within the bounds of polite behavior at least when Giles was present.

Whenever Giles was not present, however, both Honoria and Denise quizzed Merry extensively. "Do you play the harp or the piano? Neither? Why, how peculiar!"

"When were you presented at court? Never? Oh, some financial problems, I suppose. No? How strange. And you are to be in charge of Charlotte's debut?"

"Which of the hostesses at Almack's will you approach for an invitation? You cannot be serious. Poor Charlotte. Her Season doomed before it is even begun." The questions and comments continued flying like lightning bolts. "And where did you say your home was? In Bristol? How dreary."

With effort, Merry held her tongue. Her wall of calm was a barrier that infuriated her enemies. Had they realized how many of their barbs had pierced that wall they would have rejoiced.

By the time the afternoon and evening were over, Merry was looking forward to the hunt despite the fact that she was an indifferent rider. Giles too was looking forward to a brisk ride and some action.

The next morning was clear and brisk. After a hasty breakfast the company dashed to the courtyard to mount up. By the time Merry arrived, both Lady Farrell and Charlotte were already mounted, Charlotte on a docile chestnut mare and Denise on a dashing black stallion. Honoria, the reins of her horse in her hands, stood talking to Giles.

"Oh, there you are, my dear. I have just the horse for you," she promised Merry, pointing out a tall gray. "It has such a comfortable gait." Honoria smiled at Merry. "Well, let's be off."

Looking from his petite wife to the tall horse, Giles hesitated, waiting for her to comment. Taking her silence as assent instead of the fear it really was, he tossed Merry into the saddle and then mounted his own choice, a spirited chestnut stallion. With dogs baying and the horns blaring, they left the manor behind.

After a time, Merry began to relax. Her horse seemed to behave as it should. Gritting her teeth, she followed the pack across the first jump, a stream. She noticed that Charlotte, who was also at the rear, kept throwing anxious glances her way. Perhaps she is worried because she heard me say this is my first hunt, Merry thought. The idea reassured her. She looked to the head of the pack where the Master of the Hounds, Honoria, Lady Farrell, and Giles rode neck and neck behind the frantic dogs. The next jump just ahead of them looked more difficult.

Charlotte dropped back beside her. She seemed to be saying something, but the pounding of the hoof-beats and the clamor of the dogs and horns drowned her out. The leaders were safely over the stone wall. Charlotte cleared it with ease but turned anxiously toward Merry.

The gray planted its feet, tossing Merry from her precarious perch on the sidesaddle. Only her training in India saved her from serious injury as she was thrown over the wall. "Relax, go limp," she reminded herself as she shielded her head and face. Stunned by the force of the fall, she lay there for a time. In the background she could hear Charlotte's soft voice. The deeper tones closer to her ear had to be Giles's.

"Merry, Merry! Where are you hurt? Speak to me!" he demanded.

"If I could speak, I would," she tried to say, but only a few squeaks came out. A whiff of smelling salts caused her to gasp. "I'm only winded, I think," she managed to reassure him. After checking her carefully for broken bones, he lifted her in front of his saddle and mounted behind her.

"We're returning to the manor," he told the group. "You finish the hunt." Honoria and Denise exchanged angry glances. Then they insisted on accompanying the party to the house. Charlotte, who had never enjoyed hunting at any time, also turned back.

After the hot bath Giles had insisted on, Merry went to bed. By the time the fox had been caught and the hunt and breakfast were over, she awoke refreshed. Beside her, Giles sat staring at her.

"Are you certain you're all right?" he asked, his eyes worried.

She smiled up at him and moved cautiously before she spoke. "A few bumps and bruises, that's all. I could get up right now if I need to."

"No, rest at least until dinner. And no going downstairs tonight, either. In fact, I think you should just stay in bed. I'll make our excuses."

"Our excuses?" Merry looked at him questioningly.

"Well, I'm not going to leave you alone up here," Giles stated.

A scratching sounded at the door to the hall. Giles opened the door to his sister. "I just had to see how Merry is. I tried to warn her, really I did. As soon as I saw the stone wall, I remembered."

Giles frowned at her. "Remembered what?" he asked.

"Why, that the gray is sometimes skittish going over them. Remember, Merry, I tried to tell you."

Merry reassured her. "You certainly did. I wish I had heard you." Charlotte sighed with relief. Giles turned to leave the room, mentioning that he needed to speak to Honoria. Charlotte, recognizing his intent, was quick to assure him that the choice of mounts had been accidental. Merry, remembering Honoria's comments, was not so certain.

Instead of facing the quizzing she had expected that afternoon, Merry enjoyed herself. Although Giles felt committed to take tea with his cousin, Charlotte stayed with Merry. When Giles's letter had arrived and she learned of his marriage, Charlotte had been shocked. Giles marrying a tradesman's granddaughter! But Merry was his choice, no matter her own opinion. Of course, she was not beautiful like Lady Farrell, but

Merry had a delightful voice and she seemed to care about people. After three months wth Honoria, Charlotte appreciated a caring attitude. Slowly she began to relax.

When Giles rejoined them, Charlotte had just finished listing the clothes she felt she would need to begin the Season. Giles cocked an eyebrow. "Well, I see Merry's already influencing you. You have a list ready," he laughed. Merry turned pink, but Charlotte just looked at him questioningly. "A private joke," he said when he saw his sister's face. "Now, you must go and dress for dinner and the ball. I'll stay with Merry."

Charlotte had just been gone a short time when Honoria swept in, closely followed by Lady Farrell. "We have been so worried about you. Are you certain you do not need a doctor?" Honoria asked.

When Merry assured them that she only needed to rest, Lady Farrell turned her dark blue eyes on Giles. "Please come down for dinner and the ball," she drawled. "You know I simply will not enjoy one minute of the evening if you're not there." She smiled enchantingly. "I'm certain that Merry would not deny you some entertainment." Her eyes promised more than her voice.

Merry opened her mouth to assure Giles that he was free to go if he wished, but Giles answered first. "I believe that I will wait until Merry can be with me. Perhaps next time." Giles missed the flash of anger in Denise's eyes, but Merry did not. The lady was one person she would have to watch. How she hated the social whirl, with its polite manners and wicked morals.

The dinner served in their suite was excellent, though somewhat cold. From the lobster patties to the exquisite sugar baskets full of sweetmeats, Giles talked more about the places he had been. Merry delighted in the stories about Algiers, especially, but she refused to believe he had once been a prisoner in a harem. As she pointed out, sultans, or rajahs in India, were very protective of their own property. By the time the music began to drift upstairs, they were squabbling amiably and breaking into shared laughter. The thought that they were to return to London on the morrow kept Merry's spirits up.

The next morning, despite protests from Honoria that Merry needed another day of rest, Giles put Merry into the coach and surrounded her with pillows. He and Charlotte shared the opposite seat so that she could recline. The ordeal over, Merry sank gratefully into her nest of pillows and whiled away the journey by planning Charlotte's Season. Before Giles could be bored with so much social planning, they were at the London house once again.

—8—

No sooner had the knocker gone up on the Lindseys' front door, than Merry began to learn firsthand the difficulties of a London Season. Unlike Bath, where one simply paid the subscription fees, in London a hostess with a young lady to present had to make the right social contacts. Fortunately, Giles had traveled in the first circles all of his life.

For Merry, this knowledge gave her little pleasure. It meant it was she, not Giles or Charlotte, who was on trial. From the time the announcement that Mr. and Mrs. Giles Lindsey were at home and were receiving visitors appeared in the paper, Merry felt she was on display, and this time there was no Arabella to shield her.

The first to call, Lady Jersey, left her in no doubt as to why she came. Her slightly malicious voice seemed to echo throughout the drawing room. "Really, my dears, it was the least I could do for the son of my husband's closest friend." She looked Merry over critically. "Yes, she'll do. But, children, such a hasty marriage! Well, I will do my part. An invitation for our ball, of course." She paused dramatically. "And vouchers for Almack's. Or has Lady Sefton already promised them?"

"No, Lady Jersey," Merry replied coolly. Realizing her guest's displeasure, she hurried on, "You are our first visitor. We are honored with your kindness."

The acknowledgment of her importance lent Lady

Jersey more animation. "Well, Charlotte, if you mean to be first stare, you must do something about your clothes. What was your mother thinking to choose that color for you?"

"Mother didn't choose this. Cousin Honoria did," Charlotte was quick to reply.

"Well, yes, I see." Lady Jersey smiled slyly, remembering Honoria's plans for Denise. "Discard it immediately. Now, my dears, I must go." She stood. "Giles, you may escort me to my carriage." Majestically, she swept from the room.

Alone, Merry and Charlotte looked at each other, sank to their chairs, and sighed. "With Lady Jersey leading the way, the rest won't be far behind," Charlotte told Merry smugly.

Merry looked at her sister-in-law carefully. "She is right. You do need different colors in your wardrobe. Did Honoria choose all your clothes?"

"No, most of them Denise ordered from her 'gem of a dressmaker.'"

Merry nodded her head in understanding. Then she asked hesitantly, "Will she and Honoria be in town soon?"

"Before Honoria declared she would never be seen with a hoyden like me, they planned to come. However, they usually are late arrivals."

Merry smiled slightly. "That will give us a chance to surprise them." She and Charlotte exchanged meaningful glances. Over the last few days, Merry and her sister-in-law had come to respect each other. Charlotte admired Merry's organization and serenity while Charlotte kept Merry amused.

Charlotte was rarely quiet, and her keenly observant eye made her a natural mimic. When Giles reentered the drawing room a few minutes later, he paused in the doorway, entranced by Merry's laughter. Charlotte, who was prancing about the room, had captured Lady Jersey perfectly. Laughing, he cautioned, "Had the lady returned with me you would have been forced to retire to the country."

"Return? After a proper call of exactly thirty minutes? Really, Giles, dear boy, that would not be good *ton*."

Once again, Charlotte's mimicry sent Merry into gales of laughter. Giles and Charlotte herself soon joined in. Collapsed on the chairs around the room, the three of them struggled to gain control. The care-free laughter they shared was a happy memory in the hectic days that followed.

To Merry, used to the quiet business world of Bristol, it seemed as though they were never still. They were either out replenishing their wardrobes or receiving yet another visitor. Everyone wanted to see the woman who had stolen Giles from the acclaimed beauty who had made no secret of her intentions to marry him.

For Merry, it was like being in a goldfish bowl, her every movement discussed and dissected. Therefore, when Johnson announced Hugo Darryl one afternoon, she did not refuse to see him. He was not her favorite person, but he was her relative, someone who knew her as an individual and not simply Giles's wife or Charlotte's chaperone.

Hugo did all he could to maintain a pleasant relationship. After he greeted Merry, he plunged immediately into a speech so glib that Merry thought he had to have rehearsed it. "My dearest cousin, how kind you are to receive me. How can you ever forgive me? I will never forgive myself for letting my disappointment enflame me so that I almost harmed you. I am so ashamed!" He struck a pose, the back of his right hand covering his eyes.

Merry, embarrassed, urged, "Let us never refer to it again."

Breathing an exaggerated sigh of relief, Hugo sat down and allowed Merry to pour him a cup of tea. For the rest of his visit, he enlivened the time with his biting comments on the leaders of the *ton* and the latest rumors from the Exchange. Charlotte, who wandered in after Hugo had been there a short while, seemed amused by his vivid character assassinations.

But after he had taken his leave and the two women were once more alone, Charlotte said, "He may be your cousin, Merry, but I don't trust him. He can destroy you with his tongue. He may be dangerous."

Although Merry knew Charlotte was right, over the next few weeks Hugo became a regular visitor. With him, Merry talked business, and he hung on her every word. Giles, discovering him comfortably ensconced in the drawing room for the second time that week, protested when he got Merry alone, "I don't like him here. Hugo tried to kill you."

"Hugo assured me that he was overcome by disappointment. It will not happen again."

"I don't plan to give him that chance. I do not want you to have anything more to do with him. Refuse to see him the next time he comes."

It was the wrong approach to take with Merry. "Are you commanding me to refuse to see my cousin?" Merry's eyes flashed.

Giles, seeing her calm shattered, recognized the danger signs. He beat a hasty retreat. "I simply urge you to treat him with care. He's not a man I trust."

"Giles, don't you think I know that after all these years?" When he lifted his eyebrow quizzically, she continued, "Hugo is the only person in London other than you who knew Grandfather." Her voice was wistful.

Struck by the loneliness in her voice, Giles told her, "See him if you wish. But guard yourself." Merry was usually so calm he sometimes forgot she needed anyone. "Be cautious. I worry about you, my dear." His voice was soft, caressing. Shyly, Merry smiled at him, nodding her agreement.

The Season was soon in full swing. Charlotte, from her first appearance, was the center of any ball. To most young men of the *ton*, her presence was essential to the success of any evening.

The opening ball at Almack's had been her initial success. Like the other young ladies being introduced to society, Charlotte had been dressed in white, but it

vas no ordinary white. Madame Camille had accented
he blue-white tissue silk with deep turquoise flutter-
ng ribbons that matched Charlotte's eyes. Pearls hung
rom her ears and around her neck. From her high
iled dark curls to the tips of her white silk slippers
he had glowed with happiness.

When her partner led her onto the floor for the
pening set, one lovestruck young man exclaimed, "I
nust dance with that dark goddess." To Charlotte's
itter delight the name became permanent. From the
noment morning calls were proper the next morning,
he Corinthians and Tulips had appeared on their
loorstep with regularity.

Although Charlotte enjoyed her position as a reign-
ng beauty, the opening weeks of the Season had not
een as pleasant for Merry. Her capture of one of the
vealthy bachelors of the *ton* had made her the target
f many barbs from disappointed matrons and their
laughters. "What can he see in her?" Merry had
verheard more than one woman ask.

One night, as on most evenings during the last six
weeks, Merry, Giles, and Charlotte were among the
hrong of people waiting to be introduced at the latest
crush. Looking around at the others who inched their
way toward the glittering ballroom, Merry gasped in
dismay. Lady Farrell stood only a few steps above
them. Giles, already regretting his decision to act as
their escort, glanced at his wife. Merry quickly donned
her calm mask. But in the two months since their
marriage, Giles had learned to look beyond the surface.
Her hand had unconsciously tightened on his arm.

Leaning down to whisper in her ear, Giles asked,
"What's the matter? Are you ill? Perhaps we should
return home."

Taking a firm grasp on her emotions, Merry replied,
"I just remembered something I forgot to do; that's
all. We must stay. Charlotte is promised for every
set." So softly he almost missed it, she added, "But I
wish we could."

Giles's hand covered hers where it rested on his

arm and squeezed it. His eyes were warm and happy
as he said, "There at least I can hold more than your
hand." His eyes dropped to her deep neckline.

Coloring as she usually did when he began to tease
her, she started to reply. "Mr. and Mrs. Lindsey and
Miss Charlotte Lindsey," the butler announced. For
the next few minutes, polite phrases occupied her as
she greeted Lord and Lady Jersey. Her host's friend-
ship with Giles's father had smoothed her introduction to society. Lady Jersey, who enjoyed seeing the
discomfort of other ladies, turned to Giles. "Have you
seen Lady Farrell lately? When we met this evening
she asked if you would be present," she said sweetly.
"Here is Charlotte's partner for the opening dance.
I'm certain your wife will excuse you if you wish to
find Lady Farrell."

"What? And miss the opportunity to dance with
you? Never!" Giles held out his arm.

"Naughty boy, you know I cannot leave the receiving line so early. I'll find you later," Lady Jersey
promised.

As the musicians began the opening strains of the
music, Giles led Merry onto the floor. He laughed
down at her. "Thank heavens for etiquette." As he
twirled his wife through the formal measures, he took
every opportunity to flirt with her. As they came
close together, he said, "Tell Madame Camille I like
that dress. It is most becoming." He smiled.

Her blush deepened. Merry tried to ignore him. Her
dress, one of the latest from Madame Camille, was a
soft pink figured crepe trimmed with blond lace around
the deep scoop neckline and short sleeves. She had
postponed wearing it, fearing its deep neckline was
immodest. Only the repeated urgings of Charlotte and
Pilgrim had persuaded her that it was suitable. Looking around her, Merry could see that they were right.
Next to Lady Farrell's filmy dress worn over a trans-
parent petticoat, hers was modesty itself.

The dance ending, Giles led her from the floor. He
escorted her to Charlotte, who was as usual surrounded

y young men. As Merry and Giles approached, one of
he young men stepped back, landing on the hem of
Merry's gown. It tore. Making her excuses, she re-
reated to a quiet room where she made her repairs
well hidden from prying eyes. Perhaps Pilgrim had
been right when she said the dresses needed to be
shortened, she thought. Merry had finished and was
about to reenter the ballroom when she was trapped.
Two ladies occupied the sofa outside the small room.
Sending their gallants after refreshments, they began
talking. "I simply most know the modiste who dresses
the Dark Goddess and her chaperone," one soft voice
stated.

"Why?"

"Have you seen the charming dress the chaperone
is wearing? So elegant. I must have the name of the
modiste." Merry's spirits began to rise but dropped
with the woman's next words. "Dressing a beauty is
one thing, but dressing a dumpy woman takes true
talent. If she makes *her* look elegant, imagine what she
can do for me." The voices faded as the women rejoined their escorts.

Merry, laughing a little at her own vanity, left her
hiding place. "At least my dress is elegant," she
murmured. She reentered the ballroom, and her laughter died. Giles stood close to one end of the ballroom
talking to Lady Farrell. Quietly, Merry retreated to the
chairs placed against the wall for chaperones.

Although Giles returned to Merry's side when the
music ended, the evening had lost its sparkle. After
one more dance with his wife and a duty dance with
his hostess, Giles as usual retreated to the card room
to escape the gossip that was rampant at every social
event. Merry, upset by his defection, did not notice
the glow in Charlotte's eyes when she met Captain
Josiah Hunter, but Lady Farrell did. Denise smiled
lazily, enjoying the thought of Merry in disfavor with
Giles. Perhaps she could encourage the young man, a
known fortune hunter.

The ball was almost over when the Lindseys left.

As Giles helped Merry from the coach, he said, "
promised to meet some of Father's friends at White's
I will probably be very late. They want my opinion
on how to protect our West Indies trade. I'll see you
in the morning." In spite of the presence of the butler
he bent and kissed her. He whispered, "Dream o:
me."

Bemused, Merry slowly walked up the staircase
She did not notice that Charlotte was not her usual
bubbling self. Instead of relating each glowing com
ment and laughing about it, Charlotte seemed to be
dreaming. Bidding Merry good night, Charlotte driftec
to her room humming a tune.

That evening marked the beginning of a new pat-
tern in Merry's and Giles's relationship. No longer
did they share a quiet coze before drifting off to sleep.
Merry was usually in bed hours before Giles returned
from his club. Begging off from all but the most pressing engagements, Giles left Merry and Charlotte in
the hands of matchmaking mothers and dutiful sons.

Merry, relieved of his presence, felt more restrained
than usual. "Married only two months and already
abandoned," she seemed to hear the gossips whisper
as she and Charlotte were announced at yet another
ball.

Lady Farrell took great pleasure in reminding Merry
she was alone. "What? Giles is not with you? Why
I'm sure he told me he'd be here when I saw him this
afternoon," she purred. "Perhaps he's found some
new interest." She smiled consolingly.

Even that Merry could have borne. Surprisingly she
missed Giles, not in the moments they shared in public but in the quiet times. At night she rolled onto his
side of the bed trying to snuggle against him. One
night when he returned very late she even edged her
way off the bed and landed with a thump. On evenings when he returned early, Giles isolated himself
in the library, preparing the written reports he hoped
would influence Parliament. But Merry felt there was
some other reason, something he was hiding. Even

heir lovemaking was different. She could not know, nd Giles was afraid to tell her, that he was trying not o rush her responses.

It was the morning when she missed him the most. No matter how late they had stayed up the night before, they had always made time for breakfast or at east tea together. Laughing over Mathilda's letters or answering Danby's questions, they had shared ideas and dreams. Because of these moments, for the first time since her grandfather's death, Merry had begun to feel wanted, needed. But now she felt deserted.

Giles's absence was just the chance Hugo had been waiting for. One afternoon as he sat sipping tea and watching the antics of Charlotte's guests, he leaned close to Merry and said, "Quite an amusing sight, isn't it? But I fear you must miss your business involvement." His voice oozed sympathy.

"Yes, Charlotte does keep me busy. But lately I have been able to spend a few mornings a week working."

"You have? Doesn't Giles object?"

"No, he declares that my organization is what the company needs," Merry said with an embarrassed laugh.

"Perhaps you could give me some advice," Hugo suggested quietly. "I have an opportunity to make a new investment."

Just then Charlotte crossed to Merry and said, "Merry, do come over here. Lord Grayson has just returned from India. I know you will want to talk to him."

Thankful for the opportunity to escape him, Merry made her excuses. "Perhaps we can talk of this later," she suggested. Hugo frowned. Then a smile crossed his face. A few minutes later he made his excuses and left.

Thursday morning found him at the Lindsey's again, a neat portfolio clasped under his arm. Waving Johnson aside, he declared he would announce himself.

"Good morning, cousin. How busy you look. I hope I am not disturbing you."

Merry determinedly erased the slight frown from her forehead and asked, "Hugo? Did I promise to drive with you this morning?"

"No, no. When you said you worked a few mornings a week, I took my courage in my hands and decided to approach you. But if you are too busy . . ." Allowing his voice to drop, he turned as if to leave, dejected.

Before he could reach the door, he heard Merry say, "No, stay. What did you wish to discuss?"

Crossing to a low table, Hugo quickly sorted through the papers in his portfolio. "A friend has given me an opportunity to invest in a new venture. I wanted to see what you thought of it." He shoved the papers eagerly into Merry's hands. "Read the proposal."

Merry resigned herself to destroying yet another of Hugo's dreams. He had regularly sent her grandfather reports on various schemes that would make him rich overnight. As she read, a surprised look crossed her face. She reread the passage carefully. Finishing the last paragraph, she looked at Hugo. "As far as I can tell, this seems to be a very sound opportunity. Have you discussed it with your man of affairs?"

"Yes, and he too agrees." Hugo's voice was full of despair.

"Then what is your problem?"

"You know I had certain expectations," Hugo paused, his face sad. "As unfair as those plans were to you, I suffered the most from them."

"You? How?"

"Uncle Julian never mentioned Giles. Therefore I assumed, wrongly of course, that I would have certain sums of money at my disposal." His quick look at Merry's face told Hugo she was not interested in long explanations. "As a result I made certain, ah, investments that were unwise. Nothing I can't take care of, certainly. But at the moment I do not have enough cash to take advantage of this investment."

"And?"

"To invest in this project I need to borrow a thousand pounds. As you said, the opportunity is a sound one. I will pay you back promptly." His words came out in a rush. Then he paused hopefully.

Merry looked at him in amazement. Barely two months before, Hugo had been gloating over his power over her, and now he expected her to lend him money. He was an unprincipled rogue, that was certain.

Before she could issue a refusal, Hugo urged, "Don't give me your answer now. Think about it. I'll trust your good judgment." Hastily gathering his papers, Hugo minced out of the room, hardly taking time for a proper farewell.

As she climbed the stairs to her office, Merry was frowning. The investment was a good one, a chance for Hugo to make a nice return. Yet she knew what her grandfather would have done. But her grandfather was part of the problem. As much as she disliked admitting it, Hugo was right at least in one respect. Her grandfather had deliberately allowed him to hope. It would have been kinder to tell Hugo about Giles. And it wasn't as though she didn't have the money. Giles had made certain she always had a large sum of money at her disposal to use as she wanted. A few flicks of her pen, and it would be done.

Merry stopped pacing and crossed to her desk. Just this once she would help Hugo. Taking a quill, she dashed off a quick note to her cousin and wrote a draft on her bank.

As she sanded it, Giles entered, still dressed in riding clothes. "I won't be in for luncheon, my dear. Ramsey and I are driving out to talk to Greystone about the West Indies question." He crossed to stand beside her. "Don't count on me for an escort tonight either." Merry dropped her eyes to the draft, not wanting Giles to see her disappointment. As she did, Giles noticed it. "Hugo Darryl? Why are you sending Hugo a thousand pounds?" he asked angrily.

"He asked to borrow the money to make an investment, a good one."

"I forbid it. Your cousin has no right to anything." Not noticing the flash of fury in her eyes, Giles ripped the draft in half. "I knew he was visiting for some reason other than cousinly love." Then Giles's voice softened. "Come see me off."

When Giles was safely away, Merry returned to her office. What doubts she had once had were gone in her anger. Another draft replaced the first; she sealed the note and sent it quickly on its way.

Her act of defiance might have slipped by unnoticed had it not been for Hugo. That evening he was at his club, a place he had shunned for the last few weeks. When Giles and Sir Alex Ramsey entered the card room where he sat, Hugo called, "Giles, cousin, over here." Startled, Giles advanced toward him. As soon as Giles was close enough for him to whisper discreetly, Hugo said quietly, "Thank your wife for the draft. I've already invested it. Should see a good return shortly."

Giles stood as if in shock. Merry had sent the draft even after he had told her not to. Refusing all offers to play, Giles made his excuses. Returning home, he waited impatiently for Merry to arrive. By the time she entered her dressing room, his temper was ready to explode.

He dismissed her maid and turned toward her, his body tense with anger. "Well, Madame Wife, I now know how you feel about my wishes."

"Wishes?"

"Did you send your cousin that draft?"

Merry, her stomach tied in knots of fear, looked her usual calm self. She looked him in the eye and said calmly, "Yes."

"After I asked you not to do so?"

"Asked, Giles? Perhaps if you had *asked*, I might have considered your request." Her voice was as cool as she looked. "I had read the proposal, and it seemed worthwhile. On what did you base your decision?"

"That mushroom is using you, and I know it. How dare you waste money on him!"

Merry stared straight into his brilliant eyes. Her voice was as icy as the mountain streams Giles had forded in Canada when she asked, "And whose money was it?"

Stunned, Giles looked at her. "We'll discuss this later," he promised as he entered his dressing room and shut the door with such restraint that Merry could tell he was seething.

Neither slept well that night. Merry, exhausted from crying, finally dropped off to sleep in the early hours of the morning. Giles, on the narrow bed in his dressing room, tossed and turned all night. He was still angry. But now his anger was at himself. How could he have insulted Merry that way? It was her money to spend as she wanted. His guilt nagged at him constantly. If she wanted to spend it on Hugo, she had every right to do so. She would never be able to forgive him. Certain he had destroyed any good will she had for him, Giles plunged into new rounds of debates over trade, offering his expertise to those whose ideas he supported.

Giles, immersed in the world of politics, felt a power that had been missing since he had left his ship. He relished the idea that what he was doing was important to England. Like many men who were used to occupying their days in action, he had grown bored with the formality of society. Helping to thwart Napoleon was far better than pleasing a hostess. As he grew more and more involved, he also had a reason to avoid Merry. When his conscience bothered him, he told himself that she was independent and would manage. What he was doing was vital; it would help the country and their business.

In the quiet times, though, he admitted to himself that something was missing. He wanted desperately to make his peace with Merry, but he wasn't sure she would forgive him. More than once he had gone in search of Merry so that he could explain, only to find that she was entertaining callers or that she and Charlotte were out. When this happened he stormed out of the house to his club where he knew he could find someone to listen.

One day, frustrated by her absence, Giles entered Merry's office and sat at her desk. Everything was neatly in its place. He smiled, picked up a pen, and finally tried to make his peace with his wife. Confession was good for relieving guilt, he thought as he left the note on her dresser. Thoughtfully, hopefully, he left for his club, hoping to fill the next few important hours. But he would rather have been with Merry, his heart told him.

That afternoon Giles was present for tea. He had forgotten what fun it had been to share his hidden laughter with Merry as they listened to the compliments of Charlotte's admirers. The sight of the young eligibles fawning over his sister, comparing her dark beauty to the sun, almost destroyed his composure. He wondered how Merry could maintain her calm. As yet another impassioned young man declared Charlotte's skin as soft and glowing as a baby's, Giles caught Merry's eye. "Am I forgiven?" he mouthed. At her hesitant nod, Giles sent a secret, sensual smile at her, reminding her of his compliments in the throes of passion. When their guests had left and the servants had gone, Giles caught Merry to him and kissed her deeply. He released her slowly. "If I weren't promised to Lord Jersey tonight, I'd keep you awake in bed till morning," he declared. Disappointed, she pulled away. "I won't be late tonight," he said with a suggestive leer. Breaking away from him, she flounced out of the room.

Although she would have preferred to spend the evening at home, Merry knew she and Charlotte were committed to the opera, a party arranged some time before. Merry sat before the mirror staring at her reflection.

Was this the same woman who had enjoyed Giles's absence? Now, without him, her days seemed empty no matter how many people flocked into her drawing room. And her nights! No matter how late he was,

Merry only dozed until he slipped into bed with her. Perhaps that accounted for her lack of color, she thought. She remembered his words, "I won't be late tonight," and her cheeks burned. How could one man cause such raging emotions? Without him she was desolate, and with him she burned.

"Leave out my new rose nightrobe," she told her maid. "Don't wait up. I may be late." For the first time, she was anticipating their lovemaking. Usually she pretended even to herself that she was swept away by Giles. A smile crossed her face as she thought of his reaction.

As Pilgrim put the last curl in place, Merry smiled. "Get out the dress that arrived yesterday. I'll wear that tonight." Glancing curiously at her mistress, the maid opened the clothes press.

"That's the one." Merry smiled as Pilgrim dropped the shimmering gown over her head. Madame Camille was right. The sleeves and neck revealed the tops of her shoulders, and the rich green satin made her creamy skin seem to glow. She glanced hesitantly at the daring neckline of her dress, above which showed the tops of her breasts. It was really too bad Giles would not see her until the end of the evening. She glanced again at the mirror. Was she really going to wear this? Yes, she was.

When she had first seen the design, she had refused to consider it. "But, madame," said Madame Camille, "you will set a new style. Dare to be first." Charlotte, too, had agreed. "If you do not care for it, perhaps I will show it to someone else. Lady Farrell will be in tomorrow for a fitting," the modiste slyly suggested. Remembering the suggestion now, Merry felt the same anger. Her eyes flashed.

Looking at herself in the mirror, Merry smiled. As usual, Madame Camille was right. But her neck seemed so bare. "Perhaps the jade," her maid suggested. Fastening the clasp of the jade pendant hung on a diamond chain, Pilgrim nodded. "Yes, that's what it needed." Sweeping the green velvet cape over her arm, Merry descended. But tonight the usual wait for Charlotte sped by as she thought of the delights of the night ahead.

Even the caterwauling of a third-rate soprano who was noted for her body rather than her voice failed to depress Merry's spirits. During the first interval the box they shared with their host and hostess, Lord John Billingsley and his mother, Lady Billingsley, was filled with every enterprising young man who could create a message to Lady Billingsley from his mother, his aunt, or his cousin. The most resourceful produced invitations to visit during the second interval. Charlotte was in her element, basking in each outrageous compliment and accepting them as her due. Long years of hiding her feelings stood Merry in good stead. Suppressing her laughter, she extolled the virtues of Madame Camille to her hostess.

Following the practice of see and be seen, John and Charlotte chose to promenade during the second interval. Merry, the careful chaperone, accompanied them. As she sipped the punch her host had provided, Merry was an easy target. Carefully positioning herself around the corner just out of Merry's view, Lady Farrell took advantage of her opportunity. "My dear Honoria, I am so happy you have returned to town. I'm so worried about your cousin Charlotte," she drawled very quietly.

"Charlotte? Why? I understand she's one of the belles."

"But for how long? The town is simply buzzing. I don't know how long her popularity will last." Merry glanced around to see if anyone else was listening. Charlotte, John, and the rest of Charlotte's crowd were deep in their own conversation, the girls' giggles punctuating the deeper voices of the men. Merry knew that voice. It had to be Denise. The voice dropped even lower. "That poor woman. I'm glad I'm not in her position. And only married such a short time. Well, rakes will be rakes."

"Have you seen his new fancy?" Honoria asked.

"Remember that dainty blonde in the second act? Well, according to ..." Her voice dropped so low Merry could not hear it.

"Well, Giles has always gone for the beauties," Honoria reminded her. "Poor Merry. I wonder if she knows?" False sympathy simply dripped in her tones.

"I'm certain she must. What else has been occupying his time?" Denise purred.

Merry's face blanched as she realized what Denise meant. And if I didn't know, you'd be certain to tell me, she thought. What a pleasure it must have been for her. Oh, Giles, how could you? The sudden change in feeling rocked Merry; she swayed. Charlotte hurried to her side. Together, she and John helped Merry to their box.

The next act seemed endless to Merry, caught up in an agony of betrayal. Even their hostess grew disturbed as Merry began to shake. Gathering their wraps about them, the other three insisted that Merry must return home. As the next interval began, they descended the stairs. Merry was so shaken that she did not see the two men in the shadows near the head of the stairs. "Isn't that Sommerby's granddaughter?" the older man asked. "I heard she married a gentleman."

"Yes, I think you're right. Rumor has it that Sommerby left his business to her. I imagine it will be the usual case of ne'er-do-well destroying more trade than Napoleon," his friend added.

"Trade," a soft voice purred. "She's in trade." A sly smile slipped across Denise's face as she turned toward Honoria. She smiled. Then a harsh laugh broke from her. "I knew from the first moment I heard her voice this evening I would make her suffer. But trade. How delicious."

Honoria broke in. "But why keep this tidbit to ourselves? Surely the *ton* has a right to know?" The smiles they exchanged were malicious. By the time Merry and Charlotte reached home, the troublemak-

ers were hard at work. By the next day, the gossip
was one of the on-dits of the town.

Giles had been waiting for her to return. Her pallor
frightened him. Quickly and quietly, he undressed
her and slipped her into bed. He tried to persuade her
to sip some brandy, but she refused. She lay as straight
as though she were stretched on a rack, growing more
rigid as he tried to draw her to him. Puzzled, he drew
away. Both lay awake for hours.

The next morning when Giles, entering the breakfast room, bent to kiss her while the footman went to
get fresh tea, Merry sat unmoved. He felt as though
she were encased in ice. Drawing back, Giles was
reminded of the first two weeks of their marriage.
But even then she had responded. What new guilt
was she punishing herself for, he wondered. As Merry's
cold attitude continued, Giles spent more and more
time away from home. And when he did, Merry pic-
tured him in a love nest with the petite blonde. Once
again, Merry felt betrayed, betrayed by her own
weakness.

The next few days were like a nightmare to Merry. Her years of training stood her in good stead. Lady Farrell raged silently and continued her whisper campaign. Merry grew accustomed to the hush and cold stares that followed the announcement of her name. The outbreak of whispering kept her on edge. It was always low enough so that all she could hear were her and Giles's names.

Only Lady Farrell did not try to disguise her feelings. As Merry crossed to the chairs for the chaperones at Lady Cowper's rout, she came face to face with Giles's former lover. Lady Farrell, welcoming the opportunity, said, "Why, Mrs. Lindsey, where is your husband? Has he deserted you completely?" Merry pulled herself up as tall as she could, but before she could answer Denise continued, "Perhaps your business wasn't enough to warm his bed." She laughed wickedly.

Her business. How had Denise discovered that? Merry's eyes glittered, and her voice was almost a whisper as she said, "I wonder if even that would have been enough to get Giles to marry *you*." Denise drew back as if the soft ball of fluff had turned into a thistle. Turning, Merry made her way quietly across the room. Even those closest to the two had not realized the drama so close to them.

If she knows, all of London knows, Merry thought. She checked the dance floor until she found Charlotte. As usual, Charlotte was oblivious to everything but the young men, her friends, and the music. As Merry watched, Charlotte flashed an enchanting smile at her partner, a tall young man in the dress uniform of the Forty-ninth Dragoons. Relieved that Charlotte was enjoying herself, Merry sank into a chair where she could watch the dance floor.

Now the attitude of the *ton* the last few days was clear. In a society dedicated to wasting one's time in amusements and one's substance on frivolity, a person who worked was anathema. At least society did not seem to blame Charlotte for Merry's crime of birth. I knew it would be like this, Merry thought. And if I'd been younger? Thank heavens I refused to allow Aunt Mathilda to present me.

Thinking of her lively, outgoing aunt, Merry wished for her presence. Even her constant chatter would be welcome. Only when Charlotte returned to her between dances did she speak. As she watched yet another young man lead Charlotte onto the floor, she breathed a sigh. "And why are you sitting here all alone, Madame Wife?" asked Giles. He pulled her to her feet and swept her onto the floor and into a set that was forming. He was not with that blonde tonight, she thought, and smiled up at him.

"And to what do we owe your presence tonight? You said you had another engagement," Merry asked.

When Giles had seen Merry sitting there all alone, he had been worried. Now he was annoyed. "My plans changed unexpectedly. How can you show Charlotte the correct behavior in society if you sit all alone?"

"But, Giles . . ."

"No, for the rest of the evening we will repair your social errors." They finished the dance in silence.

The dance over, Giles escorted Merry to where Lady Cowper stood with her latest favorite. "My parents send their greetings, dear lady. Mother, especially, asked me to tell you that you were right. Russian sables are delightful." Giles smiled at Lady Cowper, and she, ever susceptible to flattery, dimpled back at him. A

w moments later, Giles whisked her onto the dance
oor.

For the rest of the evening Merry was escorted
om one leader of society to the next. She danced
ith Giles, but mostly she sat while he danced with
hers, everyone except Denise. Caught up in her own
elings, Merry for once failed to keep a watchful eye
Charlotte. She did not notice that although Char-
tte allowed a handsome officer only two dances, he
ent every interval beside her. But others did.

For once, Giles escorted them home. As soon as the
or to the salon closed, he said, "Merry, you must
ake more of an effort to fit in. Charlotte needs your
pport to have a successful Season."

"Leave Merry alone. She is a wonderful chaperone,"
harlotte declared. "I couldn't be more successful if I
ied."

"Oh, you couldn't, Miss Modesty," Giles laughed.
And were you born with your humility?"

Even Merry laughed when Charlotte said, "Well,
ou did tell me to enjoy myself. And I am." She broke
to giggles. Giles laughed so hard he had to hold his
ides.

Later, Merry crawled into bed still smiling. She
rifted into sleep as he bent to kiss her.

The next morning Giles, dressed for riding, looked
ondly down at his still sleeping wife. Noting the dark
hadows beneath her closed lids, he resisted the im-
ulse to climb back into bed and to kiss her awake.
miling, he hurried down the stairs. "Do not let any-
ne disturb my wife, Johnson," he told his butler.
Tell Pilgrim to wait until she is called."

He stood there in the front hallway waiting impa-
iently for his sister. Just as he was about to send the
ootman after her, Charlotte tripped lightly down the
tairs, the hem of her amber riding habit draped grace-
ully over her arm. "Isn't it a beautiful day? I can
ardly wait to reach the park. It's been so long since
ve rode together," she trilled.

"It wouldn't have been so long," Giles grumbled as

he tossed her into the saddle, "if you weren't alwa
late."

"But, Giles, I have to think of my reputation.
goddess has to be perfect." Charlotte's dimples we.
evident as she laughed down at her brother.

His muttered, "Minx," made her laugh harde
Mounting his own horse, they rode to the park. A
though they seemed oblivious to the picture they mad
the rest of London was not. More than one head turne
to look at the two laughing countenances with simila
dark curls and laughing blue-green eyes.

The scene in the park was all Giles thought
would be. All the young gallants in sight surrounde
Charlotte. No sense in trying to go too far in thi
crush, he thought. Just another chance to see and b
seen. His eye caught by a signal from Lady Sefton, h
guided Charlotte and the crowd around her to th
carriage.

Giles bent to greet her. "And how is my favorit
London Lady this morning?" He smiled down at hi
mother's friend. "I must thank you for your efforts o:
Charlotte's behalf. Did you imagine as we demolishe
your conservatory that she would ever take London b
storm this way?"

"She is simply following a tradition your mothe
and I made famous. Lud, how they still talk abou
that Season!" She smiled up at him. Then her fac
grew serious. "But that is not what I wanted to discuss
Giles, why haven't you been escorting your wife lately
Some of the tabbies are beginning to talk. And she
may hear them." He opened his mouth to answer, but
she silenced him. "No, don't say anything. I just thought
you should know." She glanced at the crowd around
Charlotte and frowned. "You had better keep an eye
on your madcap sister. Will we see you at our ball on
Friday next?" His assurances ringing in her ears, she
drove away.

Giles glanced at the group around Charlotte and
made his way next to her. Across the park, he saw
Hugo Darryl mounted on a rangy bay. His brow creased.

an effort to avoid acknowledging Darryl, he sug-
sted, "Charlotte, Serena is waving from that carriage.
erhaps you should say good-bye to the young men
d see what she wants." A few minutes later, Giles
d Charlotte were beside an elegant barouche con-
ining Lady Serena Devereaux and her mother.

"Lady Devereaux, Serena, how wonderful to see
ou. Am I to assume that the measles have left the
evereaux clan completely?" he asked.

"Hush, do you want to spoil what is left of the
eason for me?" Serena, a lovely blonde in sapphire
lue velvet, declared. "Charlotte, can you come shop-
ing with me? We have so much to talk about." Her
other added her invitation. "Tonight we go to
lmack's. Are you going?"

"I'm not certain." Charlotte began hesitantly. "Merry
sually tells me each morning what our schedule is
ut . . ."

"Oh, Charlotte, you must," her friend begged.
Please say you will."

Before Charlotte could speak, Giles said, "I'm afraid
Merry will not be able to attend. She has another
ommitment." Giles had already made his plans for
he evening.

Seeing the disappointed looks on the faces of the
wo girls, Lady Devereaux said, "Perhaps Charlotte
ould go with us? I know her presence would add to
erena's pleasure."

"Oh, Mama, could she spend the night? Please,
Giles, I need someone to talk to," the vivacious blonde
declared. His consent given, Giles and Charlotte re-
urned to Grosvenor Square. Arrangements had al-
eady been made for the Devereaux to pick up Char-
otte and her maid in an hour.

As Charlotte dashed up the stairs, Giles checked
he calendar of their obligations for the day. Entering
is study, he dashed off a few notes which he gave to
ootmen to be delivered immediately. A wicked smile
played about his mouth as he revised his plans. They
would have a whole day to themselves.

When the door closed behind Charlotte a short time later, Giles quickly mounted the stairs. Noticing his wife's maid with a tray, he asked, "How long has my wife been up, Pilgrim?"

"Just a short time, sir. She has just finished her breakfast and is at her bath now. Is that all, sir?"

"Pilgrim, you may have the rest of the day off," Giles said. Her eyebrows lifted slightly, but Giles had already entered his suite. She walked toward the back stairs. Well, it wasn't her place to question the master, she thought.

Merry, her curls tumbled on top of her head, sat up to her shoulders in warm water. Her eyes were closed as if she were asleep. As Giles watched her, she breathed deeply and sighed.

"Dreaming of me?" he asked as he dropped a soft kiss on her lips. Merry's eyes flew open. She sat up hastily and then sank back as she saw Giles's appreciative stare. Little did he know how accurate his words were. She had done little but think of him since she had opened her eyes.

"Soaking all your stiffness out?" he asked, laughing as a blush ran from her chest to her face. "Just relax." He knelt beside the tub and picked up the soap scented with her favorite sandalwood. Creating a rich lather, he massaged her back. At first his hands were impersonal. As she lay there submerged to her chin, he whispered, "Someday I'll let you give me a bath." Her eyes flew open, startled.

After rinsing her off, Giles put his hands under her arms and lifted her from the water. Picking up the towels, he pushed Merry down on the stool and softly began to dry her, starting from her feet. As the rough towels, aided by his warm hands and lips, drifted across her body, she sighed. Giles flicked the towel over her breasts and threw it down.

Merry opened her eyes. "Kiss me, Merry," Giles pleaded. Seeing the passion in his face, Merry hesitantly reached up, touching his lips first with her fingers, then with her lips. She nestled herself against him, rubbing her face against the hair on his chest. Pleased at his response, her hands drifted lower. He guided one of her hands below his waist. She could feel him throbbing against her, his warmth evident even through the fabric. He pulled her hand away and, breathing deeply, led her to the bed.

For the rest of the day, Giles delighted in Merry's wondering enjoyment of the variations of lovemaking. As she napped briefly, Giles lay on his side looking at her. He smiled as he remembered her frenzy. She was pure delight. Of course, she would never touch him unless he urged her. That would be the next step, he thought. He slipped from the bed and crossed to the sitting room.

A short time later Merry followed. A clock was chiming the hour. "Giles, the time. Charlotte will be so upset. It is Almack's tonight."

Giles smiled at her reassuringly, telling her of his arrangements. He said, "Tonight is ours. Come have some champagne." He led her to the sofa in front of which was a table filled with enticing foods. "Remember the first time we shared a quiet supper?" He smiled down at her. As they had on that first evening, her heart raced and her breath quickened. But this time it wasn't from fear. "Is it my lady's pleasure to be entertained?" he asked. Her nod was the signal for yet another adventure story. For the rest of the evening Giles entertained her, pausing from time to time for demonstrations. At last exhausted, they fell asleep still held in each other's arms.

The next morning Merry awoke and stretched. She frowned slightly as her muscles protested. Then she smiled. Giles could not be involved with someone else. Not when he made love to her as he did. She bounded from the bed.

Descending the stairs a short time later, Merry entered the breakfast room expecting to see her husband. Only her place setting remained. Johnson explained. "Mr. Lindsey asked that I give you this."

Merry broke open the wafer. Giles's bold handwriting stared up at her. "Merry, sweet," the note began. "I'm promised for a mill. I should return tomorrow. You were sleeping so peacefully I decided not to awaken you. Yours, Giles."

Merry frowned and crumpled the note. Hastily, she smoothed it out again. Although it wasn't much of a love letter, it was the first note he had written her. Oh well, with Charlotte engaged until the afternoon, maybe she could deal with some business.

The next few hours Merry spent in correspondence. Danby was working out nicely. Only rarely did he or Mr. Pettigrew need their help. But this was one of those occasions. Frowning over the letter in her hand, Merry wished for her grandfather's wisdom. She had planned to discuss the matter with Giles yesterday, but she had forgotten. Marshaling her thoughts, she jotted down a few suggestions. Until she and Giles could consult, these ideas would have to do.

Charlotte arrived home only a short time before their weekly at-home was scheduled. Her obvious delight in having her childhood friend Serena at hand again reminded Merry of Arabella. How she wished Arabella were in London this Season. Perhaps Giles and I can visit them when the baby comes, she consoled herself.

The afternoon was like most of her at-homes recently. There were plenty of young men but only a few ladies, and those were from the fringes of society. How she wished for another woman to talk to. Charlotte was such a frivolous creature. Merry gazed toward the sofa where Charlotte sat close beside a tall soldier while another young man leaned over to whisper in her ear. For a moment Merry wished she too could live such a relaxed life, worried about nothing but her clothes and her popularity. Giving herself a mental shake, she reminded herself that Charlotte was only seventeen. But even at seventeen, Merry had not been frivolous.

That evening at the musical, Merry took her place in the gilt chair beside Charlotte who, despite plead-ngs from her admirers, had declined a place on the program. Determined to make one last attempt for acceptance, Merry smiled and nodded at her acquaintances around the room. The recognition she received was slight. As Mrs. Drummond Burrell passed, Merry rose to greet the patroness of Almack's but was frozen as the lady gave her a brief nod before turning to greet Charlotte warmly. "And what do you hear from your mother, child? I do hope she will be back to escort you for the Little Season." As Mrs. Drummond Burrell continued to her seat, Merry sank back into her chair, stunned by the implications in the patroness's words.

A high-pitched voice whispered in her ear, "Good evening, cousin. Did you receive my draft?"

"Yes, I was pleased to get your note. The investment must have done even better than you expected," Merry said, happy to have something else to think about. "I am surprised to see you. I didn't know you were acquainted with our hostess."

"Well, I am surprised to see you alone again. Where is your husband? Tired of you already?" Hugo asked, settling himself in a chair beside Merry. He leaned closer to her. "You silly girl, how could you reveal your background in trade!" Merry drew back as if he had struck her. "Did you hope to bring me down as well?" Her denial did little to soothe Hugo. He continued, "If you didn't, well, I think we know who did, don't we? Perhaps he prefers a wife who won't be received in London." Satisfied with his mischief-making, Hugo Darryl turned his attention to the girl at the harp. Merry sat back, stunned. It explained so much. But would Giles jeopardize his sister's social career? She doubted it. Impatient to be gone and to confront her husband, she nonetheless clapped and smiled in all the right places. At the intermission she glanced around, startled to see Charlotte, gazing into the brown eyes of the tall captain, her hand clasped warmly in his. Merry frowned as she tried to remember his name. Seeing her sister-in-law's frown, Charlotte pulled her hand from the young man's grasp.

"You remember Captain Hunter, don't you Merry
We met at Lady Jersey's ball," she said.

Merry looked closely at Charlotte, who seemed mor
flushed than usual. "Perhaps the captain will be good
enough to get us some punch," she suggested. "Why
don't you sit on the other side of me for a while. Mr
Darryl was just leaving." Her cousin shot her a look o
pure dislike, but there was little he could do bu
leave. With luck, he would have another opportunity
to hurt his cousin. Charlotte sank unhappily into the
seat that trapped her between Merry and an elderly
gentleman with a silk handkerchief over his face to
muffle his snores. As soon as he had delivered the
punch, the captain, recognizing that he had been
outmaneuvered, retreated to the rear of the room. For
the rest of the evening, Charlotte was quiet. But that
did not save her from the scolding she knew was
coming. The ride to Grosvenor Square was an uncom
fortable one.

Merry hardly slept as she worried about what she
was to say to Giles. Awakening early, she left word
with Johnson that she was to be notified as soon as
Giles returned.

In spite of her worries about Charlotte, that morning she arranged to meet with Madame Camille and
their business agent. The meeting was extremely
satisfactory. Madame Camille rejoiced in the recognition she had found, and the agent marveled at his
clients' business sense. But between them, Merry's
already throbbing head grew worse. When Johnson
knocked on the door, she made her excuses and escaped to the quiet of her suite.

Leaving word with his valet that she needed to see
Giles, Merry sank to the sofa in the sitting room.
Giles soon entered, dressed in Court attire.

"Giles, we must talk. There are several problems I
need answers to," she stated.

"Not now, Merry. I'm due at Court shortly."

"Perhaps tonight?"

His rueful expression told her before his words did

"I may be late. You know Prinny likes to see the sun before going to bed. Maybe tomorrow."

But tomorrow never came. For days, Giles stumbled to bed at dawn and then rose while Merry escorted Charlotte hither and yon. All the while, Merry grew more and more disturbed.

—10—

By the time Lady Sefton's ball arrived, Merry had convinced herself of Giles's duplicity. Torn by her desires and her doubts, she sank further into herself. Her listlessness was a boon to Charlotte, who had decided she was in love. Although Merry kept her in sight at every ball, Charlotte delighted in the love letters Captain Hunter slipped to her. Disaster was inevitable.

The evening, like many others, began pleasantly. Merry and Charlotte dined alone and then repaired to their dressing rooms for the finishing touches. Since Giles was to join them, Merry took special pains. Her dress was the rose silk ordered for her trip to see Honoria but never worn. Pilgrim had arranged her hair in curls held by diamond stars, with soft cropped curls brushing her forehead and cheeks. More diamonds sparkled in her ears and at her neck. Taking a last look in the mirror, Merry laughed ironically. How ridiculous to dress for a man who betrays me, she thought.

She joined Charlotte in the foyer. Charlotte seemed even more beautiful than usual in her soft yellow gown with its deeper yellow ribbons. "Do my pearls go with this dress? Giles won't let me wear the topaz set Grandmother left me," Charlotte asked.

"And he is right. Young ladies' jewelry is never flashy. There will be plenty of time for colored stones when you're wed," Merry assured her. "Come, the carriage is waiting."

The ball was like many others they had attended. Only the decorations were different. Using greenery, Lady Sefton had created a forest scene. By the time the clock struck eleven, Merry decided that Giles was not coming. After watching the doorway for hours, she sank into a cushioned window seat in a small alcove. Charlotte quickly noticed her absence and slipped into the garden.

A short time later, Merry remembered her duties and returned to the ballroom. An unpleasant sight greeted her. Her husband was dancing with Lady Farrell and enjoying himself, too. The dance over, the couple crossed to where Merry stood. "Isn't Charlotte with you?" Giles asked.

Merry looked at him questioningly while Lady Farrell said, "I saw her going into the garden some time ago. Weren't you out there too, Merry?"

"In the garden?" Giles quickly walked through the open French doors.

"Have a pleasant evening, if you can," the taller woman purred viciously. She turned and left Merry alone. Giles, with Charlotte on his arm and a frown on his face, reappeared a few minutes later.

"Make your excuses and go home. We will discuss this later," he told Merry. Giles escorted the two women to their hostess and then to their carriage. "And remember, Charlotte, you are to stay in your room until we have talked." He slammed the door closed behind them.

No sooner had the horse pulled away from the entrance than Charlotte burst into tears. The short trip was punctuated with her sobs. As the coach pulled to a stop, with effort she controlled herself. She entered the house and ran up the stairs to her suite. Wearily, Merry followed.

Finding Charlotte's door barred against her, Merry retreated to her dressing room. Too emotionally drained by the events of the evening to think clearly, Merry did not resist when Pilgrim suggested a sleeping cordial.

Her first thoughts the next morning were not of Charlotte. Imprinted on her mind was the picture of Giles and Lady Farrell laughing together, laughing at her probably.

Before Merry had finished dressing, Giles was there. "You may leave us, Pilgrim," he said in a cold, hard voice. When the door closed behind the maid, he turned toward his wife. "A fine chaperone you are, ma'am. Last evening in the garden I found my sister in the arms of some half-pay officer. How could you be so lax?" Giles stormed.

"But Giles . . ." Merry began.

"You know how carefully a young lady must be guarded. And you failed me. Were you too caught up in some business scheme to care?" Giles gave little thought to the impact of his words on his wife. She grew paler. "Were you too bored with the social round to care? I've heard how you hold yourself aloof from everyone."

By this time Merry was angry. An icy calm seized her. She glared at her husband, refusing to dignify his accusations with a reply.

"Well, what do you have to say for yourself?" Giles asked.

Giving him a hard look, Merry walked to her office and opened the door. "A week ago I told you we needed to talk. Come see me in another week, Giles. Maybe then we can talk, not shout." Merry's voice was bitterly ironic. Taking one last look at her still glaring husband, she shut the door quietly behind her. The click of the lock was very clear.

"We will talk when I return," Giles said to the closed door. "At my clubs I hope to find out if the *ton* knows about Charlotte's little escapade." Grabbing his hat and cane, Giles stormed his way out of the house. From the looks on his servants' faces, he was certain this latest episode would soon be grist in London's scandal mill.

Once the door shut Giles from her sight, Merry began taking the deep breaths her ayah had taught her to restore her calm. But they did not work. "That man," she fumed aloud. "How dare he accuse me of ignoring my duties. Him. When has he been around lately? And for business. Hah! Monkey business. And his own." Muttering under her breath, Merry stalked around the room. Picking up a book, she tossed it to the floor. Delighted with the release the action gave her, Merry dropped book after book, each making a satisfying thud.

A timid knock sounded at the door. "Miss Merry, are you all right?" her maid asked. "Please let me in." Already ashamed of her outburst, Merry opened the door. Aghast, the maid stared at the disheveled room.

"Order the landau brought around. I wish to take some air. And then bring my claret cloak," Merry stated.

"Do you wish me to accompany you, ma'am?"

"No, I wish to be alone."

The bright spring sunlight was a direct contrast to Merry's mood. She entered the open carriage. "Drive around the park," she ordered.

The park was green and quiet. It was too late for fashionable riders and too early for the promenade. The stillness and peaceful surroundings helped soothe Merry. Calling for the coachman to stop, she descended and rambled on the green paths. From time to time a man or woman hurrying on an errand would glance curiously at her. Her clothes proclaimed her one of the upper class. "What is she doing in the park at this time?" their expressions seemed to ask.

As Merry drifted down first one path and then another, she did not notice the two men that followed her. The first, a young man with an honest face, stayed a few yards behind. "Turner, keep the mistress in sight," said Jem Coachman. And the young groom was careful to do just that. The second man was more furtive, skulking in the bushes whenever he thought he might be seen. His employer had been specific in his orders.

Merry wandered on, oblivious to everything but her

memory of Giles's words. He had been right. She
admitted that. It was her fault that Charlotte had
behaved so badly. How could she have been so caught
up in herself as to forget Aunt Mathilda's words?
After all, she herself was a perfect example of how
one thing could ruin a social career. As she thought
about the reaction of the *ton* the last few weeks, Merry
wondered whether Hugo had been right to suspect
Giles. Even when she was angriest with Giles, she
had had doubts. This morning he had seemed to blame
her for her social failure. Even as angry as he was, he
would not try to blame her for his misdeeds. If they
could only talk.

She sank down on a rustic bench under the shade of
a lovely old tree. It seemed so long ago since they left
Bristol. That first day of the journey, they had talked
so easily. Merry remembered Giles's words, "I don't
want to get caught up in a useless life like my friends
lead—gambling, drinking, more gambling." Was that
what had happened to him?

The last few weeks had seemed empty. But she had
rarely had a free moment. Every moment seemed
empty, though, when Giles was not around. "How could
I let my life get so entangled with his? I am an
independent person, a decision-maker. Yet I do miss
him," she said to herself.

A cloud drifted overhead, sending its shadow on
the bench. She rose. Perhaps Giles's anger would be
quick to die down. She turned and caught sight of the
waiting groom. "Find Jem Coachman and have him
meet me over there," she suggested. "Then I want to
go to Madame Camille's." The man in the bushes
smiled. He hurried away. A few minutes later, Merry
climbed back into her carriage.

After they left the park, they turned into the streets
filled with wagons and workmen. Passing a street vendor
selling fish, Merry remembered Bristol. "Jem . . ." she
began. "No, never mind. Just take me to my modiste."
The docks in London were not like those she was
familiar with. How she wished she were in Bristol.

Well, she wasn't, and wishing would not make it so. Squaring her shoulders, she reminded herself of her grandfather's teaching. "Face the problem squarely. Never run from it. Weigh the chance for success and then go for it."

She had tried. But she would try harder. Once Giles had calmed down, he would see his error. And if he didn't, she would simply have to get his attention. Merry smiled as she considered how her attitude had changed in the last few months. Logic was one means, but that low-cut silk gown she had refused earlier this week as shocking would definitely be an asset. She smiled as she thought of Giles's first glimpse of her in that dress.

Deep in her own thoughts, Merry had not noticed that the carriage had stopped. As she did, she half rose expecting to be at Madame Camille's entrance. Instead, she was in the middle of a crossroads surrounded by squabbling street vendors. Ahead of the carriage, two pushcarts had collided, littering the already filthy street with the remains of rotting vegetables. The groom plunged into the fray, trying to clear a way through the sea of humanity. "Here, now! Get away with you," he shouted. He made his way toward the two arguing peddlers. Their fun interrupted, the crowd began to drift away.

Merry settled back to wait until the street was clear. Suddenly the street filled with screams as a heavily loaded, horseless wagon plunged down the hill toward the blocked intersection below. Scrambling, pushing one another, those individuals left in the intersection darted for safety. Too startled to move, Merry watched the wagon come closer. "It's going to hit us," she said calmly. "Jump, Jem." As if everything had slowed down, she saw the coachman turn toward her. Then came the impact. The heavy load of bricks forced the tongue of the wagon through the carriage door. The heavy wooden beam struck Merry solidly on the right side. Jem Coachman was thrown clear.

The groom dived for the plunging horses. Grabbing their reins, he soothed them. As they calmed, he thought of the others. "Here, hold 'em," he told a gaping workman. Dashing to the side of the landau, he surprised a small man who had opened the door. "How is my mistress?" Turner asked. Startled, the man jumped free and disappeared into the crowd. A moan near the wheels of the carriage diverted the groom's attention. "Jem, Jem, don't move until we know how badly you are hurt."

"But, Miss Merry. What about her?" the coachman moaned.

Leaving the coachman in the hands of a volunteer, the groom dashed to the open carriage door. The sight before him made him groan. Merry lay at an angle, her right arm pinned under the tongue of the wagon. Her temple had already begun to turn blue and swell. Blood dripped from her shoulder, where a splinter of wood was lodged. For a moment Turner was frozen in horror. Then he turned to the crowd. "Who will help? The master will be generous." Selecting his assistants, he carefully lifted the wagon tongue free of his mistress. Others found a carter and a wagon with clean straw and put the coachman, his leg broken, carefully into it. Turner, worried about the blood Merry was losing and her arm that hung at a weird angle, transferred his mistress carefully to the waiting straw. He sent a small boy with long legs to prepare the household.

Still followed by a gasping crowd, the wagon stopped before the house in Grosvenor Square. Alerted by the messenger, the butler was ready. The doctor had already been sent for. Quickly and efficiently, Johnson arranged for the two injured people to be conveyed to their waiting beds. Dispensing largesse to the helpful workmen, he quickly dispersed the milling throng. As he entered the hall, he glanced at the white faces of the servants assembled there. His orders set them to work.

"Go to the kitchen. The mistress will need a sustaining broth. And you, keep watch for the doctor.

You three, go find Mr. Giles." Consulting the family's calendar of appointments, he sent them on their way. 'The rest of you, back to work." Turning to the groom, he said, "Why don't you wait with Jem Coachman until the doctor arrives. The master will also need to talk to you. You've done well, Turner." The servants once more at their tasks, Johnson went to check on his mistress. As he scratched on the door, the housekeeper answered. "Well, Mr. Johnson, she does not look good. I left Pilgrim with her. But I wish the doctor would hurry. Have you sent for Mr. Giles?" The butler nodded his head.

"Is there anything else I can do to help?" he asked. The housekeeper shook her head. "I will wait downstairs for the family and the doctor. Miss Charlotte should be home soon."

A few minutes later a carriage pulled up in front of the door. "I promise I'll see you tomorrow," Charlotte said. "Of course, I'll be all right, Serena. Giles won't beat me." She cautiously entered the hallway. Since neither Giles nor Merry had been there to stop her, she had gone shopping with Serena. But now she expected to be taken to task. "Have my brother and his wife returned, Johnson?" she asked.

"The mistress is home. But, Miss Charlotte, something dreadful has happened," the butler exclaimed in deep despair.

"What, has something happened to my parents?"

"No, it's the mistress. She was in a carriage accident."

"How bad is she?" questioned Charlotte.

"She's still unconscious. Oh, Miss Charlotte, she looks as though she's badly hurt," the butler continued.

Charlotte dashed up the stairs, opened the door to Merry's suite, and went in.

"Is that the doctor?" Pilgrim asked.

"No, Pilgrim. How ..." Charlotte gasped, seeing the blood staining Merry's bed and gown. She started to sway.

"Get Miss Charlotte out of here," Pilgrim told the

housekeeper. "Let her supervise rolling bandages if she wants something to do." Carefully, the housekeeper eased the young girl onto the sofa in the sitting room, waving a vinaigrette under her nose. Revived, Charlotte tried to rise, but the housekeeper urged her to remain seated. Charlotte, taking the glass of wine the woman offered, sat still. "Will she be all right?" Charlotte asked. "Why is that wood still in her shoulder?"

"We must wait for the doctor," the housekeeper said quietly. She too was worried about her mistress's continued unconsciousness and loss of blood.

Hurried footsteps approached the door. It opened. "Is this my patient?" a growling voice asked. The housekeeper whisked him quickly into the next room.

A short time later she returned. "Come with me, Miss Charlotte. The doctor has asked for wide bandages, and I will need you to supervise the maids rolling them." She quickly drew Charlotte away with her. Entering the small salon, she summoned two maids whom she left in Charlotte's care. As soon as they were settled, she hurried on the second part of the errand. "Johnson, I need two of our strongest young men. And they can't be squeamish. Doctor says he has to take that splinter out." Johnson gulped.

The minutes seemed to drag by. A muffled cry seemed to echo through the halls. Johnson grew whiter. Another carriage drew up before the door. Before the knocker could fall, Johnson had the door open. He stared aghast at the equipage in front of him. Two outriders, a coachman, and a groom who was letting down the stairs of the carriage stared at him. Behind that carriage was another piled high with trunks. As the butler watched, an elegant lady no longer in her youth emerged.

"So this is Giles's home. Very nice. I am certain Merry has been comfortable here," Lady Mathilda commented to no one in particular. "Don't just stand there staring. Announce me."

Johnson, already disturbed by the events of the day,

straightened and asked, "And who may I say has arrived?"

"Why Lady Mathilda Evans, Mrs. Lindsey's aunt, of course." She swept into the house followed by her maid.

Hurrying to reach the door to the small salon before she did, Johnson opened it and announced to Charlotte, "Lady Mathilda Evans." He shut the door behind her and hurried to direct her servants to their places.

"Lady Mathilda. You're Merry's Aunt Mathilda," Charlotte exclaimed. "I'm so glad you're here. Everything is at sixes and sevens, what with the accident."

"Accident, what accident?" Mathilda demanded.

Quietly Charlotte tried to explain. "Merry was in a carriage accident this afternoon. The doctor is with her now."

"Take me to her at once," the lady demanded. Hesitantly, Charlotte led her up the stairs. The scene that greeted them was not pleasant. Pilgrim, in tears, was putting down a bowl of reddened water. The housekeeper was helping the doctor wrap Merry's shoulder. "How is she, doctor?" Lady Mathilda asked.

"If you'd let me finish, I could tell you more definitely," he growled. He was worried and wanted nothing to interfere with his patient.

"We'll wait for you in the sitting room if we may," Mathilda suggested. He nodded his agreement. Drawing Charlotte to the sofa, Mathilda sank down, removing her hat and gloves. "Ring for tea and then tell me everything you know," she ordered. Charlotte obeyed.

The butler himself brought the tea tray. "Has Mr. Lindsey returned?" Lady Mathilda asked.

"No, ma'am. I've sent messengers to all his clubs. But he was not there."

"What about his friends? Surely you know who they are?"

"Certainly. I'll take care of it at once." His back was straight as he left the room.

For a few minutes the room was quiet. The door to Merry's bedroom opened. Both women sat as if frozen.

"I must see my other patient. Then I will return," the doctor assured them.

Lady Mathilda placed her cup on the tea tray, leaned back, and said, "What has been happening, my dear? Who is the other patient? And where is Giles?"

"He's Jem Coachman, ma'am. I—I don't know where Giles is. And it's—it's all my fault." Charlotte burst into heartbroken sobs.

Gathering the crying girl against her shoulder, Mathilda soothed her. "Were you in the carriage too? How lucky you escaped injury," she said.

Charlotte tried to explain. "No, I was with Serena, but I was supposed to be in my room," she cried.

"And Merry went to look for you?"

"No, Merry was already gone when I left. She and Giles quarreled, and it was my fault." Once again, Charlotte was overcome by sobs. "Giles told her she had been a bad chaperone. But she wasn't. She wasn't. She's hurt, and it's all my fault." Mathilda simply held Charlotte and let her sob.

Hurried footsteps approached, and the door flew open.

"Merry! Where's Merry? Is she all right?" Giles demanded.

"The doctor said he'd be back shortly. He didn't tell us anything more," Mathilda said.

Giles dashed into the bedroom. The sight there brought him to a halt. Merry lay there unconscious, a dark purple bruise staining her temple and the right side of her face. Her shoulder was covered in thick white bandages already speckled with red. Her right arm lay across her chest, the lower part encased in wooden planks. "Oh, my God," he whispered. He crossed to the bedside, completely ignoring the other two women. Carefully he picked up Merry's left hand and kissed it. "Merry, darling girl, I'm here. I didn't mean what I said this morning. Merry, look at me, speak to me," he begged, his eyes filled with tears.

"Hush, Mr. Giles," Pilgrim said. "She can't hear

you. Come now. Talk to Lady Mathilda until the doctor returns."

"She will be all right, won't she, Pilgrim?"

The maid lowered her eyes, not wanting to see the
pain in his. "The doctor has not said much. He'll
return from seeing Jem Coachman soon. Then he'll
tell you."

Dazed, Giles drifted back into the sitting room.
Seeing her for the first time, he hugged Mathilda
tightly. "Thank God, you're here. We need you," he
said.

The door to the hall opened. The doctor entered
and sank into a chair, taking the cup of tea Charlotte
offered him.

"Will my wife recover, doctor?" Giles asked as if
afraid of the reply.

"There are two areas of concern, Mr. Lindsey. The
first is that she is still unconscious. I have known
those who regained their wits after such a hard blow,
but others have not." Charlotte could not stifle her
gasp of dismay. Lady Mathilda's hand was shaking so
badly that she had to put her cup down. Meanwhile,
Giles's face lost all its color. The doctor continued,
"The second concern is fever, both from the blow to
the head and from the piece of wood that was in her
shoulder. If the wound becomes diseased ..." He
shrugged his shoulders.

Giles crossed to the table near the door and poured
himself a stiff brandy. Tossing it down, he turned.
"And what can we do?"

"Pray, sir. Pray and keep watch."

—11—

The afternoon had turned into evening before Merry began to stir restlessly. Giles, who had remained at her bedside, held her uninjured hand in his. Slowly her eyes opened. Her tongue touched her dry lips. "Water," she begged, so low Giles almost did not hear her. Pilgrim held a cup of honey and lemon water to her lips. Gulping greedily, she drank the entire cup.

Satisfied at last, she looked around and tried to raise her right hand. "Giles?" she asked as he gently restrained her.

"The carriage was in an accident. Do you remember it?"

"Going to Madame Camille's. Yes. Oh Giles, I'm sorry ... My head hurts so. Hold me. Make it stop hurting," she cried.

Giles, almost beside himself with worry, tried to soothe her. "The doctor will be here soon. Don't go back to sleep, Merry. Wait, darling," he begged. He replaced the warm rag on her forehead with a cool one. "Has he arrived yet?" he asked as Lady Mathilda entered.

"No, but he should be here soon," she reassured him in a whisper. "Does she know you?"

"Yes, thank God. But she's in such pain." His whisper reflected his own agony. Merry moaned as she tried to move. "Why doesn't he come?" He leaned over the bed. "Merry, don't worry. Everything will be better shortly. Here, try to drink this broth."

146

Pilgrim and Lady Mathilda exchanged a speaking glance. Taking Giles's arm, Mathilda pulled him away from the bed and into the sitting room. "Have you had something to eat, Giles?" she asked.

"Eat when Merry is in pain? I can't leave her. She needs me."

"Yes, she does. But she doesn't need your fears. We all must be calm."

"Calm? But she was almost killed. Oh, Aunt Mathilda, what would I do if I lost her?" Giles lost control for a moment, his shoulders heaving.

"If we can do anything, you won't. Now buck up, laddie. We will need your strength soon." In spite of her own fears, Mathilda smiled at him. "Now tell me what I can do to help with the contretemps Charlotte has told me about?"

"It was all my fault," he began.

"That's peculiar. Charlotte said she was to blame." Before either could continue, the door opened. The gruff doctor entered and crossed immediately to the bedroom.

As Giles and Mathilda tried to follow, he turned on them. "Let me observe my patient quietly, please," he demanded. "Her maid will help me." In front of his quiet determination, they fell back. "I will know more soon." As the door closed, they heard him ask Pilgrim, "Did she seem alert when she first awakened? Did she know everyone?"

Giles began to pace. For a few minutes, Mathilda made no attempt to stop him. But as the waiting grew longer, she finally patted the sofa beside her and suggested, "Finish telling your story, dear boy. The doctor will return when he has something to tell us. Now, how is everything your fault?" Before long, Giles had poured his story into her waiting ears.

"Then, this morning I accused her of neglecting Charlotte for business. But it was I who neglected both of them. Lady Sefton told me the gossips had begun to talk. I should have listened. If we hadn't quarreled, she wouldn't have left the house. She must

be all right! She has to be. God, why doesn't he hurry?"
He jumped to his feet again and crossed to the window.

"Lady Sefton, yes, just the person," Mathilda
muttered. "Giles, Charlotte has told me of her involvement. So you can't take all the blame. You were simply worried about your sister. Of course, you were no
gentleman to rip up your wife the way you did. I'm
certain . . ." The door opened. Lady Mathilda snapped
around to face it, revealing her own anxiety. Giles
seemed frozen.

The doctor entered. Crossing to a chair, he sank
down, a worried look on his face. He said, "Mrs.
Lindsey is a very sick woman." Giles's face grew as
white as his neckcloth. "However, one hurdle has
been passed. Her wits seem perfectly normal. It's
fever that worries me now." Mathilda let out the
breath she had been holding. "That and her pain."
Giles looked at him puzzled. "With that blow to the
head she shouldn't have any laudanum for a while.
I'm afraid that this night will be very difficult for
her."

Giles cut in. "But what can we do to help?"

"Keep her cool. And give her the cordial I left.
Sometimes it helps." He rose. "Send for me if she
becomes too restless."

That night was the beginning of a nightmare for Giles.
Refusing to leave Merry's side, he forced Mathilda
and Pilgrim to retire. Changing the damp rags on her
head, wiping her lips, he tried to make Merry comfortable. The few minutes after each teaspoon of cordial
were a welcome relief as Merry sank briefly into a
calm sleep. Then she would awaken and begin to
moan. Over and over, Giles whispered his love for her
as if that would ease the pain. As long as she could
hear his voice, she seemed quieter. Finally morning
arrived. The doctor came in, accompanied by Pilgrim.

The doctor frowned as he put his hand on her damp
forehead. After checking her head, now adorned with
a huge knot as well as a bruise, he opened his satchel.
"A few hours of quiet rest are what she needs now.

Pour a teaspoon of this in a little water and get her to drink it. I'll return later today." Between them, Giles and Pilgrim coaxed the bitter drink into Merry. A short time later she was deeply asleep. Giles, physically and emotionally exhausted, stumbled into his dressing room and fell onto the camp bed that had been set up there. His door stood open so he could hear Merry whenever she called out.

The next twenty-four hours were a time of hoping. Merry slept most of the time under the influence of the opiate. Even so, Giles seldom left her side.

Gradually, Merry grew more restless. Someone had to watch her constantly for she began pulling at her shoulder, tearing at the poultice they hoped would draw out the poison. Her skin grew hot and dry. Her lips cracked. "Cool. Make me cool, ayah," she begged. Slowly but surely she was slipping into delirium. Never far from her, Giles suffered with her. He forgot to eat or drink. One thought kept him company: "What will I do if she dies?" The world in front of him seemed bleak without Merry's laughter. Even in his sleep he blamed himself. In his dreams he was standing before a judge who accused him of his wife's murder. And he freely admitted his guilt. His punishment was to be alone forever. He would wake crying, pleading for death. Only a dash to check on Merry could relieve his fear.

As her fever climbed, her rational moments grew less. Returning to her bedside after cleaning up, Giles arrived in time to hear her ask, "Why don't they love me, ayah? No, no, don't fight. Don't hurt each other." She turned restlessly. "What are lovers, nurse? What's that man doing to Mama?" Frantically, Giles tried to soothe her. But she continued, "No, I mustn't be seen. Papa is hurting Mama." On and on went the litany of her parents' neglect and infidelities. "Does love die? Why did Mama say Papa had killed her love?" The questions drove barbs into Giles. Holding her hands, he told her that he loved her, that her parents were at peace. But his words did little to quiet her.

As she rambled on, he persuaded Pilgrim to rest. Only Lady Mathilda dared break through his isolation. Between them, they struggled to keep Merry clean and cool. Merry wandered on. "Giles. Giles. That hurts. No, please . . . No, don't leave me . . . I'm alone again. . . . He doesn't care," she cried.

"Merry, I'm here." Giles whispered, but she was oblivious to him.

"Mustn't let him see how I feel . . . I'm afraid. It's wrong. Like Mama . . . Ohhh—Giles, Giles? I need to talk to Giles. He's with his opera dancer. Want to see him. No, that's wrong . . . Denise said . . . No, Hugo? No, Giles can't have mentioned trade . . . So hot. Make it go away, ayah," she begged.

"Drink this, Merry," Mathilda commanded. Merry swallowed the bitter draught of sallow tea. "Giles, we must bring her fever down," Mathilda said. Giles, every word Merry had said imprinted on his brain, looked at her blankly.

Crossing to the bed, he was caught up once again in Merry's words. The fragments began to fall in place. Only his fears for Merry kept him from seeking out Hugo and Denise. But he would, he promised himself, he would. His own honesty forced him to accept some of the blame. He had left her to the mercies of the *ton* while he became involved with politics. She had told him she knew little about a London Season, but he had refused to listen. Or to talk, he thought. "Will I ever be able to tell her how I feel?" he asked her aunt.

Finally she was quiet. They knew the crisis was at hand. That night, Giles prayed as he had never prayed before. As a last resort, Giles, Mathilda, and Pilgrim had filled a bath with cool water and lowered Merry carefully into it. As the flush faded from her skin, they lifted her out and wrapped her closely in blankets. They began forcing warm tea and broth into her. They repeated the process several times. Finally, she began shaking, and beads of sweat popped out on her body. Carefully, Pilgrim dried her mistress and robed her in a fresh blanket. Not long afterward, Merry opened her eyes and breathed, "Giles?" After finishing a glass of barley water, she drifted off to sleep, her hand holding tightly onto his.

Sending the others to their well-earned rest, Giles sank into a chair beside the bed. Slowly his eyelids drooped, but his hand never lost its grip. Several hours later he awoke and found Merry lying quietly looking at him. She smiled weakly. His hand tightened on hers. As if afraid she was a dream that would disappear, he whispered, "Merry?" He blinked, but she was still smiling at him when he opened his eyes. "Would you like something to drink?" he finally asked. After the cup of lemonade, Merry closed her eyes and went back to sleep.

Early the next morning, Pilgrim crept in as she had for the last few days. Giles still sat there, a smile on his sleeping face. Pilgrim touched him on the shoulder. "Master Giles, go to bed. I'll watch now," she urged.

Slowly Giles stood up. Every muscle in his body seemed tired and cramped. "She smiled at me," he told the maid. "Call me when she wakes." He stretched and stumbled from the room.

But the day was almost over when his valet awoke him. Angry at first because they had not awakened him earlier, he quickly grew calm as he learned that Merry had slept quietly for much of the day and was only then being bathed. Paying little heed to his own clothing, Giles soon entered the bedroom.

"Just the person we need," declared Mathilda. "You can lift Merry while the servants change her bed." Gladly, he crossed to the bed. Smiling down at Merry, he carefully lifted her into his arms. She gasped. Realizing that every movement made her ache, he stood quietly. The bed once more pristine, he lowered her gently into it. He was as silent as if he feared a word would break the spell. Her soft sigh of satisfaction and comfort brought a smile to his face. Slowly her eyelids dropped shut again.

Satisfied that Merry was progressing well, Mathilda led Giles from the room. "Come now. The servants have prepared a special dinner. You must eat it—in the dining room. Pilgrim will call you if there is any change."

"She will be fine, won't she?" Giles asked. "She is better than she was. We won't lose her?" The farther Giles went from Merry, the more doubts he had. It took the combined coaxing of both Mathilda and Charlotte to make him settle down to dinner. From the clear chicken soup, which Charlotte assured Giles was prepared for Merry, to the trout almondine, Giles ate mechanically. Gradually, however, he began to relax. By the end of the first remove with its broiled mushrooms and asparagus vinaigrette, Giles was able to enjoy his meal. The second remove, with its baked ham and pigeon pie, captured his full attention. By the time the *crème Bavaroise* was served, Giles had begun to converse.

Although Mathilda had spent some time in the sickroom, Charlotte had not. She had made a few visits and had offered to stay, but Giles and Mathilda had felt she was better occupied elsewhere. Charlotte was put in charge of callers and thank you notes. From the moment Merry's accident became known, only minutes after she was carried unconscious into the house, the family had been inundated by the truly concerned and the curious.

During the first day, Charlotte and Mathilda received no one. The next day they felt they were ready to face the world. Beginning with Sir Alex Ramsey, Giles's friends flocked to the house to offer their sympathy and present what Charlotte called, "every flower in London." Carefully chaperoned, Charlotte thanked them all and added a few older admirers to her string of beaux. Lady Sefton and Lady Jersey set the tone for the ladies of the *ton*. After their first visit, they sent a servant regularly to check on Merry's progress. Lady Devereaux and Serena bolstered Charlotte's sagging spirits with their daily visits. Even without the fruit Giles had had sent up from the country, they would have had more than enough. Many

f Charlotte's young men arranged to have hothouse
delicacies delivered regularly in hopes of capturing
her attention.

The only visitors who were in the least unpleasant
were Honoria and Denise, and Hugo. Once after the
door closed behind Honoria and Denise, Charlotte
said, "Those two seemed as interested in Merry as
wolves chasing a sick lamb." Mathilda had to agree.
Charlotte enjoyed Hugo's calls just as little, and he
called at least once a day at first. Even Mathilda
began to doubt his sincerity, in spite of the fact he
kept her supplied with the latest gossip.

Together, she and Charlotte spent the dinner trying
to bring Giles up to date. But he refused to be parted
from Merry any longer than he had been.

The next few days, while Giles assured himself
that Merry was truly recovering, Mathilda and Charlotte rejoined the daytime social whirl. As usual, Charlotte was the center of the younger set while Mathilda
was a goldmine of information for the gossips who
declared, "Merry was dead; no, only close to dying.
Never hurt at all." While Charlotte gloried in the
flirting, Mathilda drenched herself in chatter.

And in Merry's bedroom, Giles sat reading or simply watching Merry sleep. His only exercise was his
morning gallop around the park with his sister. Sitting in the bedroom, he had ample time to remember
Merry's words in her delirium. He knew that they
would have to face those issues squarely if their marriage was to be a success. And he wanted it to be. So
many of his friends had such bleak married lives.
They went their own ways, and their wives went
another. They took mistresses. Their wives, once the
succession was secure, took lovers. The only rule they
followed was to be discreet. Well, he didn't want to
live that way. He wanted a marriage between friends
and lovers. He wanted Merry's laughter and common
sense to fill every part of his life, and his to fill hers.
Patiently, he waited. Every time Merry opened her
eyes, Giles was close by. He held her gently so the

servants could renew the linens. While she was too
weak to lift the spoon, he fed her. When she was
despondent, he told her funny stories. Gradually, Merry
began to expect him to be there.

One morning about a week after Merry had passed
the crisis, she woke early. "Giles," she called. There
was no answer. "Giles." As she waited for him, she
pulled herself up higher on the pillows. "Giles!" By her
third call, she was beginning to panic. She was alone.
After the careful attention she had been receiving,
being alone was frightening. Tears of frustration had
just begun to well up in her eyes when Pilgrim entered.

"Oh, Miss Merry, you're awake. I'm sorry I wasn't
here!" Pilgrim exclaimed. "Master Giles told me never
to leave you alone."

Merry smiled weakly. "I'm fine. I was just startled
for a minute. Where is Mr. Lindsey?"

"He's gone for his morning ride. As soon as you
began to get better, the doctor insisted that he spend
some time outside each day. Otherwise, I don't think
he would ever leave this room. Why he went for days
at a time without sleep when you were so sick. My,
what a fine husband he is."

Merry merely nodded her head. She was confused.
First he neglected her, and now he hardly left her
alone. A frown crossed her face. Pilgrim, seeing it,
hurried to her side. "Are you uncomfortable? Are you
in pain? What may I do to help you? Perhaps you
would like to freshen up. The cook promised to have
your tray ready shortly." Merry smiled. Her maid
seemed to have been around Aunt Mathilda too much
recently.

Settling back on her pillows after she had changed
clothes, she smiled. For the first time in weeks, she
was hungry.

"When may I have some regular food again. I'm
tired of custards and soup." Merry's voice was wistful.
As the door opened and a maid carried in her tray,
her eyes gleamed. "Hot rolls, cherry jam, and chocolate.
Lovely!" Merry exclaimed.

Giles entered on her last word. "Yes, you are, my dear," he assured her. "How wonderful to hear so much vigor in your voice. Too bad that's my breakfast." Merry's face fell. Giles laughed. "You are so gullible? What would a hungry man want with one egg, a roll, and jam? Sirloin is the only suitable breakfast for me. Here, let me feed you."

"No, I'd like to try it myself," she said in a determined voice. She shot him a glance from the corner of her eye. He looked so disappointed. "But I would like some company," she suggested. Giles's face brightened immediately.

The next few days were happy ones for Merry and Giles. Although she continued to improve steadily and was finally allowed out of bed for short periods, Merry and Giles spent their time in their rooms. Giles entertained her with Wordsworth's poetry. And together they tried to balance the beauty of his poetry against the sordidness of his life.

"How can he see such beauty in nature when there is so little in himself? How could he leave his daughter to face the horrors of the revolution in France?" Merry asked.

"Now, Merry, you know that his relationship to that girl has never been proved. Besides, he's a poet. You know what rascals poets are." Giles tried to soothe her.

"How could any father turn away from his own flesh and blood?" She burst into tears. Picking her up, Giles settled her in his lap, cuddling her. For a few minutes, he let her cry.

As her sobs ceased, he wiped her face with his handkerchief, handling her like a small child. "Here, blow. That's right my dear." She snuggled her head against his shoulder. After a few minutes, Giles asked, "Will you tell me about your parents, Merry?"

For a moment she froze. Then, in a wooden voice she began, "My father loved business and my mother. My mother loved my father. We lived many places in Europe. They died in India."

"Merry, I know most of that. Tell me about your parents and you." He could feel her muscles tense. "You said some things when you were ill. Tell me everything, please." She remained silent. "You asked someone why they didn't love you. Did you mean that?" He felt her nod rather than saw it. "Tell me. Let me share it with you," he begged.

Hesitantly, as if afraid her words would destroy her, she began. "The first thing I remember is a fight they had, and my father asked my mother why I was not kept out of the way." As she continued, it was as if the floodgates had been opened. She was powerless to stop the rush of memories. The neglect, the fights, the lovers, the threats, and the confrontation in India poured out of Merry. As she described the scene when her mother promised to kill her father, Giles held her tightly. By the time she finished describing the bitterness between her parents, she was weeping quietly. When her tears were over, she felt strangely relaxed. Giles's arms and quiet words soothed her. Sensing her exhaustion, he slipped her into bed. As she slept, he was deep in thought.

Over the next few days, he made Merry open up further. Her hit-or-miss schooling and her love for business were her trade for knowledge about his boyhood. Merry was enthralled with his stories of his boyish escapade when he became a woodcutter and chopped down the orange trees in Lady Sefton's conservatory and of tickling trout in his father's favorite fishing stream. Gradually, Giles was bringing her closer and closer to the topics that truly interested him: her feelings for him and her fears of society.

As she recovered, she was allowed downstairs, first for short periods and finally for the afternoon and evening. She could no longer hide from visitors. Some afternoons were enlivened by Lady Devereaux's stories about Giles and his misdeeds. She surprised Sir Alex Ramsey by beating him at chess one afternoon. Even the great hostesses stopped in once or twice to pay their respects. Seeing her quiet graciousness, Giles

vas amazed. She was neither aloof nor shy. At first,
ıe thought Merry's demeanor stemmed from the support she was receiving from her aunt.

But the day Honoria and Denise came to call on
heir newest cousin helped him to see the truth. Un-
ler polite conversation, they seemed to stab Merry
with their words. Giles came close enough to hear
Honoria say, "What a shame Charlotte's Season had to
be such a disaster. But I suppose you couldn't help
being hurt." He took quiet steps to remove her from
Merry's side.

Lady Farrell was a bigger problem. She seemed to
be so anxious about Merry. But even her mask slipped
that afternoon. She had stayed for tea. Pulling up a
chair close beside the sofa on which Merry was carefully ensconced, she leaned across and said in a low
voice, "My dear, an accident? How very unoriginal.
But didn't you take something of a risk just to recap-
ture Giles's fancy. Why, you might have died."

From behind her chair Denise heard an angry voice.
It was Giles. "Perhaps you would care to explain that
statement, Denise?" His voice was cold and hard.
Startled, his former mistress stiffened and then relaxed.

"You know I was merely teasing, Giles," she explained. For once, Giles was not deceived. The white
line around Merry's mouth told him there was more
to be learned. Sweeping Merry into his arms, Giles
bid his startled guests good-bye. Before carrying his
wife up the stairs, he told the butler, "We are not at
home to Honoria Coverly or Lady Farrell when they
call again." He entered his suite and plunked her
down on the bed. "All right, Merry, explain."

"Explain what?"

"What that cat meant a few minutes ago. And don't
try to fob me off with some lie. The truth, Merry,"
Giles demanded. A few carefully worded questions
later and the air was blistered with his curses. "Damn
it, Merry, how could you believe that of me? Ask
anyone. Look at Denise. My mistresses were all
voluptuous," he declared.

"And that's supposed to comfort me! I bet they were all beautiful, too," Merry replied.

"Hell, you know what I mean. Besides, what kind of a man do you think I am? You're as much lover as I can handle." Merry blushed and lowered her eyes.

"But those nights you came home so late?" she asked.

"I got involved with the Foreign Office. I was flattered that those in power were interested in my ideas. But I was never unfaithful, except perhaps to my own goals. Damn if I didn't do just what I said I wanted to avoid. I was wrong, I know, to neglect you as I did, but that was no reason for you to shut yourself off from the *ton*."

"Me shut myself off? I never had a chance once your explanation of my background made the rounds," Merry said angrily.

"My explanation? What are you dithering about? I've told no one very much," Giles assured her.

"Hah! Then how did they know that my family was in trade? Hugo certainly wouldn't tell them. But everyone in town knows." Giles stared at her blankly. "Why else have I been reduced to the fringes of society? At the last musicale I attended, Mrs. Drummond Burrell implied that Charlotte needed a more acceptable social companion."

Giles's face flushed with anger. "That old harridan always thinks she is better than anyone else. She almost fainted when Mother told her that my father had accepted a trade mission for the government. Where does she think her fripperies and her art come from, anyway? Let her live without her silks, spices, or tea for a while. She'd change her tune. Don't let her worry you."

"But she's one of the patronesses of Almack's! Charlotte's presentation might be ruined."

"With Lady Sefton and Lord Jersey on our side? I doubt it," he said.

Merry's face lightened. "I was so worried. And . . ."

"And I was not around to reassure you. But I will
e in the future."

Merry smiled up at him and then snuggled down
nto her pillows. Her mind at ease, she drifted off to
leep. Her last thought before she slept was that maybe
ow she would never be lonely again.

Giles sat beside her for a time simply watching her
leep. She was so important to him. Remembering his
nitial reaction when Sommerby had first proposed
he alliance, he frowned. She was warm, sensitive,
nd intelligent, and he had treated her shamefully.
Vould she ever love him as he loved her? Frustrated
y his doubts, he left the room. Remembering the
nessage he had received earlier, he headed toward
he stables.

"Here now, you polish them wheels better," Jem
Coachman was saying as Giles walked into the building.
Catching sight of his master, the man tried to heave
himself to his feet.

"No, keep your seat. You must let that leg have a
hance to heal," Giles said. "What did you wish to see
ne about?"

The coachman seemed to hesitate. Then he burst
nto speech. "Sir, I've been studyin' that accident. Me
nd Turner think something's strange about it."

Giles looked startled. "What exactly do you mean?"

"Well, sir, Turner says that the peddlars were
aughin' and jokin' about their carts. If their carts had
ruly wrecked, they'd 've been layin' into each other.
And I'd glanced up the hill. I'd a sworn the brake was
et on that wagon."

"Are you saying what I think you are?" Giles asked.

The coachman straightened his shoulders. "I think
someone deliberately sent that wagon down the hill."

All evening Giles thought about the coachman's words
Had Merry been the target, or was she simply an
accidental victim? The thought that her injuries might
have been deliberate filled him with rage. Who would
benefit at her death? Only himself. But how many
knew of their marriage settlements? Changing for
dinner, he promised himself that he would look into
the matter further. But he would let nothing, not
even his fears, disturb his plans for the evening. One
of the most enjoyable times of the day were the quiet
dinners he shared with Merry in their suite. Personally
Giles was pleased that she was still considered too
weak to dine downstairs. During the meals, they shared
memories and ideas in a way that was impossible
even around Mathilda and Charlotte. Carefully schooling his features to hide his concern, Giles left his
dressing room.

The following morning their routine changed. After
his horseback ride, Giles carried Merry to the breakfast room. The staff, overjoyed to be able to serve her
properly again, overwhelmed her with their offerings.
The freshest strawberries, the thickest cream, her tea
cup refilled every time she picked it up, eggs poached
just the way she liked them, the crispest muffin with
fresh butter—all were pressed on her. Finally taking
pity on her, Giles said, "Thank you all. We'll ring if
we need you." The servants reluctantly left. Turning
to his wife, he laughed, "I've heard of killing people

with kindness. But I never knew what it meant till now."

"They're so nice." Merry's eyes filled with tears.

"Yes, but spoiling you is my job," Giles reminded her. "And if I see a single tear fall, I'll carry you back to bed and keep you to myself."

"Giles, you wouldn't!"

"Giles wouldn't do what?" asked Charlotte as she entered the room. "'Pon rep, is the Prince coming for breakfast?" she asked as she saw the array on the sideboard.

"No, this is merely what the staff feels is appropriate for Merry," Giles told her.

"And how long do they want you to spend on breakfast? All day?"

"At least I'll have someone to share it with. Will you ring for fresh tea, Giles?" Merry asked.

"Are you certain you know what you are asking me to do?"

"Giles, ring the bell," Merry insisted.

Both Giles and Charlotte teased Merry throughout the meal. To Giles's delight, the breakfast room rang with Merry's laughter. The very sound seemed to ease his worries.

Breakfast finished, Giles deposited Merry on the sofa in the small salon. Carefully surrounded by pillows, she settled back, ready to face her first morning callers. Giles bent over her and kissed her. "I have some business to take care of this morning. I'll be back to carry you back to bed." Before she could ask him any questions, he left. Taking Turner with him, he made his way to Bow Street.

While Giles was presenting his suspicions to the Runners, Merry was caught up once again in the social scene. Perhaps because of her close brush with death, the *ton* once again tolerated Merry. And Charlotte's popularity had never waned. The conversation, the scandals—all seemed the same as at the start of the Season. Only this time Hugo Darryl was one of the players. Merry froze for a moment when

Johnson announced him, and then gave a rather strained smile.

"As soon as I heard you were better, I simply had to see you for myself," his high-pitched voice squeaked. As usual, he was dressed in the extremes of fashion. He was stuffed inside a tight snuff-brown coat trimmed with huge brass buttons and sported the latest in biscuit-colored inexpressibles. His boots were so shiny that Merry was certain he had had his valet polish them before he stepped out of the carriage. "Here, these are for you," he declared, as he covered Merry with a selection of gifts and flowers. "When they told me how ill you had been, I little expected you to look so robust. But, cousin, I am delighted." In spite of his words, his face wore an unhappy expression.

For Merry, Hugo took the sparkle out of the morning. Although others came and went, always limiting their visits to the polite half hour, Hugo lingered. When Giles returned, he was still chattering. Taking one look at Merry's pale cheeks, Giles scooped her up. "I'm certain you will excuse us, Hugo. Merry must rest now. Doctor's orders. Charlotte, please see Mr. Darryl out." Hugo's outraged gasp was quickly masked.

"Certainly, I understand," he assured Giles. "Please tell Lady Mathilda I will see her again shortly." He followed Giles and Merry into the hall. "I do hope you recover fully soon, cousin." Taking his hat and cane, he minced out of the house.

"Do you want me to tell Johnson to deny him if he calls again?" Giles asked as he put Merry onto the chaise in their sitting room.

"Giles, I can't avoid everyone who upsets me."

"At least you admit he upsets you. But remember, you do not have to receive him if you do not want to." The serious look on his face disappeared as he continued, "How did your morning go?"

"Giles, you should have been here. Lord Duncan read the most appalling poem to Charlotte's eyelashes. Can you imagine? I had to bite my lip to keep from laughing." Merry's laughter trilled through the room.

'I did so want to share it with someone. Charlotte imply accepted it as her due. To be sure, I'm not eally certain she was listening. You know that look he gets on her face. The dreamy one. Well, she sat here glowing."

"I suppose I had better be ready to refuse another offer for her hand. I wish my parents would come home and take her off my hands." Giles sounded wistful. "Then I could have you all to myself."

Merry peeped up at him from under her eyelashes. "Are you sure you are not just saying that? It seems to me that you've had me to yourself quite a lot lately. Are you trying to keep me away from the world?"

Giles looked at her sharply, not competely certain if she were serious or simply teasing. He caught a glimpse of a smile at the corner of her mouth. Mentally, he breathed a sigh of relief and continued the banter. "Perhaps I should marry Charlotte off. Who do you think would be suitable?" During the next few minutes Giles and Merry offered one ridiculous suggestion after another. Laughing so hard that neither could breathe well, they were startled by the scratching on the door.

"Your lunch, ma'am," the maid announced. She then addressed Giles. "Lady Mathilda asked me to remind you that you promised to join her for lunch, sir."

"Do go, Giles. I must rest before I see Madame Camille this afternoon," Merry said. "She will be here shortly."

Protesting, Giles left the room. As he walked toward the dining room, he thought how lucky he was that Merry had begun to relax with him. What would she do when she learned what the coachman had said? His brow creased. He had to tell her if only to alert her to her danger. But not yet.

"If you plan to frown like that all during luncheon, you may leave," Mathilda said as he walked in the door. "I will not have my digestion ruined. It is just now becoming stable again. And you must stay be-

cause Charlotte and I have much to discuss with you.'
Allowing him to seat her, she continued, "With Merry
recovering so nicely, it is time for Charlotte to reenter
society fully, don't you think? With such a short
time remaining in the Season, it is essential that we
select our engagements carefully. What do you think,
Giles?" He opened his mouth to answer, but she
continued, "It is too bad that you will have to
cancel your ball. But society will understand. Perhaps by the Little Season; yes, during the Little Season,
Merry should be completely recovered." Her light
voice flitted from one detail to another. Eventually
Giles simply let his mind wander, but it snapped to
attention when he heard her say, "I told the Prince
you would be happy to attend."

"Attend? Attend what?" Giles demanded.

"Well, really, Giles. If I didn't know better I would
think you had not been listening to me. Why the
Drawing Room, of course." Mathilda was indignant.

"Oh, the Drawing Room. And what was the date?"

"Come, Charlotte. We will discuss this matter later,
sir, when you are more attentive." Mathilda set aside
the meringue basket of sweetmeats she had been toying
with and swept majestically from the room. But when
she peeped around the corner to see Giles's reaction,
she spoiled her effect.

Giles smiled ruefully. Calling for his hat, cane, and
curricle, he decided to visit his carriage makers. With
the beautiful weather lately, Merry would soon want
to go for drives in the sunshine. She needed a new
carriage. And he knew just the one. Swinging his cane
jauntily, he tipped his hat to Madame Camille, who
was just coming up the steps, and jumped into the
curricle.

Madame Camille, her usual volatile self, first tried
to drown Merry in tears and then embraced her
warmly. "All thanks to *le bon dieu* for his mercy in
sparing you," she rejoiced, her voice quavering.

Before the modiste could once more burst into tears,
Merry asked, "And how has business been lately,

madame?" The word *business* quickly restored Madame's equilibrium.

"Oh, Madame Lindsey, you were so right. London needed me. The ladies, so kind, so ready for new ideas. I have just received the latest fashions from France. You must allow me to make up some new dresses. So healthy to look good." She chattered on.

"Perhaps one or two, madame. But truly, I need new dressing gowns and night robes." Merry held up her arm that was still encased in wood. "All my others have been split to accommodate this."

"*Oui*, madame. A problem." She thought for a moment. "But, of course. Do you have paper and pen?" Merry directed her to the desk in the office. "Ah, yes. See, madame, full, flowing sleeves in the robe ending at the wrist. And a gown in the Grecian fashion that leaves that arm free."

Merry thought of Giles's reaction and, before she could change her mind, said, "Yes, that will be perfect. In a variety of colors. I'll leave that to you."

As usual, once she had a design in mind, Madame Camille involved herself totally. Bidding Merry adieu, she left muttering, "A pale yellow, rose, a jade green. Yes, that's it."

Merry settled herself carefully on her bed. What would Giles think of her new gowns? Remembering the bow at the top of one shoulder, she imagined the ease with which the gown would fall away. For a moment she was shocked at herself. Then she laughed and settled against her pillows. She picked up the novel Pilgrim had laid beside her and selected a piece of her favorite candy. From the last interlude Giles and she had had, she doubted he would ever let her wear a nightrobe long enough for him to admire it.

A few hours later Giles burst into the room. "Aren't you ready for dinner, Merry? Mathilda and Charlotte are dining with the Devereaux. I'll have you all to myself." He took a quick look at her pale face. "But I think we'll dine here. I knew that fool doctor was letting you do too much. Now look. You're overtired. Just stay in bed. I'll take care of you."

Merry sank back into her pillows listlessly. She had been feeling so wonderful earlier, but now she felt weak and rather queasy. Her eyes filled with tears. She did so hate being helpless. Seeing the tears, Giles gathered her close. "Merry, do you hurt? Should I send for the doctor?" he asked.

"No," she sobbed, "but I want to be well. I don't like being ill."

"And I don't like it either. I'm tired of sleeping alone," he whispered in her ear. "Most of all I want you beside me all day every day. Please, my dear, rest. You've just tried to do too much too soon." He held her against his shoulder, his hands soothing her tight muscles. As she grew calmer, he settled her back against her pillows. "What would milady like for dinner?" he asked.

"Oh, Giles, I really could not eat anything."

"Merry, the doctor said you must eat properly. Let me have Cook send up some broth. Would you try to drink some?" Merry agreed reluctantly.

By the next morning Merry felt much better. Although she was still weak, she insisted that Giles allow her to get up for breakfast. This time she was very careful what she selected, limiting her breakfast to a muffin and a poached egg. Both she and Giles had decided that she had eaten something that had disagreed with her.

The rest of the day was a quiet one. Merry began to take back the reins of the household. While Merry was consulting the housekeeper, Giles visited the stables. The new carriage should arrive within the week, and he wanted to tell Jem Coachman. He also needed to talk to Turner. The Runners had promised to look into the situation, but perhaps Turner could remember more than he had told them yesterday.

As Giles described the new landau and its doors decorated with gold handles, Turner frowned. Giles stopped talking and looked at him curiously. "Sorry, sir. Mentionin' that door made me think. A strange little man had hold of the door when I got there."

"A man? What did he look like?" Giles asked eagerly. "Did you know him?"

"No, sir. He weren't nobody I knew. But he ran when I called him. Course, he might have been scared."

Giles nodded his head. "True. Could you describe him for the Runners?"

"I guess I could try," Turner said hesitantly.

"Then let's be off."

For the first time since the accident, everyone was together for luncheon. Although Giles tried to insist that Merry return to bed, her will proved stronger. Mathilda kept up a running conversation about the members of the *ton* she had seen on her morning drive. Charlotte added a bit of dash as she mimicked her latest compliments from the Tulip who had followed them all morning. "Oh, Merry. He talked so peculiarly. He lisped. 'Mith Tharlotte, you are tho thic,' he said. I could hardly keep from laughing."

"Charlotte, you must not make fun of that poor, unfortunate young man," Mathilda declared. "I'm certain that he cannot help the way he talks. Such a lovely dresser. So exquisite."

"But, Aunt Mathilda, he can. I told him how sorry I was that I did not understand him. And he became very upset and talked as plain as you or I."

"How peculiar." Mathilda had more important items to consider than a lisp. "Giles, you do remember that it is Almack's this evening? Since Merry is better, I expect you to escort us," Mathilda said.

Giles looked at Merry, but she refused to give him a chance to refuse. Merry said, "I'll go to bed early and read that novel I just began. Before you leave, Charlotte, come to my room so I can see your gown. Giles will be happy to escort you."

That evening, Charlotte positively danced into Merry's bedroom. Madame Camille had made an extra effort, and Charlotte's gown showed it. The soft gauze was an unusual strawberry pink worn over a

lighter pink crepe underslip. The deep square neckline and the bottom of the puffed sleeves were edged
with pearl and coral beads. And in her ears and around
her neck, Charlotte wore matching pearl and coral
jewelry. Her dark curls were swept to one side in a
chignon with one curl left free over her temple.

"Isn't it exciting! My first ball in so long. I do wish
you could come, Merry. Did I tell you that Serena is
going with us tonight? Her mother is going to a card
party. A card party when she could dance! Are you
ready to go, Giles?" Charlotte asked.

"I am not the person we are waiting on," he said
pointedly. Merry caught her breath. He did look so
handsome in his black satin coat with his white waist-
coat and white satin knee breeches. The only color in
his outfit was the rubies in his cravat and on his
hand. Giles urged, "Run along. Aunt Mathilda is waiting downstairs." As Charlotte left, he turned to Merry.
"Are you certain you will be all right alone? Last
night you were so weak."

"Pilgrim will be within calling distance. Go, Giles.
Charlotte needs you now." Reluctantly, Giles bent
and kissed her good-bye. "Now go. I'll just read my
book." She smiled and shooed him away.

While Merry was comfortably surrounded by pillows and entertained by gothic horrors, Giles and
Lady Mathilda were surrounded by the curious.
Charlotte, her dance card filled, escaped into the first
set. "Why, Mathilda, I had no idea that you planned
to come to London this Season. You should have
written. I would have been happy to have you stay
with me," gushed a large, buxom woman with her
youngest daughter in tow.

"You're so kind. But I prefer to stay with my niece
and her husband. You do know my nephew by marriage,
Giles Lindsey." Mathilda's voice had lost some of its
usual lighthearted friendliness. She smiled politely.
Every invitation from the woman always meant that
she and the current daughter on the *ton* would expect
to spend at least two months that summer in Bath.

"Your niece is Miranda Sommerby Lindsey?" The woman's tone was shocked.

"I thought you knew. Didn't you receive my letter at the first of the Season? I was certain you did." Mathilda enjoyed watching the woman squirm. She continued, "I am certain you've heard me mention her. My father, the Earl of Camden, regretted that his only grandchild lived so far away from him. He missed so much of her life."

Giles had to stifle a gasp of laughter. From what Mr. Sommerby had said, the earl had refused to acknowledge Merry's existence. But Mathilda had never let the truth interfere with her purpose. By the time the woman escaped, she was convinced that Merry's only flaw was family that had allowed her to become a bluestocking. Mathilda watched her head for the small cluster of older women along the opposite wall.

"Up to your old tricks again, Mathilda?" asked Lady Sefton.

"Maria, how are you? You look simply enchanting, doesn't she, Giles? Where ever did you find that exquisite dress? The color is so becoming."

"Mathilda, don't try to fob me off with compliments. I know that look on your face of old. What tale were you telling now?" Lady Sefton asked.

"You should have heard her, ma'am. To hear Aunt Mathilda tell the story, one would think that Merry was the darling of the earl," Giles laughed.

"I had forgotten. Of course, Merry is your niece and the granddaughter of the Earl of Camden. How delicious. Does Mrs. Drummond Burrell know?" she asked. Seeing them shake their heads, she suggested, "Do let me tell her . . . in my own way." She smiled a slightly mischievous smile. Mathilda and Giles exchanged a glance. Satisfied with the progress of their plans, Giles let Lady Sefton lead him to the row where those less popular ladies sat.

For the rest of the evening, Giles danced with those ladies less favored than Charlotte while Mathilda flitted from acquaintance to friend. Even Charlotte did her part in the campaign as she mentioned her new chaperone, the daughter of the Earl of Camden, her sister-in-law's aunt. By the time Mathilda gave the signal to depart, the *ton*, or at least those members who had entry into Almack's, were buzzing. With a satisfied smile on her face, Mathilda settled into the corner of the carriage. "By morning the whole town will be talking."

But by the next morning, neither Giles, Mathilda, nor Charlotte cared. Merry was growing worse again. Frantically, Giles sent for the doctor. However, by the time the doctor arrived, Merry was beginning to respond. After checking her over, the doctor shook his head. "And when did these attacks begin?" he asked.

"Two days ago," Giles said before Merry could reply. "She has complained of stomach cramps, a queasy feeling, and dizziness. Could it be her injuries?"

"Perhaps, but I doubt it. Have you eaten any seafood lately?" Both Giles and Merry shook their heads. "Well, I suggest that you stay on a bland diet for several days. Broth, eggs, a bit of steamed chicken, but nothing rich. No desserts. I will check you again tomorrow morning."

As the day progressed, so did Merry. In spite of her protests, Giles refused to let her get up or to have anything to eat but what the doctor had ordered. They spent the afternoon playing chess and squabbling until Merry's eyes began to droop. Even then, she wanted Giles's presence.

"Don't leave. Stay and take a nap with me," she begged, slightly shocked at her own forward behavior. Giles was delighted. She had asked for his company. He climbed into the bed and pulled her close, being careful to protect her right arm. She pillowed her head on his right shoulder and drifted off to sleep. Even when his arm began to go to sleep, Giles lay there. His last thought before he drifted off to sleep was how wonderful it was being close to a willing Merry.

Although Merry slept deeply for several hours, Giles

slept only a short time. After watching Merry breathe softly began to pale, he eased himself carefully from the bed and crossed to the comfortable chair by the window. He settled into it and reached for the stack of books on the table. "John Locke, Wordsworth, and a gothic novel," he laughed softly. "How very Merry." Picking up the Wordsworth, he sampled the poems, stopping often to check on Merry.

When Pilgrim came to dress her mistress for dinner, he waved her away. "I'll ring when she wakes," he promised. He lit the candles on the table and picked up his book again. As Merry slept on, he nibbled on a piece of crystallized ginger from the box beside the books. It was Merry's favorite, a treat from her days in India. It would never be his favorite, he decided.

It was almost nine when Merry began to stir. Immediately, Giles rang for the light supper he had ordered. For once, his usual hearty appetite was missing. Even the light, fluffy omelet did not appeal to him. Merry ate every bite. By the time she had finished and had taken her medicine, Giles felt exhausted and retired to his camp bed.

During the night he tossed and turned, his stomach cramping badly. The next morning he felt listless and woozy. Forcing himself out of bed and into his clothes, he entered the bedroom. "Giles, I'm ready to get up. Giles, what is the matter? You look terrible. Perhaps you should go back to bed," Merry suggested.

"No, I am already feeling better. Merry, how did you feel yesterday morning?"

"Yesterday? Why weak and dizzy and—Oh!"

He nodded his head. "We shared all our meals yesterday. Except for this." He slowly crossed to the table and picked up the box of candied ginger. "Have you eaten any of this?" he asked.

"A couple of pieces. Giles, what are you saying?" Merry's voice was anxious.

"Nothing yet, but this bears looking into."

"Well, let someone else do it. I want the doctor to have a look at you when he comes," Merry declared.

"You are staying right here until then." Weakly, Giles agreed.

Fortunately for Giles's patience, the doctor made an early visit. Like Giles, he was suspicious of a disease that struck so unexpectedly and passed so quickly. Taking Giles into his dressing room, the doctor checked him carefully and then promised to deliver the ginger to his apothecary for analysis.

As Merry had done before, Giles grew stronger as the day progressed. Like the previous day he refused to leave Merry. For once, Merry had a chance to care for him. Although she was hampered by her arm, she delighted in pampering him. When Mathilda and Charlotte visited her that morning, they even accused her of spoiling him. Giles simply sat back and enjoyed himself. But when he remembered the ginger and the accident, he worried.

During one of these intervals, he slipped into his dressing rooms where his valet waited. "Try to discover from the other servants where the ginger came from, Petersham," he ordered. "Meanwhile, I will keep a watch over my wife." Giles inspected all food they ate carefully. But mostly he basked in Merry's smiles.

The next morning he could no longer ignore the problem. According to the apothecary, the ginger was poisoned. And no one knew where it had come from.

—13—

When the apothecary's report confirmed his suspicions, Giles had to reveal the whole. Merry had been prepared for the poison, but the possibility that the wreck had been deliberate shocked her. Mathilda and Charlotte were stunned. For at least fifteen minutes Mathilda could not think of anything to say. Merry, faced with the enormity of someone's hatred for her, could only cry. Even Giles's arms around her did little to ease her pain. Once again Giles's words, "I'll protect you. No one will hurt you again," came back to haunt him. Helplessly, he held Merry until her tears slowed.

Mathilda burst into speech. "How dare anyone treat my niece so! I'll not have it. You must hire the Runners immediately and put a stop to these attacks," she demanded.

"They are already on the case," Giles assured her.

Merry drew out of his embrace. "The Runners? When did you send for them?" Both Mathilda and Charlotte looked at Giles questioningly.

"I called them in after Jem Coachman told me his suspicions. The day you received morning callers, Merry. I'll tell them about the poison later today when I check to see if they've located the man Turner described." Giles quickly related Turner's memories of the little man. "Merry, do you remember anything about the wreck?"

She hesitated. A shiver ran through her. "I remem-

173

ber the crowd and looking up the hill. A wagon moving without horses or oxen. Then I realized that the wagon was going to crash into us." Her voice was almost dreamy. "It seemed to be happening so slowly. But I knew I couldn't escape. Then the impact."

"Details, Merry. Can you remember details?" he asked.

"The sky was so blue. It was a beautiful day. I planned to order a gown I thought you would like."

"Merry, do you remember anything after the impact? Try."

"Surprise. And pain." Merry's voice began to tremble. She reached out to Giles, who enfolded her in his arms again.

"Now, Giles, you are not to upset her. Let the Runners handle the problem. That's why you hired them," Mathilda insisted.

"Can they do that, Giles?" Charlotte asked. "Have they told you anything yet?"

"Nothing of any substance. They simply say that they are looking into certain matters. But I shall continue to press them," he replied. "They told me to continue life as usual. They don't want anyone to know they are on the case."

"Life as usual? When Merry may be harmed at any moment?" Mathilda asked. "How can they be so unfeeling?"

"Now that we know for sure that someone is trying to hurt her, we will be very cautious. Merry and I are going to become inseparable," Giles assured the older woman.

"But won't people talk? A husband and wife in each other's pockets?" Charlotte asked.

"Then let them talk. They are already." He smiled down at Merry.

"Well, if you intend on cuddling in public, you will be the center of all eyes," Mathilda said disapprovingly.

"The more visible we are, perhaps the less danger there will be for Merry. Isn't that right?"

Merry's aunt nodded her head. "But I insist that you must not embrace her in public, Giles. How distressing it would be to have you labeled 'common.' And so disastrous to Charlotte."

"I think it might be fun," Charlotte replied. "Cuddling looks perfectly delightful to me."

"Charlotte Lindsey, get that thought out of your head! You will cuddle when you are married and not before," Mathilda gasped. "See what ideas you've put in her head. And she has enough of her own!" Giles could feel Merry shaking with laughter. He could barely restrain his own. Charlotte was not so polite. Her giggles started a chain reaction until all four of the family were laughing.

As they relaxed after they could control themselves, Charlotte asked, "Are you planning on attending any of the balls or other functions for the rest of the Season?"

"The doctor has said I must not overtire myself. Giles thinks we might attend one or two, but not until this comes off." Merry held up her right arm, which was still in splints. "We plan to start driving in the park soon, though."

"Just as soon as the new carriage is delivered," Giles said.

"A new carriage? How lovely. Tell me about it," Charlotte demanded.

"Later. It should be delivered soon. Aren't you promised to someone this morning?" he asked.

"Lady Devereaux's Venetian Breakfast," exclaimed Mathilda. "Good heavens, Charlotte. How could you let me forget? We must hurry and change our clothing. You know Serena will never forgive you if you are late. Have you considered what you will wear? Perhaps the white muslin with the violet ribbons. Now do not dawdle, Charlotte. We must leave within the hour." Mathilda continued her instructions until the door to her suite closed behind her. Charlotte exchanged a conspiratorial glance with Merry and Giles, and dashed away.

"How I adore that aunt of yours, Merry!" Giles said.

"She does add life to whatever she does," Merry agreed.

"And she enjoys herself tremendously. Now, how shall we spend our day?" He guided Merry into the hallway. Johnson and two footmen stood there. The footmen's arms were filled with boxes bearing Madame Camille's distinctive design.

"I shall have these delivered to your room immediately, ma'am. Shall I instruct Pilgrim to unpack them?" the butler asked.

Before Merry could respond, Giles answered, "No, not for the moment. Just put them in the sitting room." When the butler and footmen had left, he explained, "A fashion show would be just the thing."

Merry, remembering what the boxes contained, blushed. But she did not hesitate. As she had thought, Giles delighted in the design. He became quite adept in untying bows. If Pilgrim later wondered at the number of nightrobes flung carelessly over the sofa in the sitting room, she was careful to keep her questions to herself.

The next few days were pleasantly uneventful. With the doctor's permission, Giles and Merry joined the Promenade. The first afternoon they drove out, Merry dressed in a dashing yellow muslin with a matching spencer. Her bonnet was a light straw caught under her left ear in a large yellow satin bow. The day was bright and sunny, but Giles could feel Merry shaking. As he glanced toward her, he could see the white line around her mouth. Slipping her hand into his, he pressed her close to his side until he felt her relax. The sunshine and pleasant people did the rest.

After the first afternoon out, they joined the Promenade regularly. Often Charlotte went with them while Mathilda paid afternoon calls. One afternoon they were startled by a loud hello and turned to see the Devereaux's carriage close behind them. "Really,

Thomas. I am so embarrassed. Mother, make him behave," Serena declared as a blush stained her cheeks.

Even his mother's frown failed to dampen Lord Thomas Devereaux's spirits. "I say, Charlotte, how wonderful you look. I told Serena you wouldn't mind my calling to you," he said. "Have you missed me? Pater and I went to Scotland to escape the measles. Wonderful salmon up there, Giles. You must go sometime. And you must be Giles's wife. Well, someone introduce me."

"As impulsive as usual, Thomas," Giles replied. "Merry, this young scamp is Lady Devereaux's oldest son, Thomas. Thomas, my wife Merry."

"Come join us," Charlotte urged Thomas and Serena. "Tell me about your adventures."

"Adventures, maybe later," Thomas said as he helped his sister into the carriage. "I hear you are quite the belle of the season. The Dark Goddess? Really, Charlotte, it is a bit much for a brat like you." He winked at Giles.

"Well, really," Charlotte glared at him. "I'll have you know everyone thinks I'm beautiful."

"Is that new? You've been pretty from the cradle, and I should know. You've been tagging after me since you and Serena could toddle. Lord, what pests you were."

"You were no saint yourself," Charlotte reminded him. Merry and Giles sat back and enjoyed the sparring. By the time the Promenade was over, Charlotte and Thomas were friends again. Charlotte, who usually limited her partners to one dance, had agreed to open the Devereaux ball with him and had given him the supper dance, too.

Like Serena, Thomas became a part of the Lindsey household. From morning rides to excursions to the Pantheon Bazaar, he escorted the two girls. When the compliments from their suitors became too impassioned, he brought the girls to earth with a whispered remembrance of some childish prank. In spite of his lack of reverence for the position she held in society,

Charlotte enjoyed his company. Even Giles breathed easier when Thomas was present. His eagle eye kept both Serena and Charlotte in line. And his proprietary attitude kept the most obvious fortune hunters at bay.

The Season was almost over when the Devereaux ball took place. Serena had convinced her mother to turn the ballroom into a flower-filled paradise. Against the backdrop of vivid blooms, the dancers glittered. Both Serena and Charlotte had chosen to wear white. Merry, attending her first ball since her accident, was vivid in the ruby-red silk with diamonds and rubies around her throat and in her ears and hair. Mathilda had chosen a smoky blue chiffon.

When the opening strains of the music began, Thomas claimed Charlotte for his dance. Giles, taking Merry by her arm, led her gracefully into a set forming nearby. As they twirled to the music, Merry allowed herself to be soothed by the music. With Giles's presence and attention, even the presence of Honoria, Denise, and Hugo seemed insignificant.

Happy but tired after a succession of dances, Merry begged Giles to let her rest. Crossing to a chair set close beside the open doors to the terrace, she was startled to see Charlotte being led into the garden by Thomas.

"Oh, Giles," she said in a despairing voice.

"Merry, I'll go talk to her. I thought Charlotte had more social sense." A few minutes later he was back, a rueful smile on his face. "I told you she had sense. This time she organized a group carefully chaperoned by Aunt Mathilda. They plan to sit out the next dance in order to cool off." Merry relaxed once more. "Would you like some punch? Thomas assured me it was not half bad," he asked.

The few minutes Merry was alone were pleasant. Returning the nods and quiet comments of her acquaintances, Merry enjoyed the music. She wondered why she had ever been afraid of balls. Thinking back, she admitted the difference—Giles. In the last few

veeks he had become necessary to her. She who had
worn never to marry, now was only happy when
Giles was near by. But it was only because she feared
being lonely, she told herself.

"Here, Merry, take this," Giles said. Taking the
cup, she smiled up at him. Suddenly a scowl creased
his forehead. Merry turned slightly and saw Charlotte practically dragging Thomas toward them.

"Thomas, tell them what you and I heard," Charlotte demanded.

"Not here, you idiot. Giles and Merry, join us in my
father's study, please." Thomas's tone was serious.
Rather concerned, Giles and Merry followed them.

As soon as the door closed behind them, Charlotte
demanded again, "Tell them what you heard. You
were closer."

"Charlotte, you are making too much of a woman's
gossip," Thomas tried to convince her.

"Gossip, hah! I suppose it was gossip that caused
that accident, and that poisoned Merry and you too,
Giles?"

"What?"

Charlotte, her eyes very round, put her hand over
her mouth. "Giles, I'm sorry," she tried to explain.

"Tell me what she's talking about. It's only her
imagination, isn't it?" Thomas asked. Giles looked at
Merry. She nodded. Briefly, he told Thomas the whole
story, cautioning him to silence. When Giles had
finished, Thomas stood up and crossed to the table
where a decanter of brandy sat. He poured a glass and
tossed it down quickly. Turning to face them, he
asked, "Are you certain?"

"As certain as we can be without knowing who is
behind it," Giles told him.

"Tell him what we heard, Thomas. If you don't, I
will. But you heard more," Charlotte pleaded.

The young man straightened his shoulders. "Charlotte and I were in the gardens, near the fountain.
Serena and the others had gone ahead, but we had
stopped to talk." He looked toward Giles and Merry.

"I know we shouldn't have, but we did. We sat there for a while, quietly. From the other side of the fountain, we heard other people approaching. We stepped back in the shadows."

"Just take that frown off your face, Giles Lindsey. If I am not safe with Thomas, I don't know who I can trust. Besides, what we heard is important." Charlotte was not about to let her brother censure her for her actions. "Go on, Thomas," she directed regally.

He shot her a look that would have made Merry quake in her slippers. Charlotte did not even blink. "The woman."

Charlotte interrupted, "It was Denise. I saw her plainly in the moonlight."

"Lady Farrell, then, was talking to someone about you, Merry. The other person kept reassuring her that soon you would no longer bother her. She laughed loudly but was quickly hushed."

"Who was the other person?" Merry asked.

"Neither Charlotte nor I could tell. The voice was low, so low we could not tell if the speaker was a man or woman. The darkness of the hedges hid the person from view. Also, Denise was so excited, she kept babbling. She really is a malicious person. Did you know she was behind the stories about your business life, Merry?"

Merry drew a deep sigh of relief. Her instincts had been right all along. Giles was innocent. How she would love telling Hugo!

Giles leaned protectively over the back of Merry's chair. As if to reassure her, he said, "An earl's granddaughter does not need to worry about rumors, does she, Merry?" Her soft laugh lightened the atmosphere. "Did you hear anything specific?" he asked.

Both Thomas and Charlotte assured him that he knew the whole. Although Thomas was reluctant to press Giles, Charlotte refused to let him off that easily. "Are you going to talk to her tonight, Giles?"

"Tonight, no. I think I'll tell the Runner, though.

One of the men on the case asked if he could see me tomorrow."

"The Runner!" Thomas's eyes grew brighter.

"See, I told you it was important. But no. You wouldn't believe me. I'm just a girl. I don't know anything," Charlotte reminded her friend. She and Merry exchanged an understanding glance.

"No more about this tonight. Promise me," Giles demanded. Reluctantly, they promised.

"But you will tell me all about it when you can?" Thomas asked. Remembering his own love of adventure, Giles promised.

The rest of the evening was as nervewracking for Merry as those earlier in the Season. She and Giles made their excuses early, leaving Charlotte in Mathilda's care. But Merry could not relax. She tossed and turned restlessly. After her wriggling had awakened Giles for the second time, he lit a candle and sat up in bed. He pulled her close to him. Quietly he tried to soothe her fears. "This morning we had very little information for the Runners. What we learned tonight should help them. Think how shocked Denise will be when they visit her." He looked down at his wife. A faint smile tugged at her mouth. He was on the right path. "And maybe we should mention Honoria, too. I wonder how she'll like being a part of a scandal?" Merry uttered a sigh of satisfaction. Her usual forgiving nature was lost in her dreams of the conniving Denise brought before the bar of justice. Slowly, she drifted off to sleep. Giles settled himself beside her once more. A frown crossed his forehead. He hoped the Runners would have something more for them tomorrow.

The next morning his patience was rewarded. The Runners agreed to visit Denise. The report they brought furnished another suspect—Hugo Darryl.

"Hugo? What could he hope to gain?" Merry asked.

The Runner smiled as if he were amused at her naiveté. "What most criminals hope to gain—money!" he said.

"But the settlements," Giles began.

"And how many people knew of them?"

Merry and Giles exchanged a glance. "Only Mr. Pettigrew, my wife, and I," Giles told him.

"And without those, who would be the heir?" the Runner asked.

A light blazed in Merry's eyes. "If anything happened to me, the shares went to the nearest male heir," she said.

"Hugo," they said together. "Then all we have to do is tell him about Merry's will," Giles said.

"Good thought, young man. I wish it could be that simple. But . . ." The older man paused and shrugged his shoulders.

"Please tell us," Merry begged.

"Well, the problem is much bigger than we thought. Even if we had definite proof, which we don't, Mr. Darryl still might try again." Both Merry and Giles had puzzled looks on their faces. "When we searched his premises, very secretly of course, we found some very interesting information. He's really very careless, you know," the Runner paused as if to savor their puzzled looks.

"What did you find?" Merry urged.

The Runner shot her an annoyed look, but continued. "Apparently Mr. Darryl and a partner—from what we could find, a rather disreputable cent-percenter—created their own company. We found orders with their company's name to the Bristol Trading Company. And there was some correspondence signed by you, Mrs. Lindsey."

"By me?"

"Receipts for hundreds of pounds of merchandise. Looked like forgeries to us, but they probably explain the large sums of money he has been spending and receiving since the first of the year."

A curse exploded from Giles.

"That's what he wanted the money for. Or at least my draft!" Merry turned to Giles. "You tried to warn me, but would I listen? No, I had to lend him the money."

"Merry, now at least we can find ways to stop him." Giles turned to the Runner. "How does his scheme work?"

"The company is merely a front. Darryl did the ordering and saw to paying the bills. His partner got rid of the goods. Clever embezzlement scheme."

"You warned me he was an evil man. Charlotte tried to warn me. But would I listen? When I wrote that draft, I had doubts." Merry was beside herself with rage. For a moment, the threat to the company was more important than the threat on her own life.

"Merry, we will solve the problem. Together. Remember?" Giles tried to reassure her. At first his efforts showed no result. The Runner stared at Merry in amazement. The serene woman of a few minutes earlier was pacing the room like a tiger paces its cage, her hazel eyes flashing. He was astonished at the transformation. Her face was alive and almost beautiful without the mask of calm she usually wore. Giles openly and the Runner secretively were captivated by her heaving breasts.

Gradually reason won over passion once again. Merry subsided into a chair. She glared at the Runner. "What do you propose to do to stop him?" she demanded.

The Runner gulped. He took a deep breath. "You must remember that we have very little evidence against him now. Definitely not enough to bring him to trial." Merry began to stir restlessly. He hastened on. "Other men are out now trying to find more specific evidence. Also, we are watching him closely. He'll not have a chance to hurt you again."

Giles stared at the older man thoughtfully. He had heard those words before. Now they were not convincing. "Is there nothing more we can do? Must we simply wait until he tries again?" he asked.

Although the Runner tried to explain the need for patience, neither Giles nor Merry felt secure with his advice. Promising to contact them when he had further news, the Runner left. A few minutes later, Mathilda and Charlotte entered the room. At first, Mathilda refused to believe Hugo capable of any evil doing. Charlotte, on the other hand, declared, "I knew he did not like you, Merry. I could tell from the first moment that man asked about you when you were ill. Well, what are the Runners going to do about him?" she demanded. Like Giles and Merry, Mathilda and Charlotte were horrified to discover that nothing could be done.

"If he is guilty, which I am not sure I believe, he should be brought before the bar of justice. There he could answer the charges and be found innocent or guilty," Mathilda declared.

Charlotte was rather disgusted with her aunt by marriage. "Giles just told you there wasn't enough evidence. I don't want that squeaky toad to escape. We will just have to think of an idea to make him reveal his guilt." Charlotte looked thoughtful.

"For once, Charlotte, you may have the right idea," Giles said. His voice had a thoughtful tone.

"Well, don't just stand there, brother. Tell us about it," she urged.

"Not today. Let me think about it some more." Much to Charlotte's chagrin, she could not get him to say more.

"Come, Aunt Mathilda. Let's leave these ingrates to their own thoughts. I need your advice on what to wear to the picnic this afternoon."

Alone once more, Giles looked at Merry thoughtfully. "Do you plan to keep your idea from me, too?" she asked. He shook his head, a frown creasing his brow.

"This problem is that you will be in danger," he said.

"And I am perfectly safe right now? Come, Giles, you must do better than that." Slowly, she drew his ideas from him. As the plan unfolded, she too frowned. "When will this take place?" she asked.

"It will take a few days to arrange, but I believe

ithin the week." Giles smiled unpleasantly. "Hugo
, in for a surprise," he assured her.

When Hugo appeared for afternoon tea a few days
ater, all was in readiness. Mathilda and Charlotte,
rimed for their parts, helped keep him occupied
vith tea and gossip until Johnson hurried in with a
ispatch marked urgent. Hugo looked up.

"Curses," said Giles. "It's from Pettigrew, Merry.
He needs us in Bristol immediately. Some irregularity
n the books." Hugo's face lost color. "Do you feel
trong enough to travel, or should I go alone?"

"If it is business, I am going with you," Merry
eclared. "When should I be ready to leave?"

Giles glanced at the clock on the mantel as if to see
ow much traveling time was left that day. "It's too
ate to get far today. If we leave at first light tomorrow,
ve should be in Bristol early the next day."

"First light?" Mathilda asked. "Shouldn't you wait
 while? With all the crime on the highways recently,
'd feel safer if you did."

Soothing her fears, Giles reminded her that the
~oom would be armed and so would he. Hugo too
oiced his concern, reminding Giles of the robberies
ust that week. Even after Hugo realized they would
not change their minds, he stayed until the bell rang
o mark the time to dress for dinner. Refusing their
half-hearted invitation to dinner, Hugo pranced out.
As the door closed behind him, Giles and Merry exchanged a worried look. Mathilda declared, "What
did I tell you? Hugo Darryl is as innocent as I am.
You'll have that long trip to Bristol for nothing."
Giles and Merry exchanged a worried look.

The dinner that evening was a quiet one. Mathilda
and Charlotte were dining out. Both Giles and Merry
were worried, but neither wanted to discuss the
problem.

Finally Merry broke the silence. "Giles, promise me
something."

He looked at her quiet face. He hesitated and then

said, "If I can." Giles knew that look, and it worried him.

"If the person trying to harm me is not Hugo, let me stay in Bristol. Here there is always a chance that someone else may be hurt."

"Never. Where I go, you go. But don't worry. Before tomorrow is out, we will have our would-be murderer. And despite his calm this afternoon, I am certain Hugo is the one." He held her chair as she rose, and walked into the salon with her. He asked in a whimsical tone, "How shall we spend the evening, chess, cards, or bed?"

"Giles!" she laughed. For a moment the tension was broken, but only for a moment.

—14—

awn the next morning saw Merry and Giles already
tside London with the carriage swinging along at a
st clip. Neither had slept well the night before.
erry's face had lost what color it normally possessed,
d the dark blue of her cloak and hat emphasized the
rcles underlining her eyes. Giles's forehead seemed
ermanently creased into a frown. Although they said
ttle, Giles held Merry's hand tightly. After they
assed the first toll booth, the road was deserted.
here were no towns for several miles, and those farm-
s traveling to London for market were already there.

As the horses paced off the miles, Giles dropped
Merry's hand and picked up the highly polished
ooden case on the seat in front of him. Two gleaming
istols, fully loaded and ready to be cocked, lay there.
le drew one out, checking it carefully one more time.
Do you think you can fire one of these?" he asked
Merry.

As she had on all the other occasions, Merry reas-
ured him. "If I must, I will. Giles, what if Aunt
Mathilda is right?"

"You heard the Runners. He has every motive. But
f we are all wrong, you and I will enjoy a few days in
Bristol alone."

Merry smiled as he had meant her to do. However,
he was still too hesitant about her own feelings to
gree with him openly. She merely moved closer to
im. Giles closed the gun case with a snap and put it

187

back on the seat in front of him. He settled back.
few minutes later Turner pulled up the flap an
shouted, "Stand of trees ahead, sir. Could be a like
place."

"Keep a sharp lookout. And don't try to be a her
Remember, the Runners are right behind us," Gil
reminded him. He opened the gun case again. Th
first, he slipped into his own pocket. The second, h
gave to Merry, who hid it in her reticule. "No matte
what they do or say, don't be nervous." He laughed
"Why am I telling you that? Your veneer of cal
almost scared me away."

"You are simply envious," Merry said, trying t
lighten the mood. "I can hide my emotions better tha
you."

"Is that so, Madame Wife? I remember two night
ago."

"Giles," she said warningly, pointing to the ope
flap.

Just then, Turner called, "A group of men up ahead
Shall I try to outrun them?"

"This is what we have been waiting for. Pretend
is a normal robbery." As the words left his mout
Giles laughed. "Lord, listen to me. A normal robbery.
Merry too was caught up in the humor of the situation

Her giggles stopped when "Stand and deliver
reached them. The coach pulled slowly to a stop. "Of
that box, you," the leader ordered Turner and th
footmen. Opening the door to the coach, the highway
man brandished a pistol in Giles's and Merry's face
and ordered, "Out, both of you. Into the open. An
don't you try anything." Slowly, Giles left the coach
He turned to help Merry down. The closest highway
man slammed his musket into his shoulder, knockin
Giles off his feet and almost under the wheels of th
coach. Merry caught her breath in fright. "Come on
dearie. Step out and join us. Now!" a harsh voic
ordered. The hand holding the pistol was dirty an
grimy. The man behind the gun wore a black mas

covering his face as did the other highwaymen. Greasy
hair hung around his neck and ears.

Hesitantly, Merry pulled her light cloak about her
and stepped out, crossing to where Giles was getting
to his feet. Giles pulled her close against him. Once
again, Merry felt as though everything was moving at
a snail's pace. Even the highwaymen's words seemed
slow and drawn out. "Take those earrings off, missy.
And that ring. Be quick about it." Giles heard the
unmistakable sound of a hammer being drawn back.
To Merry, it was as loud as an actual gunshot. "You
there," the robber pointed his gun toward Giles, "hand
me that stickpin and studs. The ring, too!"

Slowly, both Merry and Giles complied. Each listened desperately for the Runners. As Merry struggled to remove a ring, a tall, lanky robber reached out
and ripped it off her hand. Giles started forward, but
Merry refused to let him go.

The leader pulled the tall man away from the group.
He whispered something in the man's ear. Together
they turned, stripping Merry with their eyes. They
chuckled. "No more dallying. I want that jewelry now,"
he leader ordered. "And that purse, too."

Merry shot a questioning look at Giles. Almost im-
perceptibly he nodded. Cautiously, she held her reticule out by its ribbons. As a man reached for it, she
dropped it a few inches short and drew back as if
frightened. This time the gun was not just cocked but
aimed as well. "Not yet," the man in charge declared as
he pushed the gun up. "Don't spoil our fun." He
turned back to his captives.

The action had hidden the stealthy approach of the
Runners. Suddenly, horsemen galloped through the
trees. Taking advantage of the highwaymen's surprise,
Giles threw Merry into the open door of the coach
and pulled his gun. The Runners' "Halt in the name
of the law" produced great consternation. The horses
on the carriage plunged excitedly. The leader snapped
a shot toward Giles, hitting the carriage only a few
inches to the left of his head. Horses screamed in fear

as bullets whizzed past them. It was total confusion
for a few minutes. By the time the Runners spread out
to encircle the area, all but one live and one dead fish
had swum through the net. Giles and the footmen
held the prisoner securely while Turner soothed the
horses.

Rather shame-faced, the Runners took charge of the
man. "Meet us at the Golden Bull. It's not far ahead.
And don't let him escape!" Giles ordered. He climbed
into the carriage. "Spring 'em, Turner." The chaise
set off at a fast clip to the inn where Giles often
stopped when he went to Bristol or Bath. Disturbed
by the events of the preceding few minutes, Merry
slid close to him. Her whole body was shaking. She
ran her hand over his temple, checking to see that he
was really safe. She could only whisper, "Giles."

Giles picked her up and pulled her into his lap. Her
arms went around his neck. She pulled his head down,
covering his face with quick butterfly kisses. Giles
held her tightly and caressed her back. He touched
her as though he were afraid she would disappear. As
they came closer to the inn, both grew calmer. Merry
snuggled her head into Giles's shoulder, content that
the danger was past. Giles steadied himself for the
questioning ahead.

After seeing Merry into a comfortable suite upstairs,
Giles came into the parlor he had bespoken. He told
the hovering innkeeper, "Send a tea tray to my wife as
soon as possible. And a maid if you can spare one. I
don't want her left alone." The man scurried out.
Giles turned to the men in the corner. A rather cruel
smile crossed his handsome face. Giles the adven-
turer was uppermost. And Giles knew how to survive.

He crossed to the chair where the highwayman sat
bound and gagged. "A gag?" he asked. "Perhaps that
would be better at first." He picked up a knife from
the table, running his finger down the blade to test
the edge. The prisoner's eyes widened. A look of fright
crossed his face. Giles frowned. "Have this sharpened,"

ne ordered. One Runner obligingly picked up the knife
and left the room.

Giles drew closer to the chair to which the highwayman was bound. He lifted a hand and stripped the gag
from the man's mouth. "But maybe there will be no
need for those knife tricks I learned in the New World."
The prisoner lost what color remained in his face. His
weathered complexion seemed almost gray-green.
"Perhaps this man will tell us what we want to know
without a knife's edge as persuader," Giles told the
Runners.

"I ain't tellin' you nuthin'. He'll kill me. That's
what he'll do. I dasn't." The man's voice trembled
with his fear.

"If you were safe away from him? What then?"

"No place in England I kin go. He'll find me fer
sure."

"But what if you leave England?" Giles asked. The
prisoner's face brightened. Then he shook his head in
despair.

"No press gangs fer me. And where would I git the
money to leave?" The highwayman's voice was full of
despair. His eyes shifted from Giles to the Runners
and back.

"I own ships," Giles said quietly. "Where would
you like to go?"

"No. You're just foolin' with me. Whoever heard a
man who owned ships ever offered something free."
The man's face broke into a sneer. "I knows your
kind. A slaver, that's what you are." Before the Runners could stop him, Giles stepped forward and slapped
the man across the face.

"Don't ever say that about me again."

The Runner in charge stepped between Giles and
the bound man. "Sir, go check on Mrs. Lindsey. Let
us handle this. This man is gallows meat. We'll get
the information without him. He'll be swinging within
the month." The highwayman seemed to shrink in his
bonds. Slowly but surely, the Runner edged Giles
toward the door.

The next half hour Giles spent in the common room.
The plan depended on the skill of the Runners and
the weakness of the prisoner. From what he had observed earlier, Giles was not certain of the former.
The Runners' arrival that morning had almost been
too late. His face paled as he thought about the
highwaymen's thinly veiled plans for Merry. No longer
willing to wait, Giles slammed his ale mug onto the
table. He plunged into the hall, pausing briefly to take
the knife from the officer who waited.

The prisoner faced the door. As Giles burst in with
the now sharp knife glistening in his hand, the man
halted in mid-sentence as if frozen. "Keep him away
from me!" he screamed. The Runners turned their
backs.

"Will you tell me what I want to know?" Giles
fingered the blade suggestively.

A long moment passed as the prisoner looked from
Giles to the blade. "He'll kill me," he muttered weakly.

"*He*'s not here. *I* am." Giles reminded him. His
voice was perfectly calm and icy cold. He stepped
closer and clipped a lock of hair from the man's head.

"Let us handle him," the Runner in charge urged,
crossing back to the prisoner. "A few days in Newgate
might loosen his tongue."

The prisoner looked from the Runner to the man
with a knife. "Where's those ships of yours?" he asked.

"At Bristol."

"How'd I get there?"

"Some of these men would see you on board. Any
ship I own that is leaving England." Now there was
more warmth in Giles's voice. For the next few minutes the bargaining continued.

At last the prisoner asked, "And I'll be on my way
today?"

"Today."

The story poured out. The prisoner was a member
of a gang from the slums of London. Their usual
occupation was waylaying wealthy drunks who stumbled into their paths. As though he were telling a

bedtime story to a child, the prisoner related robbery after robbery. The Runners recorded every word. Because of competition with other gangs, they had been looking for a new market. This had been their first venture into highway robbery and murder.

At last satisfied that the man had told them everything he knew, Giles shipped him off under the watchful eye of two Runners. They had instructions to shoot to kill if he tried to escape. "See Mr. Danby and give him my letter. He'll take care of the man," Giles told them as they prepared to leave.

Telling the innkeeper to provide a meal for his servants and the Runners, Giles went upstairs. Opening the door to the suite, he dismissed the maid, ordering a meal to be served when he rang. In the bedroom he found Merry, sleeping restlessly. Dressed in only one petticoat, she made a tempting picture. Although he regretted having to do it, he put his hand on her shoulder and gently shook her. With a quiet cry, she awoke and sat straight up, almost clipping Giles's chin with her head. "It's all right," Giles told her. "He finally told us everything." He sat down beside her on the bed.

"And?" Her voice was still sleep-thickened.

"He raised more questions than he answered."

"Giles, don't try to hide what you know. Tell me, please, before I go mad."

"His gang was hired in London, provided with horses and guns. They were to kill us and our servants," he said quietly. The knowledge was like a blow. Merry sank back on the pillows.

"How did Hugo find them?" she asked. Her voice had a quaver in it.

"That's what I don't understand. According to this man, they were hired by a fat woman."

"A woman?" Merry's voice was shrill. "Denise? Honoria?"

"The descriptions don't match. Besides, I doubt they would go into the section of London where this scum lived, especially at night."

"But who, then?"

"That's what I hope to find out tonight. They were to meet at the Green Gate, an inn close to here. Our man knew the signal and the time, ten o'clock. The Runners and I plan to be there," Giles said.

"I insist on going, too."

"No, my dear, you will not. You will stay right here where you will be safe."

"And what about you? Let the Runners handle it," Merry suggested.

"With their rate of success today?" Giles reminded her. "I cannot afford to take the chance. I'll take Turner with me unless you need him here." He looked at her questioningly.

"I still do not understand why it is all right for you and Turner to go to capture the woman, and I must stay here. Giles, you were almost killed today." Merry looked at him with pleading eyes. "If I have to stay here alone, I'll go mad."

"But you won't be alone. The maid will be with you. And I'll leave the footmen." In spite of his susceptibility to her pleading, he was determined not to give in. Merry would stay where she was safe, and that was that.

During that long afternoon, neither Merry's pleas nor her anger caused him to give in. Finally realizing that logic and anger would not work, Merry tried kisses. Giles received the bribes enthusiastically. For the first time Merry was the aggressor. Giles made himself comfortable and enjoyed himself. But he refused to change his mind.

Finally, Merry realized he would not give in. She flounced off the bed and crossed to the small window where she stood staring into the green pasture below.

"Cupboard kisses only, Merry?" Giles asked in a rather serious tone.

Turning to face him, Merry was struck by the rather sad look on his face. "Oh, Giles, of course not. I simply dread having nothing to do. I want to do something that will matter," she explained.

"Keeping you safe matters to me," he said, encouraged by her reply. He waited, hoping she would explain her feelings for him. She smiled but said nothing. He continued, "If you were there tonight, I would worry about you. And I need to concentrate on catching that woman. Do you understand?"

Merry nodded, too filled with emotion to speak. She crossed to the small mirror and began to straighten her hair into its usual smooth style. Giles crossed to stand behind her. For a moment, Merry was reminded of the early days of their marriage. She had been so afraid of him. Watching his face, she leaned back on his shoulder. Giles whipped his arms around her, pulling her close against him. For long moments they stood, content in the other's presence.

The afternoon shadows had begun to lengthen when Giles kissed her good-bye. "Don't wait up for me," he urged. "I promise to wake you when I return." Only her long years of practice enabled Merry to keep from bursting into tears.

"Take care," she whispered as he released her. The door closed behind him. She sank facedown on the bed.

—15—

For the first time since her marriage Merry was alone, really alone. There was no household to run, no sister-in-law to chaperone, no husband to please. As soon as her tears stopped, Merry lay there almost in a state of shock. So much had been happening in her once nicely arranged life. She who once had thought to run a successful business now allowed someone else to tell her what she was to do.

From the first, Merry had known what marriage meant. But she had had no other choice. Giles had promised an alliance—good for both of them. "How, then, have I become so involved?" she asked herself.

She flipped over on her back and stared at the ceiling. How strange it seemed, not to be enclosed by bed curtains—so open, so free. Free, that was what she had wanted to be—free of all the restrictions of her life. The thought made her restless. She rose. Looking at her rumpled dress, she smiled ruefully. She rang for the maid assigned her.

When the girl appeared, Merry asked, "Please press my dress."

"Certainly, ma'am. And would you care for some supper? Cook has a wonderful way with a joint, and there's a fresh soup," the maid said.

Merry agreed. The maid turned to leave. She was almost to the door when Merry asked, "Can you find me a pen, ink, and some paper?" When the girl had left, Merry smiled to herself. How Giles would laugh at her. Another list.

Wrapped in her light cloak, Merry finished the delicious soup and ate a few bites of the roast. Pushing the remainder of her supper aside, she picked up the pen and sharpened its point. She pulled the paper in front of her.

"Advantages and disadvantages of my marriage," she began. The column of disadvantages grew quite rapidly. From the lack of freedom to the social whirl to the danger to her life, the ideas flew. The other side came more slowly. Financial freedom from Hugo was important. So was Charlotte. Trial though she could be, she was also a joy, a truly happy, outgoing person. After the first few days, Charlotte had accepted her as a sister. What a sense of humor that girl had, Merry thought. What devils she and Giles must have been as children. Giles. Was he an advantage? Merry sat for a moment. Dropping her pen, she rose and began to walk aimlessly around the room.

Here she was safe and sound, miles from the danger. She glanced at the waning light outside. Still hours before the woman was to meet the highwaymen. Had Giles had supper? What if he were hurt? Or killed? What would she do then? The thought terrified her. Her breath came quickly, but she seemed to lack air. Growing weak and panic-stricken, she dropped facedown on the bed. Gradually her breathing slowed. She grew more controlled.

Her actions had made her thoughtful. At last she understood her fear of Denise. Merry was not frightened for herself. Denise threatened Merry's relationship with Giles. For the first time Merry acknowledged the fact. If she were to lose Giles, she would want to die.

The thought was frightening. To be so dependent upon someone else. But she was. She had to admit it. She loved Giles. She thought of the list on the table. Giles definitely belonged in the advantage column.

She smiled in the dimly lit room as she remembered her first glimpse of him. He was so handsome, and he knew it. The memory of the last time they made love was still vivid. She smiled as she remembered his passionate words. But he had never said he loved her. The thought disturbed her. He had said their marriage was an alliance, made with the mind, not the heart. Perhaps he did not want her love. The thought upset her. Once again she rose and began to pace.

A scratching at the door roused her from her despair. "May I take the tray, now?" the maid asked. Merry nodded her permission. "I'll have your dress back shortly. Supper is almost over now."

"What's the time?" Merry asked.

"Almost ten."

Ten! Giles might be in danger at that very moment. Merry waved the maid from the room. Now her worries were more immediate. Giles had to be all right. He simply had to be. The thought kept rolling through her mind. She almost forgot the danger to herself in her worries about him.

While Merry was worrying about Giles, he was thinking about her. After he had left her that afternoon, he and Turner had joined the Runners. From the information the officers had received, the problem would be explaining their presence at the inn. According to local gossip, the Green Gate was more noted for being a hideout for thieves than a place where a gentleman might go. The owners supposedly could smell a sheriff a mile off.

After much discussion a decision was made. Giles would be a young lord given to strong drink and madcap dares. The others, his servants sent along by his father to make certain he did not embarrass his family. Carefully, they put the pieces of the story together. Giles, on a dare, had driven the coach with four servants inside down the forest road. Having had too much to drink, he came a cropper near the inn. The coach had been saved by the quick actions of his groom, Turner.

Satisfied with the details, the party set off. A short
distance from the inn the plan went into motion. A
few minutes later the coach, now driven by Turner,
lumbered down the narrow road and into the innyard.

"Ostler. Hey, the house. Someone come quick," yelled
Turner. A seedy looking individual rambled out of the
stables.

"Stop bellowing. Hey now, what's a fine rig like
his doing here?"

"A room for my master, quick. And send for a
doctor. Let's get him in. Move carefully now, lads,"
Turner said.

"Well, what are you standin' about for? Tell the
innkeeper to get a chamber ready."

The stablehand stood there dumbfounded. Turner
had slipped to the horses' heads. The coach door
opened. Two of the Runners disguised as servants
stepped out.

"That's right, slow and easy. I'll not answer to the
master if anything untoward happens to the heir,"
the older Runner said as he helped lift Giles's seemingly unconscious body from the coach. By this time
the proprietor had appeared.

"What's goin' on 'ere?" he demanded. "You can't
bring 'em in 'ere."

"We can't take him any farther either. His sire
would have us drawn and quartered, he would. Isn't
that right, lads," Turner replied. "What's wrong? You
can't be full up, not with that stable empty."

The innkeeper, a surly look on his face, waved them
into the ramshackle building. "There's a room on the
first floor, second room on the right up those stairs."
The men carrying Giles quickly made their way up
the stairs. Gingerly, they lowered him on the gray and
grimy sheets that looked and smelled as if a hundred
men had slept there—with their boots on. Giles had
to work to keep his face relaxed as the smell envel-
oped him. The mattress beneath him rustled not only
from its stuffing but also from its inhabitants trying
to get away from his weight.

Below stairs, Turner lumbered in, drawing off hi
driving gloves. "A mug of your best ale. And be quic
about it."

" 'Ere now, what's all this about? What happened?"
the innkeeper demanded.

"Just another of his bloody bets. He bet Lord Harr
he could drive ten miles down any road Lord Harr
chose while standing on the driver's seat. He didn'
even go one." Turner sounded disgusted. "I tried t
tell him, I did. As soon as I saw the road, I said, 'It'
hopeless, it is. Give it up.' But he never listens t
me—no, not he. Well, lads, how is he?" he asked a
the other men entered.

"Still unconscious. Has the doctor been sent for?"
Together they looked toward the innkeeper.

"I'll send someone immediately. But it may take
while. What's wrong with 'im? He's not goin' to die, i
he?"

The older man quickly reassured him. "A knock o
the head, but mostly drunk. He'll live. He always
does." Fascinated, the innkeeper let himself drift into
conversation with the men.

While Turner and the Runners kept the innkeepe
busy in the common room, Giles was searching the
upstairs. Cautiously, he checked room after room. All
seemed in as poor condition as his. And they were all
empty. But he saw signs that they had been occupied
recently—a dirty towel, water in the bowl, a shirt
under one bed. His search completed, Giles crept
back to his own room. Deciding that his stomach would
rebel if he returned to bed, he placed a chair near the
door and sat down. At the first whisper of sound, he
would be back in bed.

Normally Giles had to be active. His enforced cap-
tivity was galling. He took his watch from his pocket.
Still at least two hours until the rendezvous. He shifted
restlessly. The floor squeaked. Giles heard footsteps
on the stairs.

Hurriedly, he climbed back into bed and closed his

yes. The door opened. "Look. I told you he'd be out or hours if not days," the older Runner said.

"I tell you, I heard footsteps up 'ere," the innkeeper protested.

"Well, it weren't him." The door slammed behind hem. Giles let out a sigh of relief. He'd best stay where he was for the time being, he decided. How hese sheets would disgust Merry. He would need a path before he could get near her again. Perhaps this ime she would share one with him. The thought of Merry in a tub with him made his heart race. She was so delightful with her hair on top of her head and her skin white and glistening. Weaving his fantasies, Giles wiled away the hours. Occasionally, one of his servants would check on him. Usually the innkeeper kept the man company.

Deciding that the time for his reappearance was close at hand, Giles broke into a loud snore the next time someone came in. "Hear that now. I told you he was more drunk than hurt," the man exclaimed. Grumbling, the innkeeper agreed. Once again they closed the door and left. "He'll sleep it off. Be up to his old tricks tomorrow. Someday he'll kill himself. Us too, if we're not lucky." The man's voice faded.

Downstairs, the party had become lively. "Best ale I've tasted lately," Turner declared as he seemingly emptied another mug. "Keep 'em comin'. Here now, what's for supper. Master's buying." His words were beginning to slur. The innkeeper disappeared into the grimy recesses of the inn. Shortly afterward a slovenly maid appeared carrying a ham, a wheel of cheese, and bread. "Just right. Put it down here," Turner demanded, taking his knife from his belt and slicing himself some cheese. The others also plunged in. While they were eating, the innkeeper, as he had done since they had arrived, plied them with questions. Apparently their answers satisfied him, for he ate with them and began to joke. When they had finished, they pushed the greasy platters away.

"Brandy! Bring me brandy, now!" Giles bellowed from the head of the stairs.

"Lord Giles," Turner said knowingly. As the innkeeper got to the bottom of the stairs, he watched fascinated as Giles weaved his way carefully from one step to the next.

As soon as his feet had hit the floor, Giles ordered, "Bring me brandy, man. None of your watered stuff. The kind that doesn't pay duty." The innkeeper drew himself up as if to argue.

Turner pulled him aside. "Just get him some brandy. He's so castaway he doesn't know what he's sayin'." Mollified, the man disappeared for a few minutes. When he reappeared, he held a bottle. Giles snatched it greedily and lifted it to his lips. His hand was shaking so badly that more went on his shirt than into his mouth.

The oldest Runner guided him to a seat near the food and hidden from the door. "Have a bite to eat, sir. 'Twill go well with the brandy," he suggested. Giles sliced a bite of cheese and ate it. He continued to drink from the bottle he held. The more he drank, the more he slumped toward the table. Finally he lay with his head on the table.

"Just leave him for now. We can carry him up when we finish," Turner suggested. Just then a coach pulled up at the door.

"Who'd be stoppin' 'ere at this time of night?" the innkeeper wondered. Before he could reach the yard, a short, fat woman swept in. Brown curls jiggled under the broad brim of her dark brown hat.

"Innkeeper?" a high-pitched voice whined. "I was to meet some people here. Have they arrived? Is the Green Room ready?" The words "Green Room" set the room in motion. Turner, who had followed the innkeeper to the door, slipped behind the woman. The Runners took positions to each side of her. The innkeeper blocked her view of the common room.

From behind the burly innkeeper came a quiet voice.

"I'm afraid the men you were expecting will not be coming."

The woman paled at the sight of Giles. The innkeeper, almost as startled as she, backed to one side, giving Giles a frightened look. The woman whirled to escape, her cloak billowing behind her. Directly in front of her stood Turner, his arms folded across his sturdy chest. The woman frantically looked from side to side. Realizing her escape was blocked, she rushed forward, taking Turner by surprise. Her hands outthrust before her, she rammed the startled groom, knocking him to the floor of the passageway.

"After her! Don't let her get away!" Giles shouted. The Runners made a somewhat tardy grab for her, but she eluded them. Giles chased her into the innyard. She had her foot on the step of her coach when he caught her by her skirt. Turning, the woman brought her fist up, catching Giles on the chin. He fell back. As he fell, he kept his grip on her dress and pulled her down with him.

The woman flailed wildly, landing several good punches. Giles tried frantically to capture her hands. As they struggled on the ground, the woman lost her hat. Next to go was the wig.

"Hugo Darryl," Giles shouted with satisfaction. He pulled back his fist and connected with a strong right cross.

"Gad, a man!" the innkeeper muttered, looking at the unconscious figure. "What's goin' on 'ere?"

"Get him tied up securely," Giles ordered. "And bring the coach around. I've had enough of this place." Within a few minutes, the bill had been paid, an unconscious Hugo had been dumped on the floor of the carriage, and they were once more on their way.

—16—

The trip back to the Golden Bull seemed much shorter than the one that afternoon. With two Runners on top with Turner, Giles and the other two Runners were comfortable. Only Hugo, trussed like a chicken for the spit, complained.

From the moment he recovered consciousness, Hugo had tried to weasel his way out of his predicament. He was a dupe of Lady Farrell, he said at first. When that did not work, he blamed Merry. "If she had only married my brother, I would not be in trouble today. It is all her fault. That headstrong, conniving woman turned Sommerby against me. All she's interested in is the business. You had better watch out, Lindsey, or she'll destroy you too."

At first Giles simply allowed him to ramble, hoping that Darryl would admit his guilt. Surreptitiously one of the Runners was recording Darryl's words. Then Giles began asking leading questions. "When did you begin to embezzle money from the company?" he asked.

"Embezzle? Hah, it was mine, and she was stealing it from me! Merry might inherit the company, but I would have the money. Look how long it took her to catch me. One of the cent-percenters I owed money to suggested it. With my knowledge of company agents, it was easy." Hugo seemed to have forgotten that he was being held prisoner in his eagerness to explain how clever he was.

"What made you decide to kill Merry?" Giles asked quietly.

Before Hugo could answer, the coach drew up in the innyard of the Golden Bull. "Tie him securely to a bed, and then you get some rest," Giles suggested. Three of the Runners led Hugo away. The fourth, a frown on his face, remained.

"Mr. Lindsey, I fear we still have little evidence on which to convict Mr. Darryl." Giles raised his eyebrows inquiringly. "Oh, not the theft charge. For that we have his confession. For the attempted murder. May I remind you that you allowed our only witness to go free."

Giles considered the idea thoughtfully. "Tomorrow, take him back to London. Perhaps the threat of Newgate will encourage him to reveal everything, especially if you suggest a possible arrangement I might be willing to make. For now, get some rest. Ask the innkeeper for a conveyance in the morning. I'll see you in Bow Street tomorrow."

The Runner left. Giles started toward the stairs and then paused and entered the common room. Catching the eye of a servant, he asked, "Can you send a man up with a tub and water immediately? I need a bath." Giles held his odoriferous shirt gingerly away from his neck. His once polished Hessians were grimy with mud. He made his way toward the stairs.

Reaching the two rooms where he had left Merry, he opened the door quietly. He crossed the sitting room and entered the door of the bedroom. There was Merry, asleep. A few tears were drying on her cheek. Quietly, Giles pulled the door between the two rooms closed. He had stripped to his pantaloons when the man with his bath arrived. After he helped Giles with his boots, the man removed Giles's offensive clothing, promising to return it the next morning.

Giles made quick work of his bath. His dressing gown lay folded next to Merry's nightrobe. Putting it on, he opened the door to the bedroom and entered. A candle guttered on the table. Giles crossed to blow it

out. As he bent down, he glanced at the paper that lay
there.

Another list, he thought. Smiling, he held it closer
to the sputtering light. When he saw the title, his
breath almost stopped. He lit a second candle. All his
pleasure, all his hopes seemed dead. He reread what
Merry had written. Slowly, he crossed back to the
sitting room. For almost a half an hour he sat on the
settee with his head in his hands. Then he put the
crumpled list on a table. His shoulders straightened.

"Merry," he called as he reentered the bedroom.

"Giles?" Her voice was happy. Then she looked at
her husband carefully. "Giles, what happened? Are
you hurt?" He shook his head. "Did she escape?"

"No, Hugo Darryl is in custody," he said.

"It *was* Hugo! How upset Aunt Mathilda will be."
She smiled up at him as if asking him to share the
joke. He avoided her eyes. "What is wrong? Was Turner
hurt?"

"No, everything went well."

"Tell me about it," she suggested, hopping off the
bed and crossing to him. Giles, who had been avoiding
looking at her face, now stared at the low neckline of
her chemise where the tops of her creamy white breasts
showed. Gulping, he turned away.

"Come into the sitting room. I'll tell you there." In
a voice almost devoid of emotion, Giles covered the
hours they had been separated. Merry kept glancing
at him as if she could discover what was wrong from
his face. From time to time she asked him to explain
something.

As he related the comments the Runner had made,
she asked, "And what other options do we have?
Shall we let him go free?"

"No! He must never have the opportunity to harm
you again." Giles's tone was determined. "Together
we will think of something." He got up and crossed to
the window. His back was ramrod straight. When he
spoke again, his voice had once again lost all its emotion.

"Go back to sleep, madame. We will think more clearly in the morning."

At first, Merry just stood there looking at him. Then she crossed to stand next to him. Overcoming her fear of confrontations, she demanded, "Giles, what is wrong? You must tell me."

"We can talk in the morning."

"No, now. I must know what the problem is."

Giles turned to face the small, determined figure of his wife. This time it was he whose face wore a mask. He glanced at her and then turned his face back to the window. Slowly he said, "Merry, you agreed to marry me because you had no other choice."

"Yes, but . . ."

"Hush. Just listen." His voice was once again almost emotionless. "When we married, it was advantageous to both of us. It was to be an alliance between business partners. Do you remember?"

Merry nodded her head, too disturbed to trust her voice. Giles was trying to tell her he did not care for her; he was tired of the constant problems. The hopes that had been so strong earlier seemed dead. A heavy lump filled her throat.

Giles continued. "I promised you safety, but I failed miserably."

"Giles, neither you nor anyone else could have known what Hugo was willing to do. If I had only told him of the settlements, none of this would have happened," Merry said, trying to reassure him.

"Even before the accident you were not happy. You wanted to be free, but I trapped you in society you disliked." Giles refused to allow her to soothe him. "You wanted freedom, and all I have given you are problems, Merry," he paused.

She braced herself for the blow she knew was coming. Her hands were tightly clasped to still their trembling. Her face, although pale, was calm. But her eyes were full of despair.

"Merry, I will agree to your living in Bristol if that is what you want. You can live your life as you choose."

Merry, her eyes glazed with tears, stumbled to the settee. She was too heartbroken to speak. As Giles waited for her answer, his shoulders slumped. When he had waited as long as he could, he turned to face her. His eyes widened at the sight of Merry curled into one corner of the settee, her head bowed, her shoulders shaking with sobs. The hope that he had thought dead blazed once more. He crossed to the settee and picked up her hands.

She pulled away. Trying to smooth her face into its usual serenity, she whispered, "When you return to London, please have Pilgrim pack my things and come to Bristol."

Once again, Giles captured a hand. "Merry, is Bristol what you really choose?" he asked as he kissed her hand. "Look at me, my dear." She raised her tear-drenched, red-rimmed eyes to his and sniffed. Giles, using the sleeve of his dressing gown, rubbed the tears from her face. In a deep, passionate voice, he said, "Before you make your choice, you deserve to know everything." Once again her hopes began to dwindle. "I want you to be happy, my dear. But I shall miss you. Oh, Merry, I love you so."

For a moment she sat bemused. Then she was in his arms, her arms tightly wound around his neck. She covered his face with kisses until he captured her lips with his in a deep kiss that seemed a renewal of their marriage vows.

After a short while, he released her and sat back. "Well, Merry?"

She blushed a deep rose. Then, gazing deep into his eyes, she said, "I love you, my dearest, darling." With a whoop, Giles gathered her back in his arms, crushing her against him. For some time, Merry leaned against him, happy to be where she wanted to be. Then she drew back. "Giles, what upset you this evening?"

"That's nothing to worry about now," he assured her.

"But there was something. What was it?" Reluctantly, Giles picked up the crumpled list and gave it to her. Merry's eyes widened. "Because of this?"

Giles's frown had reappeared. "Charlotte is there, but I am not."

Merry smoothed his tousled hair back from his forehead. She smiled up at him. "I was afraid to admit how much I loved you even to myself. Will you forgive me?" She put her arms around his neck again and drew his lips down to hers. There was nothing more wonderful than loving Giles.

His arms closed tightly around her. He picked her up and carried her to the bedroom. "Shall we go to bed?" he whispered in her ear. As they neared the bed, Merry reached down and untied the sash on his dressing gown and pushed the garment off his shoulders. Giles stood her up beside the bed.

"But don't you have too many clothes on?" he asked as he let his dressing gown fall to the floor. For a moment Merry just stood there enjoying the sight of his muscular body. Then she raised her hands and ran them over his chest.

Giles captured her hands in one of his. "No more of that until we get rid of these," he said as he untied the bows on her chemise. As he pushed the straps off her shoulders, his hands cupped her breasts. Merry caught her breath. Giles's hands drifted to her waist and the laces that held her petticoat in place. As he nuzzled her neck and nibbled her earlobe, her petticoat drifted to the floor. Stepping out of it, she kicked it out of the way and pressed herself against him.

Giles encircled her with his arms, holding them so close that they seemed imprinted on each other. Passionate sighs and whispered endearments created a special song of love. His arms dropped lower. Giles cupped Merry's buttocks in his hands and lifted her off her feet. Laughing her delight, she encircled his neck and captured his lips. Her legs straddled his hips. As she felt him hard against her, her eyes widened in delight. She wiggled to get even closer and then giggled as Giles gasped.

For a moment Giles allowed her to take the lead. Then, slowly, he put her gently on the bed. Merry looked up at him, pouting. "There is no rush. We have a lifetime," he said smiling down at her.

Merry reached out and pulled him down beside her.

He bent and savored her lips. "Slowly, Merry. Ah, you are so sweet." He buried his head in her full breasts. His hands caressed her stomach and thighs.

Quickly their passions grew. Unable to wait longer, Giles raised himself over her and made them one. As the dance of love continued, the movements grew wilder, faster until both exploded in a crescendo of passion.

As she lay there under him, listening to his heartbeat slow, his breathing become regular, Merry rejoiced in Giles. As he rolled on his side, she kept her arms around his neck and snuggled close. "I love you," she whispered.

"And I love you, my dear." Giles bent and kissed her. The passion they thought extinguished flared quickly. It was a long time before they slept, wrapped closely in each other's arms.

—17—

Although they both had awakened before eight, it was almost eleven before Giles and Merry were ready to leave the inn. The Runners with their prisoner had left hours earlier. Turner and the footmen had spent the time cleaning the coach.

"London, Turner," Giles ordered as he handed Merry into the equipage. He settled himself beside her and pulled her close.

"Giles!" she said warningly, pointing to the open flap in front of them. Giles pulled it down and tied it securely.

"Now, Madame Wife?" he said as he kissed her thoroughly. Laughing at her blushes, he picked her up and put her on his lap.

"Giles, behave!" she laughed, struggling to regain her seat beside him. Once more on the soft cushions, she settled her skirts and smiled. "Giles," she breathed.

He looked down at her inquiringly, but she simply rested her head on his shoulder. For a few minutes there was silence. Then the doubts began. Had this been the way her parents' marriage had begun, she wondered. What had gone wrong? Would it happen to their marriage? For once her worries showed clearly on her face.

"Merry?" her husband asked.

His question was the opening she needed. Instead of keeping her fears inside as usual, she let them burst forth. "Giles, I'm so happy. Yet I am afraid," she explained. "What if our marriage is like my parents'?"

Realizing the depth of her feelings, Giles was honest in his answers. "Merry, we are not your parents. I cannot make any guarantees. All I can say is that I love you, and that I'll try my hardest to make our marriage work."

Merry cuddled closer to him. "And I love you. But will that be enough?"

"During the six months we have been married, our problems have come from not talking to each other, not sharing our doubts and fears. If we always find time to share, maybe that will help," he suggested.

"Sharing. I like that idea," Merry mused. "Not just the good things, the bad ones too."

"Especially the bad ones," Giles agreed. "My parents have succeeded. We will too." He dropped a kiss on her forehead.

Merry was almost asleep in his arms when she said dreamily, "I suppose in a way we should be grateful to Hugo." She bolted upright. "Hugo? Oh, Giles, what are we going to do about Hugo?" She looked him in the eye. "I shall positively hate having him stand trial. And if I have to be a witness, it will be even worse. Think of the scandal. And his poor family!"

Merry twisted a corner of her cloak in her hands. "There simply must be some other way. Oh, if that upstart Napoleon had not stirred up the continent!"

"Leave England? Yes, that would be just the thing. But where?"

"And what will he do when he gets there? If he will agree to go," Merry added doubtfully.

"There will be no chance of refusal. A choice between a public trial or emigration? He'll go." Giles's voice was hard. "Let us think about it." By this time the sounds of London surrounded them.

"London. I never thought I would be happy to see it again," Merry said. "Everything seems brighter."

"Mayhap it is the viewer's attitude?"

"Giles, you wretch. Just let me be happy."

"Oh, I will. I will. And I know how to keep you happy." He bent and whispered in her ear.

A blush colored her face with a soft rose. She simply moved closer and whispered back, "That sounds delightful." His smile made her catch her breath.

The coach pulled to a stop. Before the footman could let down the steps, the front door opened. Aunt Mathilda, Charlotte, and the two Devereaux stood there. Giles could almost feel his sister's impatience. Before the front door closed behind them, Charlotte pulled them into the small salon.

"Tell us everything!" Charlotte demanded as she settled her figured muslin skirts around her.

"Perhaps we should tell them our news first?" Mathilda suggested. Giles and Merry nodded, but Charlotte would have none of it.

"I refuse to wait a minute longer," she declared.

Giles laughed and began. His listeners moved to the edge of their seats as he described the attack by the highwaymen. "Even the best laid plans sometimes go wrong," he explained as he described the way the robbers had separated him from Merry.

"I would have fainted. I know I would have," Mathilda declared. Both Serena and Charlotte nodded their agreement. "How you remained conscious I'll never know, Merry. I suppose you have your grandfather to blame." Giles and Merry exchanged a look. His eyes brimmed with laughter, and hers echoed it.

"Thank heavens she didn't," Giles exclaimed. "They might have killed us on the spot."

"As it was, they tried to kill Giles," Merry added.

"Who did? Was it Hugo? Well, I shall certainly have something to say about that when I see that odious, little man." Charlotte jumped from her seat and hovered close to Giles as if to protect him.

"No, my dear, it was not Hugo. At that time we did not even know Hugo was involved," Giles explained.

"I told you he was much too refined to be involved in such a dastardly deed," Mathilda declared.

"But he was!" Merry exclaimed. "We simply did not know it until later."

"I don't understand," Charlotte began.

"If you would stop interrupting, we will tell you everything," Giles reminded her. She sat down, her face in a pretty pout.

"Well, tell us," she said.

"Yes, do. It's so thrilling," Serena urged. Thomas nodded his head in agreement, his eyes bright with excitement.

"Giles made me stay at the Golden Bull while he and the Runners followed the trail," Merry complained. Although Mathilda nodded her approval of his action, both Charlotte and Serena shot him a baleful stare.

"I'm glad you were safely away from there. The Green Gate was the rankest place I have ever entered." Thanks to Giles's colorful descriptions, even Charlotte agreed that it was no place for a lady. "I only hope I did not bring home any vermin," Giles added. All the women shuddered at the thought.

"But Hugo. What about Hugo?" Mathilda asked.

Giles returned to his story. The excitement in the room built as he related the long wait. "Finally a coach drew up, and a short, fat woman entered the inn."

"It was Hugo. I just know it was," Charlotte exclaimed.

"Hush. Let him continue," Mathilda ordered.

Rather than the flat statements that Giles had used the evening before when he had described the scene to Merry, his words sang with action and suspense. Even Merry held her breath as he described the way the woman was surrounded. His account of her attempted flight caused a gasp and a chorus of moans. "But I caught her," Giles continued. The story of the fight and the loss of the wig shocked Mathilda.

"I knew it was Hugo all the time," Charlotte said smugly. Both Thomas and Serena shot her a look of disbelief. "Well, I did."

"So it *was* Hugo. How depressing," Mathilda seemed to shrink back into her chair.

"You couldn't have known. As much as I disliked Hugo, I never dreamed he would try to kill me," Merry tried to reassure her. She gave her aunt a quick hug.

"And what will happen to him now?" Thomas asked.

Giles looked at Merry. His forehead creased into a frown. "Neither of us want to have to go through the trial. But we cannot allow him to go free. We thought of sending him away from England. But where?" Everyone nodded in agreement.

"India, perhaps?" Thomas suggested, his face thoughtful.

"No, I want to return there someday." Merry decided.

"Australia," Charlotte suggested. But no one else agreed.

"He's no political prisoner. Besides, his family could not accompany him," Giles told her.

"I suppose that only leaves the American colonies?" Mathilda suggested.

"Canada or the United States?" Merry asked.

"I understand a gambler can make his way easily in the South. Perhaps he and his family would enjoy the Carolinas." Giles grew very thoughtful. "The Carolinas or Georgia. Yes, that would be just the place." The decision already clear in his mind, Giles looked at Merry. She nodded.

Only Mathilda seemed disturbed by the idea. "But his property in Yorkshire? And his brother? What will become of them?" she asked.

"Mere details," Giles assured her. "Our lawyers can settle that. Now what about your news."

Charlotte, Serena, and Thomas exchanged glances and burst into laughter. Even Mathilda uttered a twitter or two. "Oh, Merry, I wish you and Giles had been there," Charlotte exclaimed. Every curl on her head seemed to be dancing in delight. "It was grand."

"Don't keep tantalizing us. Tell us your story," Merry urged.

Still giggling, Charlotte began. "Last evening we were invited to a ball at the Russian embassy." Both Giles and Merry nodded. "I wore my new gown shot with silver with the silver ribbons. You know the one."

Thomas interrupted, "And what does that have to do with anything?"

Charlotte shot him an angry look but continued. "Lady Farrell and Honoria also attended. I simply do not know why Honoria insists on wearing purple. She looks horrid in it."

"Charlotte, if you cannot keep to the story I will tell it," Thomas threatened.

She hurried on. "As the hour grew later, we could tell from the way she constantly watched the entrance that Denise was waiting for someone. When midnight had passed, she seemed almost frantic. Taking pity on her," Charlotte paused with a smug look on her face, "I sent her a note.

"You sent it? I was the one to write it," Thomas declared.

"Well, we sent her a note asking her to come to the garden." Charlotte and Serena smiled mischievously. "Several couples of our friends persuaded Mrs. Drummond Burrell to provide us an escort through the gardens."

"Mrs. Drummond Burrell? How did you manage that?" Merry asked.

"It is simply amazing what flattery will do," Serena declared. The three young people laughed delightedly.

"We were most circumspect, Giles. We were never out of Mrs. Drummond Burrell's sight. We were also quiet." Charlotte reassured him, breaking into giggles again.

"Well, go on," Giles urged.

"There in the center of the garden was Lady Denise captured in a passionate embrace with a tall man. She was struggling a little, but I don't think anyone else noticed that. As he realized our presence, the man released her. She broke free, and Mrs. Drummond Burrell saw them clearly. Lady Farrell had been kissing Mrs. Drummond Burrell's footman." The conspirators broke into gales of laughter. "And, Giles, I told him you would find him a job," Charlotte concluded, still giggling.

"And how did you arrange this?" Merry asked.

"My maid's cousin is the footman in Mrs. Drummond Burrell's household," Serena explained. "You know how particular she is about having handsome, educated servants? According to my maid, this man had grown tired of her pickiness and was looking for a new position. He also likes a bit of fun."

"When Thomas suggested the plan," Charlotte smiled at him, "at first we thought to hire an actor. But when Serena and I were discussing it, her maid overheard and made an improvement. And it worked perfectly."

"I knew nothing about it until it was over," Mathilda declared self-righteously. "I am certain I would have had a spasm. But I do wish I could have seen Mrs. Drummond Burrell's face!"

"It was a rare study. At first she went white and then a deep red. In the coldest voice imaginable she said, 'Jackson, you are dismissed. I expect you to be gone before I return home.' Lady Farrell looked as though she were going to faint. Mrs. Drummond Burrell gave her a scathing look and then turned and left without saying another word," Thomas said.

"And Denise? What happened to Denise?"

"I understand she had to return home because her mother is ill. It is possible they will need to move to a warmer climate," Mathilda exclaimed solemnly.

Merry had to smile as she thought of Denise bearing the censure of society. The conspirators were ecstatic with glee. Even Giles let a smile play about his face. Only the scratching at the door brought a semblance of calm to the room.

"Are you at home, Miss Charlotte?" the butler asked.
"Some callers have arrived."

"Callers! Shall we discover the latest on-dits? I
wonder what it will be." Thomas Devereaux held out
his arms to his sister and to Charlotte. Mathilda,
never one to forego gossip, tripped behind them.

Merry released the yawn she had been trying to
stifle. Giles pulled her to her feet and smiled down at
her fondly. "Go take a nap," he suggested. "You may
need it later," he said suggestively. She snuggled close
to him and pulled his head down, planting a sweet
kiss on his welcoming lips. "I must visit Bow Street,
but I will be right back," he promised. His gaze followed her until she disappeared into their suite. Giles
sighed and then reclaimed his hat and cane.

Slowly and surely the problems were resolved. Two
weeks later, Merry and Giles stood on the steps of the
house in Grosvenor Square, waving good-bye to Aunt
Mathilda and Charlotte. The Season was over. Most
houses on the square were empty once more, the knock-
ers removed from the doors.

"Are you certain your parents will not mind Charlotte's visiting Aunt Mathilda in Bath?" Merry asked.

"After sending her to stay with Honoria? Besides,
Charlotte deserves a reward for ridding us of Denise."
Giles chuckled softly.

"But is Bath ready for Charlotte?"

"The Devereaux will arrive shortly. Thomas knows
how to repress her when necessary. Besides, your
Aunt Mathilda is awake on every suit," he reassured
her.

The knocker sounded. "A dispatch from Bristol,"
the butler explained as he handed Merry the message.
She tapped it lightly on the table and looked at Giles
inquiringly.

"Well, go ahead and open it," he said.

"What if it is a problem?" Merry asked.

"We will take care of it. Give it to me." Giles
ripped the letter open. "They are gone! They sailed
yesterday."

"Hugo? Really?" Merry breathed a sigh of relief.

"Mr. Pettigrew arranged everything. You are now the proud owner of a Yorkshire estate."

"And you are the guardian of a lunatic," Merry reminded him.

"As long as he stays in Yorkshire, there will be no problem. The estate should support him admirably." Giles assured her.

"Maybe someday the doctors will be able to help him," Merry suggested wistfully.

"Let us talk of happier things, my desirable darling. We are alone at last." He reached out an arm and pulled her close.

"A month in the Lake Country with you." Merry sighed blissfully. "And then to Bath."

"Arabella's and Brandon's son will have the most delectable godmama ever," Giles declared, bending down to kiss her. One caress led to another. Finally Giles broke away. "Shouldn't we be preparing for our journey or something?" he asked as he led her up the stairs. Merry agreed. The "or something" won.

About the Author

Barbara Allister is a native Texan who enjoys reading and traveling. An English teacher. Ms. Allister began writing as a hobby after experimenting with techniques to use in her creative writing class. THE PRUDENT PARTNERSHIP is her first novel.

JOIN THE REGENCY READERS' PANEL

Help us bring you more of the books you like by filling out this survey and mailing it in today.

1. Book title:_____

    Book #:_____

2. Using the scale below how would you rate this book on the following features.

Poor	Not so Good		O.K.			Good		Excel- lent	
0 1	2	3	4	5	6	7	8	9	10

	Rating
Overall opinion of book.................................	_____
Plot/Story	_____
Setting/Location	_____
Writing Style	_____
Character Development	_____
Conclusion/Ending	_____
Scene on Front Cover	_____

3. On average about how many romance books do you buy for yourself each month?_____

4. How would you classify yourself as a reader of Regency romances?
   I am a ( ) light ( ) medium ( ) heavy reader.

5. What is your education?
   ( ) High School (or less)   ( ) 4 yrs. college
   ( ) 2 yrs. college   ( ) Post Graduate

6. Age_____   7. Sex: ( ) Male ( ) Female

Please Print Name_____

Address_____

City_____State_____Zip_____

Phone # (   )_____

Thank you. Please, send to New American Library, Research Dept, 1633 Broadway, New York, NY 10019.

RAPTURE ROMANCE
BOOK CLUB

Bringing You The World of Love and Romance With Three Exclusive Book Lines

RAPTURE ROMANCE • SIGNET REGENCY ROMANCE • SCARLET RIBBONS

Subscribe to Rapture Romance and have your choice of two Rapture Romance Book Club Packages.

- **PLAN A:** Four Rapture Romances plus two Signet Regency Romances for just $9.75!

- **PLAN B:** Four Rapture Romances, one Signet Regency Romance and one Scarlet Ribbons Romance for just $10.45!

Whichever package you choose, you save 60 cents off the combined cover prices plus you get a FREE Rapture Romance.

"THAT'S A SAVINGS OF $2.55 OFF THE COMBINED COVER PRICES"

We're so sure you'll love them, we'll give you 10 days to look over the set you choose at home. Then you can keep the set or return the books and owe nothing.

To start you off, we'll send you four books absolutely **FREE.** Our two latest Rapture Romances plus our latest Signet Regency and our latest Scarlet Ribbons. The total value of all four books is $9.10, but they're yours **FREE** even if you never buy another book.

To get your books, use the convenient coupon on the following page.

YOUR FIRST FOUR BOOKS ARE FREE

Mail the Coupon below

Please send me the Four Books described **FREE** and without obligation. Unless you hear from me after I receive them, please send me 6 New Books to review each month. I have indicated below which plan I would like to be sent. I understand that you will bill me for only 5 books as I always get a Rapture Romance Novel **FREE** plus an additional 60¢ off, making a total savings of $2.55 each month. I will be billed no shipping, handling or other charges. There is no minimum number of books I must buy, and I can cancel at any time. The first 4 FREE books are mine to keep even if I never buy another book.

Check the Plan you would like.

☐ **PLAN A:** Four Rapture Romances plus two Signet Regency Romances for just $9.75 each month.

☐ **PLAN B:** Four Rapture Romances plus one Signet Regency Romance and one Scarlet Ribbons for just $10.45 each month.

NAME _____
(please print)

ADDRESS _____ CITY _____

STATE _____ ZIP _____ SIGNATURE _____
(If under 18, parent or guardian must sign)

RAPTURE ROMANCE

This offer, limited to one per household and not valid to present subscribers, expires June 30, 1984. Prices subject to change. Specific titles subject to availability. Allow a minimum of 4 weeks for delivery.